R.D. Parsons.
3 - VII - 88   Oxford.

CHRISTOPHER MARLOWE AND CANTERBURY

CHRISTOPHER MARLOWE
AND CANTERBURY

William Urry

Edited with an introduction
by Andrew Butcher

faber and faber

LONDON · BOSTON

First published in 1988
by Faber and Faber Limited
3 Queen Square London WC1N 3AU

Phototypeset by Wilmaset Birkenhead Wirral
Printed in Great Britain by
Richard Clay Ltd, Bungay, Suffolk

British Library Cataloguing in Publication Data

Urry, William
Christopher Marlowe and Canterbury.
1. Marlowe, Christopher, *1564–1593* —
Biography 2. Dramatists, English —
Early modern, 1500–1700 — Biography
I. Title
822'.3   PR2673
ISBN 0–571–14566–3

CONTENTS

I first met William Urry in the summer of 1964 at the bus stop at the corner of Giles Lane, just outside our old school, Kent College, in Canterbury. We had both been attending the school's Speech Day. We rapidly fell into conversation, and he became excited to discover that I was reading history at university and had become interested in what we then still called the ' "Peasants" Revolt of 1381'. The bus was not long coming but before it arrived William had already invited me to the cathedral archives to look at the manuscript materials held there which cast new light on the revolt in Canterbury. When the bus came William insisted that we sat on the top deck and from there he conducted an animated lecture on the history of Canterbury as revealed by the first floors of its buildings in St Dunstan's and the High Street. I took up his invitation, learned to read medieval manuscripts under his direction (never admitting the inadequacy of my Latin as he read for me at break-neck speed), and have been concerned with Canterbury, its history and its archives, ever since. In helping to bring this book to publication I hope I have gone some way to paying the debt of gratitude I shall always feel.

The text of *Christopher Marlowe and Canterbury* has been prepared from a number of drafts of the book which remained among William Urry's papers. For access to these and other relevant papers, as well as use of William Urry's library, I am grateful to Mrs K.

Urry without whose patience and generosity the work could not have been done. In the process of editing and streamlining a large manuscript there have, inevitably, been losses of tone and, above all, of inimitable personal touches conveyed in the discursive style of a more leisurely treatment, but I hope and believe there have been no losses of substance though many details of the people of sixteenth- and seventeenth-century Canterbury and many good stories must be left untold.

I am indebted to the staff of Canterbury Cathedral Archives and of the library of the University of Kent for their assistance, and to members of the research seminars at the University of Kent for their criticism and encouragement as well as the opportunity to share in their work on related matters. In particular, I have been sustained by the kindness and learning of David Birmingham, Christine Bolt, Peter Brown, Kate McLuskie, Marion O'Connor, Diana O'Hara and David Nightingale – to say nothing of the tolerance of Alice, Matthew and Mary.

Andrew Butcher
Eliot College
University of Kent at Canterbury

1 *William Urry and Canterbury*

When William Urry died in 1981 the greater part of his researches remained unpublished. A lifetime's work on the history of Canterbury had produced in print a number of learned papers, as well as his doctoral dissertation, but the wide range of his scholarly investigations was known to the general public only through his many brilliant popular lectures and through locally published occasional or popular pieces. To an enormous number of fellow scholars his erudition had been known through passionate and amusing conversation or letters, especially during that period in which, as Cathedral and City Archivist at Canterbury, he generously shared his incomparable knowledge of these archives. Born and bred in Canterbury, and powerfully influenced by its history and traditions, he worked as antiquarian, archaeologist, topographer and local historian, with an unashamed chauvinism to recover its past. But for serious illness which dogged the last twenty years of his life, he might have published the major works on Thomas Becket and Christopher Marlowe which he left fully drafted in manuscript, as well as the general history of Canterbury which it had long been his ambition to write.

Born in the parish of St Mary Northgate, Canterbury, in 1913, William Urry was educated at a number of local schools before going to Kent College on the northern outskirts of the city, though it seems likely that by far the greatest influence on his educational development came from a remarkable home and perhaps particularly from his mother, whose historical and literary interests were to prove a great stimulus. In the 1930s he furthered his education by working for a BA General followed by a History Honours BA at Birkbeck College, University of London. On his return from the war in 1946 he was appointed assistant to the Honorary Librarian of Canterbury Cathedral Library, William Blore, and two years later, after Blore's death, he took over the management of the cathedral's archives and library. To this onerous task was subsequently added his appointment as Archivist to the City of Canterbury in 1951. During the two decades of his work at Canterbury he not only collected, organized and arranged the repair of the substantial archive collections at Canterbury with very little assistance, but he also served the considerable demands of a rapidly expanding readership of students as well as those of his native community, and still managed to publish his doctoral researches as a two-volume book on *Canterbury under the Angevin Kings* (London, 1967) which, along with the Revd H. Salter's work on the city of Oxford, stands as a pioneering study in urban archaeology and topography. His work in these years was recognized in his election as Fellow of the Society of Antiquaries and as Fellow of the Royal Historical Society. In 1968 his career underwent an important change of direction when he went first as a visiting fellow to All Souls College, Oxford, and then in 1969 when he was appointed to the Readership in Medieval Western Palaeography in the University of Oxford and was elected Fellow of St Edmund Hall. On the point of beginning what he hoped would be another fruitful period of his life – in retirement in his beloved Canterbury – he died, in February 1981.

As Archivist at Canterbury, in contact with a wide range of scholars, William Urry's interests grew and were influenced by the inquiries of a generation of postwar historians, though his surviving papers suggest that it was the 1930s and 1940s that were critical for his development as a historian. Inspired no doubt by parental encouragement, the support of the Revd Claude Jenkins and the stimulus of some of his teachers, especially at Kent College, and excited by his reading of Somner and Gostling, he discovered an ambition to follow in the footsteps of Canterbury's former antiquaries. It is striking, indeed, to find him writing on 1 May 1932, when living in London and in the initial stages of degree work at Birkbeck College: 'I am determined to write a survey of Canterbury.' By 6 February 1937 he had produced a still more ambitious programme. Now he had a ten-point plan: '1. History and Antiquities of Canterbury; 2. The persecution in the dioceses of Canterbury and Rochester; 3. The persecution in the rest of England; 4. The Probate Courts of England; 5. A life of Somner; 6. An edition of his works; 7. Letters of Sir Philip Sidney; 8. Lives of Early Antiquaries: Leland, Speed, Camden, Somner, Gibson, Sammes, Foxe, Battley, etc., etc., Hall, Languet, Cooper; 9. Archdeacons of Canterbury; 10. Una cum Matre *Historia Familiae*.' And though he might later have looked back ruefully on this list, it is clear that he set to work to accumulate materials for all of these areas, reading prodigiously, transcribing a whole range of documents and collecting manuscripts and archaeological remains. From these early researches came materials which contributed to what were to become the principal focuses of his later work on city and church in twelfth- and thirteenth-century Canterbury, on the life and times of Thomas Becket, and on the biography of Christopher Marlowe.

The 1930s, however, were far from being simply a happy, formative period in which William Urry developed his historical interests at university. Lectures and classes at Birkbeck in Anglo-Saxon, English, Latin, French and History were in the evenings. During the day he worked in the university library in a three-year employment, cataloguing, dealing with the mail, binding, typing cards and chasing queries. However useful the training proved to be, the conditions were far from congenial to a young man who did not suffer fools gladly and resented being treated as a dogsbody. Lodgings in Brixton provided few home comforts, were cold, and served cold boiled beef, roast mutton ('of which I am sick') and boiled pork ('which I don't like'). Long hours working in the university library were often accompanied by academic work before breakfast, in lunch hours and late into the night. Anxious about examinations, underestimating his own ability, often tired and with aching eyes, his eventual achievement is all the more remarkable.

Visits home to Canterbury were times of great relief and relaxation. Whatever the pleasures of life in London, his powerful identification with Canterbury made comparisons inevitable and provoked dissatisfaction with his surroundings. In a note which helps to explain his commitment to Canterbury's history, he wrote in May 1932: 'I wish my job were in Canterbury. There they all have much more fun than I do. More seeing each other, more social interests, more happiness than I do. They have the land, the sea, and the air all fresh and almost unspoiled. They have the plenty of all. If you wish for country life, there it is. The sea is only 1½ hours' walk away; the air is pure and undefiled. Sport for the athlete, beauty for the artist, company for the lonely, solitude for the weary. In trouble, sympathy, in joy, praise and congratulation, in work, anticipation of a good relaxation, in all things, charity. But I have none of these. I work, work, work, by day, by night. I walk through a wilderness of yellow brick as lonely for me as a desert. The air is foul, and the land and sea are virtually gone, for I see none of either except in parks where each plot has a fence round it . . .' Not that London was all bad. When the regular postal orders from home had been cashed there were a variety of trips to be made, sights to be seen, and purchases which, even within modest means, might include books or, as in April 1932, 'a 1567 shilling' bought for 1s. 6d.

But the delights of Canterbury were simple, obvious and very different. Home for Whitsun in 1932, William Urry was quickly 'down the town, through Mercery Lane, into Cathedral, into Nave, into Cloister'. Later he went to pick bluebells in Whitehall and then 'went again into Cathedral'. On Sunday there was cathedral Communion and then Matins followed by a visit with his father to see the tulips in the cathedral garden. In the afternoon at Chilham he watched the presentation of the troop colours and dedication in Chilham Park; after tea they returned home and then went back to the cathedral, later visiting friends in the Whitstable Road. Monday was spent camping at Chilham, 'in shorts and khaki shirt', and watching races at the sports ground in Chilham Park in the afternoon. In the evening all the guides and scouts 'went into the swimming bath for about an hour and had a good time'. Travelling back by bus to Canterbury they were home by about ten o'clock. Writing the day up later, Urry concluded: 'It seems that at Canterbury they have a happier time than we do here in London for no one is ever jolly in London.' It was as if they spoke another language.

For all this, and perhaps because of it, Urry's development as a historian took shape under the influence of his teachers and studies at Birkbeck while reacting with passionate commitment to Canterbury's past. The second and third items of his 1937 plan were symptomatic of this stage. His interest in sixteenth-century religious persecution stimulated extensive study of Foxe's *Book of Martyrs* and its application to Canterbury and Kent. From at least as early as August 1935, Urry began to collect and transcribe biographical materials to this end, along with the transcription of wills and other local documents which filled his notebooks. And it was no doubt an encouragement to discover from his father that there had been a 'Foxe' in his family home in Chichester. He began to think in terms of publishing an edition of the wills he had transcribed and, in drafting part of this used a sentence which recurs among his papers and distinguishes him as a developing local historian when he wrote of 'the trivial details which are really the important things of life'.

Other projects soon suggested themselves. From 1935 onwards he became concerned with the destruction of Canterbury's more ancient properties – in Beer Cart Lane, Stour Street, St Radigunds, North Lane, White House Lane, Castle Row and Pound Lane, for example – a concern which persisted for the rest of his life and made him an important guardian of the city's environment. He planned an essay on Canterbury's seventeenth-century Dick Whittington, Mr Alderman Sabine, but inevitably his attention was soon drawn to his antiquarian hero, William Somner. In 1940 he was invited to speak to the Canterbury Archaeological Society on William Somner and, after many years of intermittent study, he wrote an introduction to the Scolar Press reprint of Somner's *The Antiquities of Canterbury*, published in 1977.

The early years of the Second World War were greatly to stimulate the archaeologist in William Urry. He was a frequent visitor to the archives and museum of the Beaney Institute in

Canterbury, making it gifts of some of the archaeological finds which he collected. He began making detailed drawings of buildings in the city, exploring trenches dug in the town and measuring and studying existing ruins. Among his notes at this time he recorded, with obvious relish, an extract from White Kennett's *Life of William Somner*: 'At the digging up foundations, and other descents into the bowels of the earth, he came often to survey the workmen; and to purchase from them the treasure of Coins, Medals, and other buried reliques, of which he informed us, that many were found in almost all parts of the City, some of which came into his hands.' Urry was no less assiduous. At the same time he was closely involved with the packing up and removal of the cathedral archives to safety, which was under way in August 1939. With great delight he recorded the manuscripts which he personally had 'handled': chapter acts, priory treasurers' accounts, the twenty volumes of the Somner manuscripts, etc. With fellow historians and antiquarians he explored the city and the countryside: with Blore, the Cathedral Librarian, Mrs Gardiner, Higginbotham of the Beaney Institute, F. Jessup, G. Webster, K. Pinnock, K. Burrows, W. Pantin, R. A. L. Smith and many others. They went to the Barham and Kingston Downs, to Tonford, Ickham, Patrixbourne, Rochester, Godmersham and elsewhere. The discovery of 'Jutish' jewellery at Bekesbourne was especially exciting. No wonder that Urry was called 'the archaeologist' by Canon Crum, a description which was recorded by him with, presumably, some pleasure.

Joining the army in November 1940 restricted his activities in Canterbury. By that time, however, Blore had introduced him to the early Christchurch rentals which were to be fundamental to his pioneering study of his native city, *Canterbury under the Angevin Kings*, and this, combined with his archaeological investigations, may have changed the course of his studies from the fifteenth, sixteenth and seventeenth centuries to the twelfth and thirteenth centuries. As Cathedral Archivist and Librarian from 1948, and City Archivist from 1951, his range of knowledge grew perforce, though his own researches now centred upon the earlier period. Above all his knowledge of the historical topography of Canterbury came to be unrivalled and unlikely ever to be equalled. Increasingly Becket became an object of fascination in his early work, and only later did Christopher Marlowe occupy his attention.

Although Urry was fascinated by topography and archaeology, he also delighted in the 'trivial' details of the lives of ordinary people in the past. As Archivist at Canterbury he discovered for himself in the ecclesiastical and urban court proceedings a veritable mine of such biographical detail and, in parallel with other social historians, though free of their influence, he worked to recreate the texture of social life in sixteenth- and seventeenth-century Canterbury, eventually finding a focus for his studies in the life of Christopher Marlowe. For Urry, Marlowe was the product of the city which had been the object of his life's work, and Marlowe's poetry and plays were imbued with the genius of the cathedral city.

Urry's development as a historian gives his analysis of Marlowe and Canterbury an especially personal conviction. By the age of twenty-seven he had made for himself a range of discoveries in Canterbury's antiquities which were to provide stimulation for the rest of his life. The demands of his job as archivist were to broaden and deepen his understanding of the city's past, though those demands combined with serious illness were to prevent the publication of his major studies. His ambition to write a full-scale survey of Canterbury's history was never realized, though he may well be the last historian in modern times who might, single-handed, have contemplated such a project. *Christopher Marlowe and Canterbury*, however, is perhaps as close as he came.

2 *The biography of Christopher Marlowe*

In recent years there has been a reaction against literary biography. The detailed study of the author's life as a key to the understanding of his work has been replaced by a greater concentration upon audience, reading and the social construction of the text. Part of the reaction has been against a facile psychologizing, a crude psycho-historical approach, and part has been prompted by the sheer difficulty or impossibility of recovering sufficient biographical data, especially the further back in time the historical inquiry must go, to make a worthwhile investigation. Indeed modern textual criticism, when not positively ahistorical, is prepared to countenance consideration of the influence of traditional literary forms, iconographies and bodies of philosophical, ecclesiastical and political theory, yet is reluctant to consider the role of the specific context on the individual. But the relationship between artist and culture remains crucial.[1] The problem of determining how the production of a particular work of art came about at a particular time is still a vital issue in coming to an understanding of that work. If literary biography and historical method have failed to satisfy, it may be because they have failed to ask the appropriate questions of the appropriate evidence.

One particularly scathing review of biographical and historical method concluded that the 'everyday supports of scholarship which one may expect with other writers or periods, do not exist for Marlowe'.[2] The order of composition or production of his works is unknown and the degree of authenticity of the surviving texts is uncertain. Little is known about the direction, acting or décor of his plays, or even the stage on which they were performed. The players for whom he wrote are shadowy figures, his relations with the professional companies are unclear and their composition uncertain. Of his audience and its response nothing is known. The lack of manuscript evidence makes it very difficult to assess Marlowe's contribution relative to the moral interludes, academic drama and court and civic pageantry of the 1580s and 1590s. In such a position recourse to biographical method is not surprising, but in Marlowe's case the fragments of evidence which survive are of doubtful value. The evidence supplied by Kyd, Baines's deposition, the deposition against Cholmley and the testimony of those involved in the Deptford brawl is scarcely adequate to provide insight into Marlowe's works. 'Our entire knowledge of Marlowe's mind and character outside the uncertain texts of his contradictorily interpreted plays, springs directly from Kyd's frightened attempts to clear his own name by accusing someone else. His letters are a hotchpotch of uncorroborated and shifty accusations, supported only by the smears of informers, given spurious credibility by the shocking nature of Marlowe's plays, and his convenient death by violence, in a violent age, which removed all possibility of reply.'[3]

However partial and reductive this analysis may be, it is a valuable corrective to the excessive associative ingenuity of some critical work in this field. This work, at best, has resulted in three contradictory images of Marlowe: the youthful and iconoclastic free-thinker, 'the embodiment of Renaissance individualism'; the 'orthodox Christian moralist'; and the 'ambivalent, disillusioned ironist, sceptical of the conventional attitudes and beliefs of his day'.[4] To some extent these images have developed progressively, by reaction, but they represent also changes in the use of evidence. Informed by a romantic view of the individual, the artist and the sixteenth century, a naïve description emerged, the product of an interaction between the biographical fragments and certain elements in the plays. Work on the various strands of contemporary thought and doctrine and the inheritance of dramatic forms uncovered a writer working squarely within an orthodox Christian tradition. Closer textual analysis of the plays and a new attention to dramatic technique restored something of the rebellious spirit of the early image but increased the sense of ambiguity, modern criticism being largely unable or unwilling to resolve the question of Marlowe's moral and religious commitment. The direction which criticism has taken, however, involves a progressive abandonment of the biographical method.

Though strongly influenced by the romantic image of Marlowe, Urry's work does much to stimulate a new kind of approach through biography. Direct evidence of Marlowe's activities and opinions is now unlikely to be discovered, but it is none the less possible to recover in some detail the experience of social groups with which he was intimately involved. Whether in Canterbury, Cambridge or London, in family, neighbourhood, town, craft association, school, college and university, aristocratic household, company of actors, ale-house or tavern or other distinctive social entity, evidence survives which enables the biographer to assess the collective experience of Marlowe and his contemporaries and to begin to set limits to the ways in which the individual might absorb and express that collective experience. For Canterbury, in particular, Urry's exploitation of every available kind of documentation and his detailed topographical knowledge makes it possible to begin to reconstruct the contingent, formative pressures acting upon the young Christopher Marlowe which arguably shaped his identity and attitudes. It is not simply that Canterbury, for example, might have provided specific materials which were to be incorporated into his poems and plays, but rather that his whole sense of personal relationships, of religion and of politics, were significantly determined by his upbringing in that small provincial town and by his acquired sense of individuality. Thus if we wish to consider Marlowe's 'sexual politics', as one recent study has done,[5] then we might be led by Urry's investigations not only to examine the portrayal of Dido, Zenocrate and Abigail but also to examine gender relations as they were expressed in the social, economic, political and religious institutions of sixteenth-century Canterbury and especially in the family and household to which Marlowe belonged. Such an investigation might begin to provide a description which would fully reveal the shallow incomprehension of those seeking to explain Marlowe by ill-defined reference to homosexual compulsion.

Traditional areas of investigation by English historians, such as topography and genealogy, may therefore be put to new use in the cause of literary biography in the light of modern developments in historical and sociological methodology. In the time it has taken Urry's work on Christopher Marlowe and Canterbury to be published, literary criticism has first announced 'the death of the author' as an analytically useful concept, and then come to the conclusion that the verdict was premature or much exaggerated. If the centrality of the author in the determination of textual meaning is still highly debatable, there is an increased necessity for the detailed examination of the way in which an author is produced within society. As never before the need to identify the social and ideological factors that shape the consciousness of the author is apparent if there is to be a 'move away from a conception of the author as a fixed and monolithic originator of meanings, whose identity lies in a supposed or projected biographical trajectory'.[6] In the particular case of Christopher Marlowe, the examination of the origins of a system of values in his native city, and a knowledge of the circumstances which determined his reception of those values, provide the basis for an understanding of the interaction between those values, developments in Cambridge, London and elsewhere, and the immediately contingent matters of religion and politics which assumed national and international significance. The complexity of such a historical investigation is, perhaps, as great as the complexity of the author's works themselves. All that can be achieved by such an approach is a significant limitation of possibilities in the interpretation of the works, though at the same time it may enhance an awareness of the contribution of both author and audience, illuminating the nature of their dialogue. The work of the local historian engaged with the apparently trivial details of the lives of ordinary women and men becomes of crucial value.

Recent work on social and political developments in English urban society in the sixteenth century, for example, has emphasized the degree of conflict, informed by religious issues, which pervaded civic life from the 1530s to the 1590s.[7] When Christopher Marlowe's father, John Marlowe, came to live in Canterbury in the mid-1550s, he entered a community which had already experienced three decades and more of Reformation turmoil. In the 1520s, as earlier, there had been popular unrest in the city as well as attacks on members of the governing élite; at the same time political attitudes were characterized by a powerful anticlericalism, and urban privilege became a frontier of conflict with local monastic houses; and, among a small circle, humanist ideas continued to have an influence. Conservatism, however, was still strong, especially when aroused by Elizabeth Barton, the so-called 'Nun of Kent', yet following her downfall Cranmer's reformist activities encouraged the growth of religious radicalism and ushered in a period of division and confusion. The 1530s were to witness in Canterbury an increase in civic disorder with further attacks on the governing élite as well as conflict and division in its ranks. The city continued to find itself in opposition to the cathedral priory, and as attempts were made to reform the traditional religious and political structures of the town so iconoclastic attacks on churches and shrines increased, culminating in the suppression of Christchurch Priory in 1540. There emerged, it seems, a coherent and effective radical party as partisan politics developed, party strife intensified and conservative reaction grew. The middle years of the 1540s were an interlude of fragile political stability which disintegrated under the strains of warfare and social distress and, from 1548, an increasingly ascendant Protestantism was accompanied by disorder and rioting. Though political lines were never as clearly drawn as this summary would suggest, these were matters which affected town and country alike, placing an almost intolerable strain upon those social mechanisms normally competent to cope with adaptation to change. Individual, family and community values were severely tested.

Arriving in the mid-1550s, John Marlowe had to adapt to a highly volatile community which had not only endured the see-saw of recent conservative–versus–radical Protestant politics but had witnessed a remarkable *volte-face* among its governing élite which, after 1553, was able 'to embrace with alacrity the restoration of Romanist ceremonies, many of which they themselves had helped to overturn in Henry VIII's reign'.[8] The abundant surviving litigation in local lay and ecclesiastical courts gives testimony to the struggles among the people of Canterbury to recover and maintain social, political and religious order. If John Marlowe was among the crowds which saw the Protestant martyrs put to death just outside the walls of Canterbury in 1556, he was also one of those who had to accommodate the consequences of those executions within his own family, neighbourhood, parish and city community.

Urry's reconstruction of the Marlowe family and its world permits a special examination of Reformation society in an English provincial town which throws light not only on the social and psychological pressures acting upon the family, thereby suggesting much that may have influenced the developing attitudes of the playwright, but also upon the potential audience for Marlowe's work. If the confused and often violent religious and political history of Canterbury in the first fifty years of the century was the bequest to Christopher Marlowe's generation, life in the city under the new queen was to provide little respite. The accession of Elizabeth ushered in another decade of upheaval with radical lay and clerical Protestants seeking to eradicate what they saw as the measures of Marian betrayal. But conservative resistance was strong and it was only the intervention of the Privy Council which gave the Protestant element the advantage with the suppression of leading Marian clergy in the city and the reinstatement of Edwardian Protestant clerics. The families of the governing élite, however, made only token concessions and encouraged popular resistance so that only external governmental intervention was able to secure the election of a Protestant mayor in 1562, though by 1563, with the fear of Catholic invasion from France, city Protestants were strong enough to assert their control. By 1569, however, when Christopher Marlowe's father had established himself as a shoe-maker and had perhaps begun to enjoy some prosperity and respect in the community, the political and religious wheel had again turned. Conservative, Catholic families had launched a counter-attack and successfully removed leading Protestants from office. To succeed in any career in these years required considerable negotiating skills.

As John Marlowe's family grew and his business expanded in the period before Christopher Marlowe went to the King's School, during years in which subsistence crises and the threat of Catholic invasion frequently coloured popular politics, the struggles between Protestants and conservatives continued, with the queen's government often prepared to tolerate the resistance of the conservative element for the sake of a reasonable degree of civic order. In the early 1570s, however, the Protestants acquired an ascendancy in Canterbury which they were to retain for the rest of the century. Conservative petitions to the queen in 1573 against the city's governing Protestants resulted only in the imprisonment of members of the protesting opposition, and Archbishop Parker's new severity against Kentish recusants helped to confirm conservative defeat. A period of relative economic revival before the 1590s, stimulated in part by the arrival of French and Dutch refugees in the city, furthered the Protestants' control, enabling them even to impose a stern Sabbatarian regime in the 1580s.

The struggles between conservatives and radicals pervaded all aspects of town life. The traditional order of late medieval Canterbury was systematically subverted in the declared interests of a Protestant vision of a godly religious community working in civil harmony and wholeness and employing the surplus resources of a secularized church to revitalize the city to the benefit of all its citizens. But, in seeking to achieve such ends, radicals in Canterbury and elsewhere were bent upon the destruction of that popular culture which expressed the traditional order and was deeply integrated with every aspect of the life of the community. From 1532 they tried to stop the city's marching watch, held to celebrate the Translation of St Thomas, with its display of civic organization and office-holders, of military strength and the religious tableaux of the Martyrdom of St Thomas, St George and the Dragon, and the Annuniciation, Nativity and Assumption of the Virgin Mary. Despite acts of suppression, the pageant was remarkably resilient, but after substantial revival during Mary's reign was finally abolished in 1559. In the 1530s and 1540s iconoclastic attacks were part of the reforming programme. The worship of saints was condemned; images were torn down in the churches of St Mary Northgate and St George; plate, ornaments, jewels and vestments were looted from Christchurch; Becket's shrine was sacked; and the property of chantries and chapels was appropriated to finance increased civic expenditure. A whole panoply of feasts, ceremonies, processions, rituals and customary and seasonal pastimes, intimately associated with the church calendar and inextricably involved with the maintenance of the social and economic structure, were slowly eradicated. And as they were purged so they became the focus of conflict: conservative leaders in 1559 encouraged the playing of May-games, the lighting of bonfires in the streets on Midsummer's Eve and the activities of a bawdy jester who, with a crowd of boys, made a great fire outside the main gate of the cathedral on St Peter's Day – all to humilate Protestant reformers; in the 1540s the reformers sought to enforce the law relating to images by detailed investigations of the St George's Day solemnities entered into by the mayor, the aldermen and their wives; and repressive legislation extended to popular dancing, alehouses, gaming and the performance of plays on the Sabbath. To be raised in such a world and hope to make sense of it encouraged either a dangerous commitment to the extremes or a cautious ambivalence in the interests of self-preservation. For an immigrant family seeking to establish itself in the community the latter course might seem more prudent.

What we now know of the history of John Marlowe's family, and perhaps especially its history during the lifetime of Christopher Marlowe, once set against a background of urban social upheaval, begins to suggest the possibility of a more sophisticated approach to the dramatist's work through personal biography. The problems of settlement and family formation in such a society were many. The winning of respect as craftsman and neighbour in the parish of St George, a parish at the centre of religious and political conflict, was no easy matter. Entry into the ranks of the freemen, moreover, in a city such as Canterbury which possessed a relatively restricted franchise, gave John Marlowe a significant political status which necessitated his involvement in the important affairs of the community and lent some weight to his opinions. Because he was an immigrant, of modest means, and yet of the privileged, small group of Canterbury's citizens, moreover, his negotiation of the religious and political minefields would have to have been particularly sensitive if his family were to prosper. No doubt the anxieties of his early years in the city were passed on to his children.

Between 1562 and 1576 his wife, Katherine, another immigrant to the city, gave birth to nine children of which only five lived beyond the age of fourteen years. The size of this family is perhaps some testimony to an increasing prosperity and confidence, but as John Marlowe reached his forties the growing needs of his family must have begun to cause some strain. Christopher, with four younger sisters and until the birth of Thomas (II) in 1576 the only male child, must have known special responsibilities within the family which would have sharpened his sense of personal difference. As the son of a freeman, moreover, with an automatic right to enter the ranks of the freemen of the city, by the time he went to the King's School at the age of fourteen he must have developed a sense of his possible position in Canterbury society and the issues with which he would be concerned.

For John Marlowe the marriage of his daughters was no doubt as pressing a problem as the career of his first son. In sixteenth-century Canterbury, marriage, especially the marriage of a freeman's daughter, might prove to be a crucial exercise in the continual and complex process of social adjustment in a small, intimate and turbulent society. The daughters of Canterbury freemen, moreover, were an especially valuable commodity for they carried with them the benefit of a near-automatic access to the ranks of the city freemen for their husbands. They might become, therefore, a precious asset in the enhancement of personal and family status. Though Christopher Marlowe left Canterbury for Cambridge before any of his sisters found husbands, the marriages of his twelve-year-old sister Jane and his twenty-five-year-old sister Margaret, the only two to take place before his death, and the courtship of his sister Anne, must have been subjects of concern to him, especially on those occasions when he returned home. In the event the Marlowe sisters were all to marry outsiders or men from families of recent arrival in the city, families in many ways similar to their own. Their marriages all conferred freedom on their husbands, the early marriages of Jane and Margaret benefiting the family less than the later marriages of Anne and Dorothy, which were to men of probably greater substance and ability. Noticeably they did not attach the Marlowe family to that inner core of the wealthy élite which was involved with town government and the affairs of the wider world. John Marlowe and his family were to remain at the fringes of such activity though its consequences determined their daily actions.

Though John Marlowe was to take important office in the Shoemakers' Company and to serve his parish church and city ward in official capacities, there is little in the biography which William Urry recovered to suggest a significant upward social mobility. It may be, however, that John saw such an opportunity for his son when he permitted him to go to the King's School. There Christopher was among the sons of local landowners, local clergy, professional men and royal servants, as well as farmers, tradesmen and artisans. But if the school provided new social perspectives through its pupils, it probably also heightened political and religious awareness through its teachers. From the time of the appointment of John Twyne as headmaster by Archbishop Cranmer at the school's foundation, a succession of Protestant masters maintained the ideal of the town grammar school as a crucial institution in the establishment of a godly commonwealth. Anthony Rushe (1561–5) and John Gresshop (1566–80) were both committed to this cause, and Gresshop especially may have influenced the young Marlowe. The strict Calvinist education experienced by the radical preacher Josias Nicholls as a schoolboy at the King's School in the 1560s seems likely to have affected subsequent scholars in the 1570s. As the son of a respectable Canterbury tradesman, 'a city councillor, and a member of that small group of second generation Protestant leaders which had risen to prominence in the city during Edward VI's reign', Josias was born into the inner core of governing families.[9] Just as Nicholls's acquired social status may help to explain his response to his education and upbringing in Canterbury, so Christopher Marlowe's peculiarly ambivalent, uncommitted social position helps to explain his special sensitivity to the language of social, political and religious discourse. And at a time when the traditional language was attacked all around him and the power of an old symbolism and iconography was challenged, the King's School provided a classical education which supplied a new vocabulary and a new range of images with which to come to terms with contemporary upheavals; and it also introduced the performance of plays in Latin and Greek which might be compared with the popular drama and entertainments of courtyard and street. Gresshop's library perhaps supplies some indication of the potential range of that education, with works by Vives, Ascham, Elyot and Sadoletus indicating the Renaissance educational theories which may have been put into practice. It is difficult not to see the impact of such a school in such a city as being a powerful and even a transforming one. The intimate interpenetration of school and city life for a young shoemaker's son must have intensified his self-awareness and increased his perception of the significance of his own world relative to national and international affairs, while giving him an additional depth of historical perspective. Yet at the same time it was an education which was clearly partisan, the education of godly activists struggling 'with Catholics or crypto-Catholics in their own streets or market place'.[10]

In Urry's view, Christopher Marlowe's experience of Canterbury, reinforced by that of Cambridge, where divisions within the university would have been all too familiar as he prepared himself, ostensibly, for a career in the church,[11] inevitably found its way into his writing. His language made use of such Kentish colloquialisms as 'trot' (meaning an old woman) or 'ringle' (for 'ring' in describing harness). Childhood impressions of ceremonial splendour in school and town might influence the choice of 'scarlet roabes' in *Tamburlaine* (I:v.i.524).[12] His knowledge of the archaeology and topography of Canterbury and its environs, and of Dover, might be drawn upon in describing water supplies in *Tamburlaine* (I:III.i.59 and II:III.iii.29) in leaden pipes like those constructed in Wibert's priorate around 1160 for the Canterbury Cathedral Priory, which were still in use in the sixteenth century in the King's School; in speaking of 'Two lofty Turrets that command the Towne' in *The Jew of Malta* (v.iii.11) in such a way as to recall Canterbury's St George's Gate; in referring in the same play to 'a darke entry' (III.IV.79) and thereby echoing the name of a passage running close by Marlowe's schoolroom; or in the inclusion of a nunnery converted from the private house of Barabbas (I.ii.129, 256, 278, etc.) when in Canterbury the reverse conversion occurred in the transformation of St Sepulchre's nunnery into a private dwelling. For his *The Massacre at Paris*, Urry suggested, there were plenty of sources among Canterbury's own refugee population, while the image of papal towers kissing the ground which occurs in both the *Massacre* (ll.1214–15) and *Edward II* (ll.396–7) may have contained the memory of the attempted demolition of the enormous, southernmost tower of the west end of St Augustine's abbey church which took place in the early 1540s.

In *Hero and Leander*, moreover, when Marlowe wrote (I.3)

> In view and opposite two cities stood;
> Seaborderers, disjoin'd by Neptunes might

it seemed to Urry that he was on the cliffs above the English Channel looking at Calais and Dover; when Hero sings

> Upon a rocke and underneath a hill,
> Far from the towne (where all is whist and still,

> Save that the sea playing on yellow sand,
> Sends forth a ratling murmure to the land . . .
> My turret stands . . .

Marlowe has in mind the town of Dover lying 'in a deep cleft between vast cliffs, the northernmost of which is crowned by the Castle and the Roman pharos and the lower cliff opposite forms a spur upon which, in Marlowe's youth there stood at the apex a tall, slender turret, another Roman lighthouse, which must have been evoked by the description of Hero's tower standing above the sea, found in Musaeus or his translators'. Furthermore, it seemed to Urry that the detailed local knowledge of East Kent which occurs in *Henry VI* Part II was certainly of a kind which Marlowe might have possessed and used. In describing Alexander Iden, Best, Wingham tanner, Emmanuel, the clerk of Chartham (or possibly Chatham), and Dick, the Ashford butcher, the dramatist seemed to be drawing on a knowledge of individuals who were demonstrably known to those living in Canterbury and its hinterland. Similarly, the local knowledge incorporated in *Arden of Feversham* was such that, for Urry, if Marlowe's 'name appeared on a title page it is unlikely that anyone would have argued against inclusion of *Arden* in the Marlowe canon'.

Such an approach, however, yields only small rewards. Marlowe, as Kocher observed, 'is anything but homely', and his imagery is drawn much less frequently from the common details of life than is that of many of his contemporary dramatists.[13] To move from such a recognition, however, to assert that he possessed 'a temperament unusually remote from the world of men and their affairs',[14] is to swing the argument too far in the opposite direction. More profitable, perhaps, is to begin with Greenblatt when discussing *Tamburlaine*, by acknowledging that 'despite all the exoticism in Marlowe – Scythian shepherds, Maltese Jews, German magicians – it is his own countrymen that he broods upon and depicts'.[15] And in exploring his treatment of those countrymen and their concerns it becomes possible to trace the sources of his treatment and the mental structures from which they derive.

For Kocher, in search of the particular constitution of Marlowe's psychology, the author's works provided 'a record of the discovery and expanding perception of the world outside the self, accompanied by an increasing identification of the self within that world'.[16] In *Dido*, he argues, 'the idea of the self has not definitely emerged into consciousness' and it is only in *Tamburlaine* that we see its emergence, an emergence which must have taken place in Cambridge during his student days and not, *pace* Tucker Brooke, as the turbulent life of London provoked wilfulness and iconoclasm.[17] In an approach which argues for a more or less unmediated projection of the author's self through the construction of dramatic 'character', Kocher argues that 'We find in all four of Marlowe's chief dramas this opposition between a central figure, with or without a few supporters, and the system which hems him in. With Tamburlaine, Barabbas, and Gaveston, moreover, the social iconoclasm is intensified by the fact that they, like Marlowe, are of base or detested lineage. It is difficult not to conclude that this was the attitude of Marlowe himself and that he felt in varying degree not merely an aloofness but a positive enmity to the generality of mankind . . . this feeling was mollified as he grew older'.[18]

Kocher examines the hero and the minor characters in *Tamburlaine* as individual constructions which reveal the author's personal qualities, and in the treatment of minor characters concludes that at this stage Marlowe is little more than 'a recorder of his own inner experience, which he distributes among his dramatis personae without transmuting and individualizing it as a dramatist should'.[19] Marlowe, he judges, at this stage 'knew little about human beings other than himself' and was 'primarily self-sufficient, remote from both God and man', yet was, at least, developing human sympathy and showing an awareness of the transitory nature of human power. In *Faustus* the transition from a drama of exultation to a drama of spiritual death marked a shift of emphasis from the strength to the weakness of the self before God, and the failure of ambition, signalling an advance towards a greater fellow feeling for mankind even though *Faustus* remains essentially unsocial. Only with *The Jew of Malta*, in Kocher's view, does Marlowe give proper emphasis to society, the world of men rather than the world of imagination. It is 'thus a symptom of the rise, both psychologically and ethically, of the idea of human society in Marlowe's perception'.[20] *Edward II* continues this development, engaging with political issues which remained significant for Marlowe's age, revealing in the treatment of character a conflict of sympathy which indicates that alongside the 'worship of selfish power' that remains in Marlowe's nature there is 'the new realization of the evil it entails'.[21] Dismissing *The Massacre of Paris* as of little significance biographically, Kocher sees *Hero and Leander* as an uncharacteristic interlude which cannot deny that 'fundamental strain of solitary and ruthless aspiration' which 'will return to its own in those moods of bitterness when circumstances may cause Marlowe again to defy the world'.[22] This, of course, is the judgement of a writer who saw in the Baines note 'that master key to the mind of Marlowe', the quintessence of revolutionary dissidence.[23] But it is also the view of one who believed that 'In some degree most sensitive men have the same experience. Their youth is a time of storm and stress when they see nothing clearly, being rapt away in dreams and transports. Increasing maturity brings them a more stable and objective philosophy. The difference is that Marlowe's greater spiritual energies have carried him farther away and made more difficult his return.'[24]

It is easy to see why such a thorough-going romantic treatment should no longer seem adequate, dependent as it is upon both literary and psychological naïvety and with little sense of historical difference, though it should not lead to the abandonment of the biographical project. The dating of Marlowe's work alone is insufficiently secure to permit a ready acceptance of Kocher's conclusions. The potential circularity of his argument, moreover, prevents any testing of the hypothesis unless by references to that highly dubious collection of stories about Marlowe which seem, in any case, to have already informed the analysis. Personal development itself is posited in terms which themselves are questionable – the emergent self, the growth of tolerance and sociability, a progress 'towards health, sanity, and a social sympathy which is itself the highest kind of spiritual activity'[25] – and all takes place within a dozen years, rather too conveniently reflected in the surviving texts. The argument from dramatic character to personal psychology seemingly neglects dramatic convention or particular textual strategy and takes at face value narrative and personal representation without accommodating, for example, a sense of irony or satire. And finally, in making his author sole producer and arbiter of meaning, Kocher ignores that productive conflict between author and audience/reader without which, indeed, his view of Marlowe's psychology would not exist.

If, through the exotic material of his works, Marlowe broods upon and depicts his own countrymen, then those countrymen were to recreate those broodings and depictions in terms which they partly shared with the author but were their own. In a society in which matters of church and state were rapidly assimilated in personal relations, the audience's access to Marlowe's works might well be by way of the political issues they raised. The examination of political relationships portrayed within the plays and the consideration of the playtexts as the vehicles of political ideas and theories has demonstrated how much the immediately contextual provides a stimulus for dramatic production and consumption. Thus it is useful, with Belsey, to consider *Tamburlaine* as a play which is content to pose, 'with a certain sharpness to an Elizabethan society preparing to embark on a series of colonialist adventures', disturbing questions about the nature of its conquering hero;[26] or to go further with Shepherd in discussing the way in which 'Turkishness' disguises a range of contemporary issues in plays which 'publicly discuss the problem of the relation of ruler, counsellors and army that was endemic to the absolutist project of the Tudors'.[27] More obviously, *The Massacre at Paris* has great topicality, drawing closely upon contemporary sources and transforming them by means of irony and satire so that they disturb the consciences of an audience already sympathetic to the Huguenots.[28] Pursuing the 'politics of Elizabethan theatre', Shepherd suggests that *Edward II* should be seen as questioning 'the rhetoric of both sides in the foreign policy debates of the late 1580s', and that the significant context of *Faustus* is 'reinvigorated state repression' in the same years as 'show trials of puritan activists' and 'the breaking up of presses'.[29] The danger of such an approach is that it results in the text being mined for simple correspondences or crude reflections of reality, ignoring 'the fact that the text works actively on its audience, bringing ideas to their notice, situating them ideologically, making problems of concepts that might usually have been taken for natural or commonsensical'.[30] For Shepherd, however, the politics of Elizabethan theatre resides in 'the relationship between dominant ideologies and the questioning/affirming strategies of the individual text'.[31] For the biographer of Marlowe the political problem is more complex. The relationship between dominant ideologies, contemporary events and the strategies of the individual text has to be seen as part of the constant process of the development of the author. It must be related to the changing system of values which historical investigation has already uncovered if some attempt is to be made to assess its precise dimensions. And the more Marlowe is seen as exploring and testing the dangerous ground of contemporary politics the more the process of his development needs to be examined so that both the production of his work and its consumption may be more fully appreciated.

If Marlowe's work is understood to be intimately concerned with the construction and development of himself as author in response to both the course of contemporary events in the 1580s and early 1590s and the systems of values he was to confront in Cambridge, in aristocratic households, among companies of actors, intellectuals, and members of the underworld of spies and informers, then the biography of Marlowe must seek to recover those systems of values, if not directly (because of lack of surviving evidence), then at least by analogy and comparison. Such a project would, of course, be a substantial one, but nothing less is required if the challenge of the decentralization of the author is to be taken seriously – and the implications of such an analysis may imply a radical re-examination of the history of texts within society.

What Urry's work suggests is a way in which the crucial early stages of the construction of the author, and by analogy of other authors also, may be approached through the investigation of those sources, available for the first time in England in abundance for the sixteenth century, which reveal social structures and their accompanying mental attitudes. For Urry this was the stuff of his early chapters on Marlowe's life before his departure for Cambridge, and similar materials might be employed for the later years. A lifetime's work among the financial records of Canterbury and its Dean and Chapter, among chapter acts and the proceedings of the Borough-mote, among quarter sessions and city court papers, and especially among the depositions of the ecclesiastical courts, gave him an unrivalled knowledge not just of the activities of the Marlowe family but of that rich and changing complex of formative tensions with which Marlowe's identity was inextricably involved.

For Urry, the discovery of such evidence among the depositions of the ecclesiastical courts was a delight because, while illuminating the dramatist's career, it also provided a fund of wonderfully intimate and often scurrilous stories which gave a remarkable insight into the community while enabling the reader to take vicarious pleasure in what must have circulated as gossip. It was easy to see, moreover, a relationship between this deliberately recorded gossip of the courts and the work of Elizabethan drama-tists. Particular favourites from cases in the 1560s and 1570s were those which possessed a striking resemblance to episodes in *A Midsummer Night's Dream* and *The Merry Wives of Windsor*.

In 1564 a young woman called Dorothy Hocking lived in the parish of Holy Cross, close to Canterbury's Westgate, with her mother and stepfather, next door to a tailor's shop and house belonging to a former Yorkshireman by the name of Robert Holmes. Between the two back yards of these houses was a wall, probably one of those walls made up of stones and earth, bonded with hair and coated on the outside with lime or roughcast, while a capping of thatch kept out the wet. But the wall had developed a hole, and through that hole the dog in Dorothy Hocking's house had come into the Holmes's back yard and stolen a piece of conger fish. Dorothy was unhappy and in love. Her parents were cruel to her, confining her to the house, forcing her to do all the housework and treating her like a drudge. She had managed, however, despite these difficulties, to form an attachment to a young man called Richard Edmundes, and it seems that Robert Holmes's wife decided to encourage a match between Dorothy and Richard. 'About five or six of the clock in the afternoone', on the pretext of discussing the dog and the conger fish, she drew Dorothy from 'her mothers busynes in hir mothers backsyde' to speak with her secretly at the hole in the wall. Soon they had agreed to send for Richard Edmundes and Robert Holmes found him, playing bowls, in 'the backsyde of goodman podiches house', and took him at once to talk with Dorothy. Holmes's wife took Dorothy's hand through the wall and made Richard take it by the finger, asking 'knowe youe who this is that hath youe by the finger', and Dorothy answered 'no not yet'. Robert Holmes said 'it is Richard Edmundes' and Dorothy asked 'what . . . he wold have with her'. Richard first asked whether her father and mother were in the house and, learning that they were not, he said, 'well my wench I beare youe good will and if thow canst find in thie harte to love me and wilbe ruled by me I will delyver thee out of thye miserie. And she answered she could find in her hart to love him above all men. Then Edmundes axed her howe ould she was, saieing, I thinck you bee neere hand 16 or 17 yeares of age, and she said yea that I am, for I am neerer 20 yrs ould but my age is kept from me. Then Edmundes said unto Dorothee have youe made any contract before this tyme to anye others so that we can laufully go together, and she answered no. Then said Edmundes, can you finde in your harte to forsake father and mother and all men lyving for my sake and she answered yea.'

Then Robert Holmes called his journeyman, Harry Jenkinson, recently come from London, to come out of the house where he was working and act as witness to the betrothal of Richard and Dorothy. 'Where and whan, Edmundes toke Dorothie by the hand throughe the hole in the wall and then said Dorothee unto Edmundes these words, viz. I Dorothee take youe Richard to my husband forsaking all other for your sake and thereuppon I give you my faith and trouthe. Then said Edmundes, in faith wench, I were too blame if I would not speak the like woords unto thee', and when he had done so he 'called for drinck and dronck to Dorothie' and gave her 'an ould angell' in token of their betrothal which Dorothy received thankfully but, for fear of her parents discovering it, asked Robert Holmes to keep for her and after a few words concerning the speedy dispatch of their marriage, they departed. Later, when circumstances changed, Dorothy was to deny the betrothal and Richard Edmundes was to bring a case against her in which he defended his own reputation and that of Robert Holmes and his household, and exposed the domestic tyranny under which the stepdaughter suffered. The case is far more than a bizarre tale with Shakespearian echoes, since the depositions it gave rise to provide evidence of the functioning of neighbourhood and household and the role of the ritual of betrothal at a time when those social institutions were under strain and the assertion and maintenance of the norms of community behaviour were complicated by divisive ideological issues.

The story of William Darrell, one-time vice-dean at Canterbury, which brings to mind *The Merry Wives of Windsor*, has similarly interesting social implications. A member of an ancient Kentish family of Cale Hill, near Ashford, Darrell was made prebendary of Canterbury Cathedral by Queen Mary in the spring of 1554, later retaining his position under Elizabeth and being one of the four members only of the chapter who assembled to elect Matthew Parker as archbishop. In favour at court, he became chaplain to Queen Elizabeth but failed to gain further promotion following allegations of sundry misbehaviours. Despite his emoluments as a pluralist, he fell into debt and his colleagues were constrained to pay off his creditors, who actually came down to Canterbury to recover their money, and arrangements were made to deduct the cash from his canonical salary. His appearance in the ecclesiastical courts is in the unlikely company of Clemence Ward, a woman of 'suspect behaviour' living in the parish of St Alphege, close by the cathedral precincts. Early in the 1570s her reputation was repeatedly impugned and when she brought along neighbours to testify to her virtue it was adjudged that they were of insufficient substance to act as compurgatrices. The court required that she should undergo penance by appearing clad in a white sheet, standing in the church porch of St Alphege in the forenoon before service on Sunday, and remaining on bended knees throughout the service; and when she failed to comply she was declared excommunicate. Finally she was expelled with her husband from her lodgings.

At about harvest-time in 1575, one Goodwife Thomasina Newen went round to the Northgate ward of Canterbury to the house of Goodwife Pratt, and sat working with her at her door. Near by a new-made widow, Goodwife Culverhouse, gave milk to her child. They gossiped of Clemence Ward, saying 'Yt is a pity she is not carted out of the town.' One story which they told about her was repeated a few months later with slight variations in the kitchen of the house of Goodwife Joan Moyse, a widow and 'impotent woman' aged fifty, when Clemence Ward's landlord, John Foster, kindly went to see if Goodwife Moyse lacked for anything. As Goodwife Moyse rambled on, retelling a story told previously by a Mrs Hunt, as she recalled, she conjured up a scene of two people staggering through Christchurch Gate into the cathedral precincts on the way to Canon Darrell's house at the far east end, by the city wall, carrying between them a laundry basket over which a coverlet was spread. They went along the great length of the 'Centuary' or cemetery of Canterbury Cathedral, through the Norman gateway to the inner cemetery until they came to the Oaks in front of Canon Darrell's house. There they set the basket down, in among the oak trees. The laundry basket was going, said Goodwife Lea, 'to Mr Darrell's chamber'. Before long either Mr Whyting or perhaps Mr Wade, one of the cathedral lay clerks, approached with some foreknowledge of what was in the basket. He drew out his dagger and plunged it into the basket and, with a wound in her arm from the dagger, out leapt Clemence Ward. For unrecorded misdemeanours Darrell was eventually suspended from his canonry.

Regardless of the facts, the role of the story and, indeed, the case concerning Darrell and Ward in mediating the political and religious tensions which surrounded the canon are fascinating. Few stories, so told by such witnesses, could be better designed to destroy Darrell's reputation. And such evidence, intimately linking the struggles of the Reformation with the control of the lewd, disorderly, and ungodly poor, and placing such emphasis on the proper behaviour of the respectable, the landlord and the lay clerk among them, begins to indicate the formative pressures of those decades and the ways in which social change in the urban environment might readily be translated into issues of national and international moment while helping to explain how such issues came to be understood in such communities.

The trouble caused by Simon Oudart's daughters was another case which led Urry to compare the descriptions of the courts with the work of contemporary dramatists or songwriters. 'A few deft touches', he wrote, 'would turn the story of the "Maiden Strangers" into an Elizabethan song.' Simon Oudart was a Huguenot who, in 1597, lived in the parish of St Alphege with his two daughters, Rebecca and Hester. The assimilation of the refugees was a very slow process and most preferred to maintain as separate a life from the English citizens as possible, but Rebecca and Hester were courted by two English boys called John Jackson and Stephen Strong. Witnesses gave evidence that the partners were seen out together, that Rebecca and John had once met in Simon Oudart's garden, that Rebecca would stand in her father's back yard signalling to John Jackson as he looked out of his chamber window over against her father's house, indicating that he should write to her, and that she would send him tokens and letters. The two couples met in narrow lanes in the town or talked secretly together in the more private glades around the Ridingate. John and Stephen finally invited these daughters of a strict Calvinist family to a banquet in their chamber in St Alphege parish. They came, determined to become betrothed to their partners, and John Jackson went to find witnesses in Canterbury High Street and returned with Goldwell Roger (aged twenty-six), Anthony Webb, gentleman, and Bartholomew Salmon, the saddler, a respected man of forty-eight years, whereupon, in a simple ceremony, John and Rebecca and Stephen and Hester became betrothed, speaking words of mutual agreement, taking each others' hands and kissing. For Simon Oudart, however, such betrothals were not to be countenanced and, in the case of Rebecca and John, he took action in the courts to prove the betrothal invalid.[32]

In a community where Protestant refugees had been finding a home for twenty years and more, Simon Oudart struggled to maintain a separate cultural identity, which must have fostered an ambivalence among the native population, especially among traditionalists and in those more marginal social groups who sought to find a *modus vivendi* among the conflicts of the warring factions. Yet, as nothing escapes the neighbour's eye in such a community, the case itself, the rumour of the case, and the observed and reported antics of the children promote a change which is subversive of traditional identities. To the observer of such processes of adaptation, particularly to the participant observer, they may well provoke a scepticism or even cynicism about contemporary values.

In a final case, not used by Urry, that of *Lobly v. Yetman* in 1574,[33] the importance of such evidence for the biographical project emerges still more forcibly. A case of slander seems to have begun unremarkably, with a nineteen-year-old domestic servant named Kemborough Usburn in the parish of St Alphege accusing one Juliana Lobly of being a whore, but progressively it comes to examine the testimony of a number of witnesses about matters which affect the development of reputations and relationships over a period of eight years. The instigator of all the trouble, however, appears to have been Margaret Bland who, realizing the implications of what she has done, comes to confess as much to William Yetman, a minor canon of the cathedral, in his house in the cathedral precincts. It was from Yetman that she first heard stories about Juliana Lobly, but he turns on her in anger saying that 'she was to blame to make any talk therof privatlie or openlie seing the matter was done and past so long ago'. Margaret confesses, significantly, that 'she thought the devell was in her to tell it so' and that if she had thought it would come to this she would never have mentioned the matter. None the less, it was she who had told Kemborough Usburn 'in privat talk betwixt them two' 'how Juliana Lobly was take in playing the naughty pack in carnall copulacion with one of Mr Kings serving men named John Ellis when she was King's maid'. And though she had wished that Usburn might conceal what had been told to her in private it was because of their conversation that Usburn had called Lobly a whore and said that though unmarried she had a child.

Lobly, however, soon settled with Usburn but turned upon William Yetman and brought him to court as the true source of the slanders. William Yetman and his wife Johanna, it emerged, had been servants in the precinct house of prebendary King and his wife at the same time as Juliana Lobly and John Ellis, though Yetman might claim that Mr King was his 'uncle'. Furthermore, whatever else may have been going on in Mr King's house between Ellis and Lobly, according to the testimony of Elizabeth Pashelie of St

George's parish, and fifty-four years the wife of John Pashelie, when she was attending Mrs King in childbed, she discovered in the same house Lobly and Ellis and William Yetman and Johanna, later his wife, all lying naked in bed together. It seems, however, that William Yetman, having found Lobly and Ellis together again 'suspiciously', in Mr King's parlour, 'in suche beastlie sort as this deponent is almost ashamed to depose', then reported Lobly to Mrs King's daughter, grieving 'that his uncles house . . . should be so ill spoken of by suche a fact'. Informed by her daughter, Mrs King confronted Juliana and, when weeping she professed her belief that Ellis meant to marry her and pleaded 'good mistress for gods sake forgeve me and let not my Master know of it for then I am utterly undone', gave her a stern warning. When later it was discovered that Juliana, fearing herself pregnant, had tried to induce an abortion by drinking some special preparation, Mrs King's reaction was to rebuke her for a harlot and a beast as she 'wept, being also sick upon her bed', then to send for her mother, and finally to 'put her awaie'.

As the case unfolds and Yetman endeavours to protect his own precarious reputation against the attacks of a woman who presumably held him at least partly responsible for her disgrace, the role of female sexuality in the construction of honour and reputation becomes increasingly apparent, as does the double standard which applies in the morality of honour and shame. In a range of witnesses from casual female domestic servants to Elizabeth King, the prebendary's wife and her daughter, now married to a citizen of London, the workings of a complex social hierarchy in the struggle to maintain or establish status are very clear, as is the crucial distinction between private and public, seen and unseen in this society. What is more, as Yetman tours his witnesses and we hear their admissions we become party to a world of overheard conversations in houses with thin walls and open halls, and the discussion and confrontation of these vital issues of public morality in the street, in doorways, in the butcher's shop and in the yard of the Chequers tavern. And while the matter under discussion may at first sight appear to be the raking over of an old dispute between former servants in the same household, it rapidly becomes involved with sexual politics and the influence of kinship and its codes within the urban social hierarchy. And, as in the discussion of the previous cases, what begins as gossip almost inescapably comes to have a bearing upon the standing of a leading representative in the ideological struggle within Canterbury and its practical resolution.

Gradually, though imperfectly, the accumulation of such evidence enables the literary biographer to differentiate the structural constraints upon his subject's development and the work he produces. Once the collection of such materials has been made the next stage is to identify the contingencies which determine the internalization of those structures. Building upon this examination of the crucial, formative, early years it should then become possible to consider the repeated reconstructions of the author and in that way contribute to an understanding of the author's work and the ways in which his audience/reader assimilates that work.

Raised in the profoundly turbulent Reformation city of Canterbury, Christopher Marlowe, it might be argued, fashioned dramatic and poetical works out of the materials of a disintegrating traditional culture, transforming them so that, at least in the short term, they operated successfully to enter into a critical dialogue with an audience that shared a sense of political and religious crisis and an uncertain grasp of values. His experience of Canterbury and Cambridge gave him a sense of difference and distance and perhaps even ambivalence, and his education provided him with the means of locating the microcosm of his home community in such a way that its significance, and the significance of communities like it, might be employed by himself and his audience to better comprehend those manifestations of change which took place at national and international levels. The question of whether the interaction between the Christopher Marlowe of Canterbury and the experience of his years after Cambridge directed him towards an outrageously radical iconoclasm, as some surviving fragments of evidence would suggest, is unlikely to be resolved, though the romanticism of such a possibility will never fade away. The possibility now exists, however, if social and literary historians will co-operate on the project, whether for Marlowe or for other authors whose works are a product of this highly documented society, for the biography of the decentralized author to play an important role in the understanding of literature. The achievement of such a project is still a long way off. What Urry's work does is to stimulate such an endeavour.

Andrew Butcher

CHAPTER ONE

'An old city'

When Christopher Marlowe was murdered in 1593 he was only twenty-nine years old and had spent most of his life in Canterbury. He had grown up in this small Reformation city on the main route between London and the Continent, which had experienced all the religious and political turmoil of its age. As an ecclesiastical capital and provincial centre the city, with its clusters of towers and turrets rising above the city walls, and dominated by the cathedral, international centre of pilgrimage, had inherited a splendid medieval past. Drawing upon a rich agricultural area, the influence of Canterbury reached deep into the countryside and neighbouring towns, its craft and industry supplying regional as well as local needs. If the destruction of monastic dissolution had thinned out the towers, destroying much of St Augustine's abbey, causing St Gregory's priory to be cleared away and three friary churches to disappear, there was much that remained. Though the monks had gone from the cathedral priory there was, in the New Foundation, considerable continuity. In its popular culture and its schools, always in contact with external developments, the traditions of the community continued to influence its citizens.

'An old city somewhat decayed yet beautiful to behold', Canterbury was only a small town at the time of Marlowe's birth.[1] On 9 July 1562 a letter from the Privy Council instigated a household

for notes see p 145

1

survey in the city. When the survey was completed in 1563 the total number of households recorded came to 700.[2] In 1569 a further household survey, though incomplete, gave 845 households, and if this is modified on lines suggested by the 1563 returns then a total of some 900 households is indicated. Figures for numbers of communicants in 1569 give an approximate total for the population above the level of adolescence of 2,341.[3] The population of Canterbury in the 1560s was probably somewhere between 3,000 and 4,000 persons. It was a city close to the countryside. Green meadows came right up to the walls. Cows grazed within a hundred yards of John Marlowe's shop and local women went milking every morning. Gleaning went on at harvest-time in Barton Fields, stretching into St George's parish.[4] Fifteen minutes' walk would have taken the young Marlowe far out into the meads, the orchards and primrose lanes. His contact with the open countryside was as close as that of the boy Shakespeare.[5]

This small population, however, possessed great ethnic diversity. Men and women came to the city from all over England. There was also a strong Welsh contingent, represented by families of Davys, Joneses, Vaughans, Williamses and Evanses, some of whom still spoke their native language among themselves.[6] And there were migrants too from Scotland and Ireland.[7] From elsewhere in Europe came German, Italian, Spanish, Dutch, French and Walloon settlers, providing a wide range of experience in the small community.[8] In Marlowe's childhood the most significant element among such migrants must have been the Protestant refugees from France and the Low Countries. There had been an early wave of refugees by 1540, but the main flood poured in after the St Bartholomew's Day Massacre in 1572, increasing steadily until the vast cathedral crypt, which had been allocated to them as a place of worship, was scarce large enough to contain 'such a swarm'.[9]

The newcomers were not unwelcome for they maintained their own poor and gave jobs to unemployed denizens. They gratified property-owners, indeed, by taking over the numerous empty, tottering houses throughout Canterbury, often packing themselves in at the rate of three or four families to one house. Many of the Marlowes' new neighbours would have been able to provide first-hand accounts of the atrocities in France. Increasingly these immigrants came to play an important part in town life, men like the prosperous merchant Laurence des Bouverie, and Dr Gerard Gosson whose extensive practice and extortionate medical fees became the subject of the courts' interest. Most distinguished, perhaps, was the Cardinal de Chatillon, Odet de Coligny, who arrived before the Massacre and lived, for a time, with one of the cathedral canons.

Such distinguished immigrants and many more humble trades-men, craftsmen and labourers swelled the population of the grow-ing city, which for all its beauty and proximity to the countryside was dark, dirty and disease-ridden. The houses of Canterbury were mostly framed of wood, jutting out at each storey, almost meeting each other at the top in a narrow street like Mercery Lane. Roads were mostly well, if roughly, paved though vulnerable to heavy rainfall. A kennel or central gutter ran down each street. Posts and rails gave pedestrians their only protection from lurching wagons and laden animals. Often the streets were choked with filth or blocked by rubbish or abandoned loads. River and side-street would frequently become the dumping place for sewage from citizens' overflowing cess-pits, which were often dug no more than a few feet from wells. Members of the Marlowe family circle such as John Cranford and Thomas Graddell, the sons-in-law, were more than once offenders in this respect.[10] John Marlowe's friend, Laurence Applegate, the tailor, simply let his pit and privy overflow into the neighbouring Iron Bar Lane.[11] The parish of St George in which John Marlowe's shop was situated must have been particularly malodorous for it lay between the cattle market on the one side and the butchers' shambles on the other. Disposal of blood and offal from the shambles was a perpetual problem and even the tough stomachs of Tudor citizens were turned by the tubs of blood and entrails trundled past their doors on summer evenings. A dominant sound of Marlowe's youth must have been the screams of cattle driven to slaughter only a few yards away.

In such circumstances the prevalence of epidemic disease was only to be expected. Between 1563 and 1565 Canterbury experienced high rates of mortality during a nationwide outbreak of plague,

St Mildred's and St George's parishes being most severely affected.[12] In 1575 another outbreak occurred, and deaths in St George's parish, compared with average levels, more than doubled in the plague months of May, June, July and August, with groups of two, three or four identical surnames pointing to stricken households.[13] Again in 1593 Canterbury was struck by epidemic.[14] And these were only the most dramatic episodes in a period of high mortality rates. Natural disasters and the minor calamities of accident and illness loomed large in such a society. The notes made by a contemporary shopkeeper recall drought in 1567, early and heavy snowfalls in October 1575, storms and floods in May 1576 with cellars swamped and the streets awash between the King's Bridge and the old Greyfriars' Gate, a blazing star on 11 November 1577, a tempest of wind and snow in February 1578 so that the highways were stopped with snowdrifts, and earthquakes in April and May of 1580. There were other frightening manifestations: on Sunday 14 November 1574, when Christopher Marlowe was ten years old, there were seen around midnight in south-east England 'diverse strange impressions of fire and smoke', proceeding south from a black cloud in the north, continuing till daylight next morning. The following night the heavens all round seemed to burn 'marvellously ragingly', and flames rose from the horizon all round and met overhead, 'and did double and roll in one another, as if it had been in a clear furnace'. This was a grand and abnormal display of the aurora borealis. In the latitude of Canterbury lesser displays are occasionally to be seen, and sometimes on a winter's night Christopher Marlowe might have beheld long red streamers in the sky far to the north above the cathedral, hanging in the dark firmament like streaks of blood.

Whatever its former importance this diverse and vulnerable small community was not a thriving centre of industry and commerce. There were prosperous manufacturers like Alderman John Rose, the woollen-draper, and Alderman Thomas Bathurste, who started a cloth manufactory in the Old Blackfriars precinct, but the main economic activity was in the hands of craftsmen and shopkeepers of middle rank. There was the usual range of occupations to be found in a sixteenth-century provincial town: grocers, shoemakers, blacksmiths, tanners, dyers, saddlers, carpenters, builders, limeburners, linen-drapers, butchers, fishmongers, bakers, apothecaries, victuallers, and so forth, all of them making or preparing their products in shops or workyards around the city.[15] Among the professional men were clergy, lawyers, schoolteachers, physicians and surgeons. With a dozen parish churches and a cathedral staffed by twelve senior canons, six minor canons and part-time clerics such as the 'Six Preachers', the clergy were numerous. Leading lawyers dealt with the business of town and country families and among them the Railtons and the Gaunts were well known to the Marlowes. Extensively intermarried, their families formed a very tight and closed group. Others within the legal profession included such men as the serjeant-at-law William Lovelace, attorneys in the courts such as John Smith and Giles Winston (with whom the Marlowes were to become involved) and office clerks turning a penny by writing wills. Schoolteachers ranged from unqualified and unregistered men instructing a handful of children in some small room to the distinguished graduates at the King's School.[16] Medical men such as Dr Gosson probably tended to the needs of the more affluent. Further down the social scale a surgeon such as Mr Russell of St George's parish might carry out an amputation or other brutal operations.[17] And the activities of witches and cunning men were widespread. Among the poorer sort were those who worked at small scale, domestic by-employments such as 'Agnes that makes strawen hattes', beggars like Mother Bassocke going from door to door holding her apron out for scraps, and others occasionally whipped out of town.[18]

The popular culture of Tudor Canterbury and the amusements of its citizens were much the same as elsewhere. The citizens danced indoors and outdoors. They sang and played the virginals, the lute, the rebec, the recorder and other instruments. They gambolled round the maypole on the Dane John field until the moral zealots cut it down. At butts in the city or out in the countryside they shot with the longbow. They rode out hunting and beagling, or watched bull- and bear-baiting. They quarrelled incessantly, exchanging abuse and blows, and even litigation seems to have been a major form of public entertainment both for participants and observers. They played at dice and shovegroat, at shootball and football, and even at some form of cricket.[19] Most notably, however, there was a long theatrical tradition at Canterbury. From at least as early as the thirteenth century the monks at the cathedral and St Augustine's abbey invited in actors and other entertainers to perform on festive occasions. The city authority organized and financed religious drama and there was a cycle of biblical plays based upon St Dunstan's church outside the western city walls. As late as the 1540s the corporation was subscribing to the support of a religious play in paying for shoes and clothes for 'tormentours'. In almost every year of Marlowe's boyhood there is a record of travelling players coming into Canterbury. They performed in the Guildhall and no doubt in the yards of the great inns. Certainly they played at the Chequers inn in 1546–7 and again 1608–9. Groups of actors with aristocratic patrons are frequently recorded and it seems probable that Marlowe saw some of their performances. Some evidence exists for dramatic performances in private houses in the city. In the case of slander in 1561 brought by old Bishop Bale, spending his last days as a canon of Canterbury, there is evidence of Bale's plays being staged in the house of Alderman George May who lived in the precinct of the dissolved priory of St Gregory.[20] The same case involved Bale in a violent quarrel with Alderman Okeden, who persisted in his Catholicism right into the reign of Queen Elizabeth. Okeden, it seems, had attempted to interfere with the manufacture of friars' garments for one of the plays in a tailor's shop beside the cathedral gate.[21] At the King's School too there were dramatic shows, considerable sums being spent in 1562, for example, on plays. There was still a tradition in the later eighteenth century that a building north of the cathedral had been pulled down by the 'zealous puritans' for being profaned by plays acted there by the scholars.

The pageantry of politics and status was also part of Marlowe's boyhood as it was of that of children growing up in almost any provincial town. All ranks of society and many nations were involved. Besides the usual calendar of civic ceremonial, ambassadors came riding by, with sometimes a prince like John Casimir, leader of Protestant armies, who met 'Mr Philip Sidney Esquire' in Canterbury in 1579.[22] There were also merchants, mariners, soldiers and foreigners in strange costumes such as 'the man that caeme

out off the land of Babyllond' in 1564.[23] But the greatest of the
visitors during Marlowe's youth was Queen Elizabeth who celebrated her fortieth birthday in the city in 1573.[24] She arrived on 3
September and attended the cathedral service amid a blaze of scarlet
from civic and ceremonial robes. Wednesday 7 September was her
birthday and the occasion for a great feast held in the hall of
Archbishop Matthew Parker's palace. Ordinary people were
allowed into the hall to stand gaping at the galaxy of nobles, both
French and English, presided over by the queen. John Marlowe may
have found a place with his nine-year-old son. The queen's progress
through the city streets and the sight of the banquet would have
made a profound impression upon the boy, the triumphal ride
through the ancient ecclesiastical city being a magnificent demon-
stration of the power and splendour of monarchy. Even to look at
Canterbury through the window of his father's shop window in St
George's parish would have been to observe the endless and
fascinating spectacle of the year-long procession.

The parish of St George in which Christopher Marlowe grew up
accommodated some 208 communicants in 1569.[25] It was a parish
dominated by some conspicuous landmarks. The church was a
Romanesque building with a heavy nave arcade.[26] Gothic windows
had been pierced through the southern wall in the later Middle Ages
to relieve the gloom. At the western end stood the square embattled
tower with a circular staircase projecting out into the street and
impeding traffic. Here was the great waking bell for the whole city,
and ringers slept under the tower and rose to toll it at four o'clock
each morning.[27] Equally impressive was the city gate called Newingate or St George's Gate, rebuilt about 1470 and standing at the
highest point in the circuit of the city walls.[28] Spanning the parish
boundaries of St George and St Mary Magdalen was the notable
block of apartments built by Stephen Thornhurst, the property-
developer in Burgate Lane. At the end of the parish was the hideous
landmark of the gallows, erected there in about 1575 after removal
from another site. The young Marlowe must more than once have
seen a dismal procession passing by his father's shop as a malefactor
was carted to his death at Oaten Hill.

The names of the Marlowes' neighbours may readily be found.

On the corner of Iron Bar Lane stood the Vernicle Inn.[29] Next door, towards the church, lived Laurence Applegate the tailor, John Marlowe's friend.[30] A few doors farther down the High Street lived Alderman Rose the woollen-draper, also well-known to John Marlowe.[31] Opposite Alderman Rose lived Gregory Roose the capper, husband of Goodwife Roose the local midwife, who may have brought Christopher Marlowe into the world.[32]. Next to Roose lived John Smith the attorney, and just beyond Smith, on the corner of Rose Lane, dwelt Alderman Nutt from whom John Marlowe rented a house in 1585.[33] Almost opposite the church, near the gateway of the Austin Friars, was the house of Harmon Verson, the immigrant glazier, in whose house Laurence Applegate made bawdy remarks in 1564, resulting in a lawsuit in which John Marlowe became involved.[34] Near at hand lived Alderman Gaunt whose wife Dorothy might have given her name to Dorothy Marlowe, Christopher's younger sister.

In a small parish a clergyman may figure large and greatly influence the rising generation. But the parson of St George's in Marlowe's youth was a pathetic and ineffectual creature. The rector, the Revd William Sweeting, was originally a tailor by trade and in the reign of Queen Mary had acted as parish clerk.[35] Evidently not too literate, he left his parish register in a great muddle.[36] Desperate to find men who could somehow fill the ill-paid church vacancies, Archbishop Parker had conducted mass ordinations. Sweeting had been hastily invested at Lambeth with the rank of deacon and priest in rapid succession and then thrust into the living of St George the Martyr.[37] In the record of a Visitation in 1564 it was mentioned that Parson Sweeting could not preach and that while four sermons a year were customary at St George's the new rector had been able to organize only two, and then only by bringing in another clergyman to preach for him.[38] He did, however, encourage his flock to go to the cathedral and listen to the sermons there. In 1569 the Visitation reported that the Revd William Sweeting was hospitable according to his means but was not a graduate and had taken up the additional office of curate of St Mary Bredin near by, enjoying the modest combined income of both churches.[39]

To judge by his will, Sweeting was a poor man. He was buried at

St George's on 3 May 1574 and bequeathed pitiful legacies of single groats to the members of his family.[40] Of his several children one deserves special mention here. Leonard Sweeting, born in 1563, became a scholar with Christopher Marlowe at the King's School. When Marlowe went to Cambridge, however, Leonard Sweeting became apprenticed to a local ecclesiastical lawyer. One of the witnesses of William Sweeting's will is named as John Pashley, who had earlier been a fellow tailor with Sweeting and was probably father to Christopher Pashley, Marlowe's predecessor in the scholarship at Cambridge.[41]

Within the small parish of St George's connections were close and influences many and various. Marlowe grew up in a talented generation among talented neighbours. Close to St George's church dwelt city councillor Thomas Bull, cathedral organist and trainer of the splendid choir there. He took pupils, some of whom became resident in his house.[42] Next to Laurence Applegate lived John Johnson the artist, who was sometimes glad to eke out a livelihood by painting derisive paper labels to stick on punished witches. Another musician, at a humbler level than Thomas Bull, was William a Lee, the taborer, often to be heard banging and piping away for halfpence before he died in 1567 or 1568.[43] One character left over from what seemed a remote age was 'Sir' John Heaviside, called 'old Heaviside the priest', whose burial service was held a little way down the street at St Andrew's church in August 1566.[44] His alternative surname was Dygon, which probably identifies him with the Tudor musician John Dygon.[45] He had been professed a monk of St Augustine's abbey about 1498, was turned out at the dissolution of his monastery forty years later, and had hung around in Canterbury for nearly thirty years after his expulsion, evidently the last of the local monks.

Christopher Marlowe may rank as Canterbury's most distinguished son by birth, but there were others in his time who were to become well-known men of letters or of action. One such was Stephen Gosson (1554–1624), who was to become an influential figure. It is striking that the greatest innovator in the drama and this well-known opponent of the theatre should not only have been born in the same city but even in the same small parish. Baptized at

St George's on 17 April 1554, Stephen was the son of Cornelius Gosson, a joiner by trade.[46] His mother was Agnes Oxenbridge, daughter of Jerome Oxenbridge, the grocer. Stephen's reference to himself as a 'mule' has been taken to indicate that he was half foreign by birth, and the description of his father as 'alien' in local tax lists now confirms this.[47] The son became a scholar at the King's School at Michaelmas in 1567 and was admitted scholar at Christ Church, Oxford, in 1572.[48] He failed to complete his degree procedure and went off to London where he wrote plays and, in 1579, his best-known work, the *Schoole of Abuse*, a violent attack on the theatre as a training-ground for evil coupled with a lament over the decay of the English spirit. Dedicated to Sir Philip Sidney, this work may have provoked Sidney to write his *Apologie for Poetrie* (1581). The Puritan opponent of the drama turns up later, however, in Rome in 1584, as a student at the English College, preparing for the Roman priest-hood.[49] Making an excuse of poor eyesight, Gosson slipped back to England, re-entered the Anglican church and died in 1624 as rector of St Botolph's, Bishopsgate, in London.

Probably born in Canterbury in about 1555, John Lyly, son of Peter Lyly, also occupies a notable position in English literary history.[50] His father came to hold the position of registrar in the Canterbury Consistory Court in 1551 and had lived at first in the southern parish of St Mildred. By 1562 he had moved to St Alphege, near the cathedral gateway, where the family lived in a large wooden house bearing the sign 'Splayed Eagle', later known as the Sun Inn, in Sun Street.[51] The upper windows of the house still command a splendid view of the cathedral, which perhaps inspired a lyrical passage on Canterbury in John Lyly's *Euphues*.[52] Peter Lyly's other children can be traced in the St Alphege parish register and two of them, Peter and William, appear on the scholars' list at the King's School. John Lyly reached Magdalen College, Oxford, by 1569, in the year of his father's death. To assure his son's future Peter had secured from Archbishop Parker a grant, dated 3 February 1569, of the reversion of office as actuary or scribe of the Court of Arches, and a confirmation of 31 March 1598 made by Archbishop Whitgift to Fulk Broughton, gent., his *famulus domesticus*, grants the same office now occupied or exercised by 'John Lyllye, gent.' – John no doubt relinquishing an interest in an office exercised through substitutes.[53] When his father had prudently bought the position nearly thirty years before he had, of course, no idea that his son would become a celebrated poet, dramatist and novelist, and author of the popular *Euphues*. Lyly stands now for the courtly, indoor drama performed in London by boys of both St Paul's and the Chapel Royal, as opposed to the rough and tumble of the inn-yards or open-air theatres. Children of neighbouring families in this small provincial city, John Lyly and Christopher Marlowe at the same time headed two major manifestations of theatre life in the capital.

If Canterbury was to make an unusual contribution in the realms of literature and drama it was not without its men of action. Richard Boyle, for example, the 'Great Earl of Cork', proves to be the son of Roger Boyle, clerk in the employ of William Lovelace, serjeant-at-law.[54] The future colonizer of Ireland was about eighteen months younger than Christopher Marlowe but shared a similar childhood. Not many yards from the Marlowe's dwelling there lived and worked in St George's parish a grocer's assistant of puritan views named Robert Cushman.[55] Returning from Holland to England after long years of exile for his beliefs it was this same Robert Cushman who was mainly instrumental in 1620 in hiring the ship *Mayflower*.

The common experience of sixteenth-century Canterbury seemed to provide for its children an environment and opportunities which encouraged a distinctive response from its more talented members. The effect of religious and political turmoil upon this ecclesiastical capital and provincial centre, with ancient traditions and a rich medieval inheritance acting through new and reformed institutions, was to give Canterbury an influence and importance which transcended local boundaries. Christopher Marlowe was, perhaps, the most talented young man to benefit from this environment in the sixteenth century, but to understand his development it is necessary to begin with that most formative institution, his family.

CHAPTER TWO

Family, kin and neighbours

Just as the story of Christopher Marlowe's childhood and youth was the story of sixteenth-century Canterbury, so his family circle and connections parallel the city's extensions into the surrounding region. Most of the links were local, within a radius of twenty or thirty miles, but occasionally the Marlowes were in touch with more distant communities, in London and beyond in Cambridge-shire, Oxfordshire and Lancashire. Their world was that of small tradesmen and craftsmen, but it embraced a wide range of exper-ience derived from distant connections and information passing through the busy local ports of Faversham and Dover.

John Marlowe, Christopher's father, grew up at a time when the great abbey church of Faversham was being demolished and its stones shipped to strengthen the defences of Calais, and when the murder of Thomas Arden by his wife, Alice, in 1551 became a matter of notoriety. John's origins have been the subject of debate,[1] and he himself gave varying evidence on four separate occasions in the local courts as regards his age and life history. He was, however, certain of one thing, that he was born in the village of Ospringe beside Faversham.[2] When his friend Laurence Applegate, the Canterbury tailor, was charged with slander in 1566, and in a case concerning Mrs Benchkin's will in 1586, John Marlowe's testimony indicated that he was born in 1536. Giving evidence in 1593

12

For notes see p. 149

regarding a visit to his supplier of leather, Leonard Doggerell, and later in a tithe case brought by the parson of St Mary Breadman in 1603, his autobiographical sketch suggested dates of 1543 and 1537. The evidence from apprenticeship records, however, tends to confirm the earliest date, 1536, and it seems probable that he came to Canterbury about 1556, becoming one of the crowds which, in the reign of Queen Mary, flocked to the sandy hollows at Wincheap half a mile away to watch more than forty Protestant martyrs dying at the stake for their beliefs.

Sometime in the financial year running from Michaelmas 1559, John became apprenticed to Gerard Richardson, a shoemaker, who paid the city chamberlains the statutory 2s. 1d. for his enrolment in that year.[3] The evidence of John Marlowe's deposition, made when he was about thirty years of age in 1566, suggests that he arrived in Canterbury when about twenty years old and, from 1561–2, had lived in St George's parish.[4] If this is so he may have been as old as twenty-four when he became apprenticed. No more than four years later, in April 1564, he became a freeman of Canterbury.[5] His age and the speed with which he became a freeman suggest that there was more to his progress in Canterbury than the officially recorded details indicate. Indeed, since he married in May 1561, the length of his official apprenticeship to Gerard Richardson may have been no more than two years.[6] In all probability, however, John had already acquired his skills before coming to Canterbury in 1556 and finding a job as a shoemaker's assistant for four years, perhaps with Gerard Richardson. His apprenticeship has the familiar appearance of a fiction designed to enable an individual, already working in the trade, to circumvent the stringent demands of full apprenticeship and to make a back-door entry into the city's freedom. Within about eight years from the time he left Ospringe for Canterbury, John Marlowe had made his way into the narrow ranks of privileged citizens. He was now an established craftsman and, having met and married Katherine Arthur, had a growing family making demands upon his time and income.

Katherine came from the Arthur family of Dover. Her brother, Thomas, in the testamentary case over Mrs Benchkin's will in 1586, declared that he was about forty years of age and had been born at

Dover.[7] Earlier, in 1575, this same Thomas was specified as the son of William Arthur of Dover, and other members of the family may have been associated with the St James area of the town, close to the harbour front under the castle cliffs.[8] Katherine, therefore, spent her girlhood among the colourful surroundings of the busy port and great stronghold of Dover.

The Arthur family does not appear to have ranked very high in the town. They seem not to have risen into the ranks of freemen.[9] No particular trade has been recorded in the case of Katherine's father, who died in 1575,[10] though an earlier William Arthur, who died in 1558, seems to have carried on a precarious livelihood in small-scale farming by hiring dead- and live-stock, with a sideline in occasional brewing.[11] When this same William died in 1558 three Canterbury men had claims upon his property. He was in debt to Thomas Applegate, father of John Marlowe's friend Laurence, Stephen Thornhurst, the property-developer in St George's, and Thomas Pelsham, 'spiritual son' to Thomas Whittals, alderman of Canterbury.[12] Such connections may help to explain the fact that Katherine Arthur was married in the parish church of St George the Martyr at Canterbury and not in her native town and parish. Her brother Thomas also found his way to Canterbury: born in Dover in about 1545, he had moved in the 1570s a few miles away to Shepherdswell before living in Barham for a year and moving into Canterbury. He lived in the parish of St Mary Northgate until late in 1584 and had moved into the adjacent parish of St Alphege by 1586 before a further move into the extramural suburb of St Dunstan's.[13]

John and Katherine Marlowe were to produce nine children of whom Christopher was the second. Their first child, Mary, brought for baptism at St George's church in Canterbury on 21 May 1562, died young and was buried in the graveyard on 28 August 1568.[14] Christopher was brought for baptism on Saturday 26 February 1564 and died in 1593.[15] The third child, Margaret, was probably christened on 18 December 1565, again in St George's.[16] Margaret married John Jordan, a tailor, on 15 June 1590 at St Mary Breadman church in the High Street of Canterbury, her family then living in that parish.[17] When she died she may have been seventy-six years old, living right up into a different world on the threshold of the

Civil War.[18] The second son born to John and Katherine was baptized at St George's, but with no mention of a Christian name, on 31 October 1568.[19] The child lived only a few days and was buried on 5 November following.[20] Within a few months they had lost two children.

Jane Marlowe was christened in St George's on 20 August 1569 and, less than thirteen years later, married John Moore in St Andrew's church, Canterbury, on 22 April 1582.[21] She became a mother by 13 January 1583 and most likely died in childbirth, possibly followed by her son.[22] In 1570 the Marlowe family lost another infant son, the register of St George's recording a baptism of Thomas Marlowe on 26 July followed by his burial three weeks later on 7 August.[23] Christened at St George's on 14 July 1571, Anne Marlowe was to live to make her presence felt in her native city.[24] She was already expecting a child when she married John Cranford, a shoemaker of Canterbury, at St Mary Breadman on 10 June 1593, only twelve days after her brother Christopher was slain at Deptford. The child was baptized Anne, daughter of John Cranford, on 6 January 1594.[25] Only at the age of eighty-one, on 7 December 1652, was she laid to rest at All Saints in Canterbury.[26] Her sister, Dorothy, was christened at St George's on 18 October 1573, and on 30 June 1594 at St Mary Breadman she married Thomas Graddell, glover and later vintner, innkeeper and hackneyman in Canterbury.[27] Outliving her husband, who died in 1625, she may have married again, and died under a different name, and cannot, therefore, be traced in the local registers.[28] The last child born to John and Katherine was baptized Thomas (II) at St Andrew's church, Canterbury, on 8 April 1576.[29] Listed as a choirboy at Archbishop Whitgift's Cathedral Visitation in 1589, he otherwise fails to be noticed by the Canterbury records.[30] Since he was not mentioned in his mother's will it is possible that he was dead by the time it was drawn up in 1605.[31] Or was he the Thomas Marloe, one of the governor's men at Pashehaighs, beside 'James City' in Virginia, said in a list drawn up in 1624 to have arrived in the ship *Jonathan*?[32]

The eldest son and, after the death of Mary in 1568, the eldest child of John and Katherine, Christopher Marlowe grew up in a household in which he had four younger sisters at the time of his departure for Cambridge in 1580. Margaret, only a little more than a year his junior, was probably just fifteen years old when he left. For her and for the Marlowe family, the ramification of family connection was still to come through the daughters' marriages in the 1580s and 1590s. For Christopher immediate family influences must have come from Marlowe and Arthur kinsmen, from neighbours and from John Marlowe's fellow tradesmen and craftsmen.

What is known of the career of Katherine's brother Thomas Arthur illustrates one aspect of the connections within the Marlowe family circle. Thomas, though not resident in the city until the 1570s, was to be found in St George's parish as early as 1564 when he was about nineteen years old, and it becomes possible to describe his activities in more detail after his marriage to Ursula, daughter of Richard Moore, the blacksmith of Ulcombe (twenty miles west of Canterbury), whose family had moved into the parish of St Mary Northgate in about 1573 when Richard bought his freedom of the city.[33] The marriage must have taken place some time between the early months of 1576 and late in 1581.[34] Dorothy Arthur, child of Thomas and Ursula, was baptized in St Mary Northgate church on 18 September 1582, the first of five children to be born to the couple between 1582 and 1593: Joan was baptized in 1586, Daniel in 1588, Elizabeth in 1590, and William's date of baptism is unknown.[35] In these years, if places of baptism are a reliable guide to place of residence, the family seems to have moved in Canterbury from St Mary Northgate to St Alphege to St Dunstan and to St Mary Magdalen.[36] Ursula, moreover, mother to this mobile and growing family and aunt to Christopher Marlowe, though only a few weeks his senior, had a brother, John Moore, who would seem to be the same man who took as a bride the twelve-year-old Jane Marlowe in April, binding the two families still more closely together.[37]

Thomas Arthur was a literate man who, in 1586, enjoyed the modest but responsible position of joint bailiff of Canterbury's large extramural suburb of Westgate.[38] In 1592 the local branch of the much-hated Court of High Commission was in session at Canterbury, meeting in the Dean's house, and Thomas was acting as gaoler of the Westgate prison, perhaps as deputy to the keeper, Clement

Gasken, or, more likely, in charge of the lock-up a short distance outside Westgate which catered for delinquents in the suburb.[39] His job as gaoler would have taken him well beyond Canterbury, as it did in 1591 when a Privy Council warrant was passed for payment of £5 for the trouble and expense of Thomas Arthur and three others bringing up prisoners from Canterbury.[40] And all this at a time when his nephew's voice was at its most strident against religion and right order.

The plague which raged in London and the south-east in 1593 probably wiped out the whole Arthur family in Canterbury apart from the ten-year-old Dorothy.[41] Thomas Arthur died on 17 August, his son John was dead by 29 August, on 6 September his daughter Elizabeth died and the following day so did her brother William.[42] Ursula Arthur was buried on 13 September and the child Daniel on the next day.[43] The Marlowes at once took Dorothy into their care and swiftly sought to secure the administration of her father's property.[44]

On 15 September 1593, two days after Ursula's funeral, John and Katherine Marlowe, on Dorothy's behalf, were bound for proper performance of the administration of Thomas Arthur's estate along with their faithful friends Thomas Plessington, the baker of St Margaret's Street, and Laurence Applegate, the tailor of St George's Street. Bound in the large sum of 200 marks, they were all instructed to exhibit an inventory by the first court after Christmas following. But the inventory was not forthcoming and only after pressure had been brought to bear was it produced on 22 April 1594 with a total value of £56 7s. 6d., a not inconsiderable sum for the time.[45]

Dorothy Arthur survived her dreadful bereavement by only four years; when only just fifteen, she too lay dying in August 1597.[46] Described at this time as *ancilla* or maid, perhaps made to work for her living in the Marlowe household, she pronounced her will verbally in their favour as the family gathered around. It was claimed that when asked by her aunt Katherine if she wished to leave anything to her aunt Barton, born Agnes Moore, sister to Dorothy's mother Ursula Arthur, and wife of Solomon Barton the pailmaker, she had said she wished to give her nothing and did not even want her to be sent for. She spoke her will on 21 August 1597 and was

dead by 26 August, being buried at St Dunstan's.[47] Two obscure
and illiterate women, Margaret Crosse, wife of Nicholas, and
Margaret Coxe, wife of John, were produced to attest the validity of
the verbal will and probate was granted on 27 August.[48]

Pursuing Thomas Arthur's assets, the Marlowes found liabilities.
They were successful in their action against one Richard Quested
who admitted to having entered into a bond to pay Thomas Arthur
£10 but was equally able to prove that he had settled the debt.
Thomas Arthur's creditors, indeed, began to look to the Marlowes
as administrators of his goods and chattels. John Taylor, for
example, sued for 50s. 4d.; John Boys, Esquire, a leading Kentish
gentleman and lawyer, claimed that Arthur had owed him £30;[49]
and a dreadful demand was made as late as 1596 by George Byng,
Esquire, late sheriff of Kent, for the enormous sum of £500 claimed
as owing from Arthur's estate.[50] The outcome of these cases is
unknown and, fortunately for the Marlowes, they may well have
been dropped. In the sole verdict surviving in their favour in these
matters, John and Katherine Marlowe won their case against
Thomas Beake of Fordwich for a debt of £10 to Thomas Arthur,
though they did not secure satisfaction through the Fordwich court
until 1596.[51]

The Moore side of the family was also involved in a vexed
administration of family goods in what must have been an object of
vigorous discussion in the Marlowe household. This time Ursula
Arthur (née Moore), Christopher Marlowe's aunt, was involved in
the improper handling of goods and chattels after the death in 1582
of her father Richard Moore, the blacksmith and freeman of
Canterbury.[52] Court action was instigated by George Aunsell, the
grocer, brother of Mary who had married the blacksmith's son
Thomas and, after his death, remarried to become Mary Collyn. As
uncle to Richard Moore (II), the son of Thomas and Mary, George
Aunsell sought to protect his young nephew's inheritance.
Thomasina Moore, widow of the blacksmith and grandmother to
the young Richard, together with her daughter Ursula, became
involved in the improper handling of the estate until in 1583, at the
court held in the White Hart Inn opposite St Margaret's church,
George Aunsell was appointed the boy Richard's guardian with the

2

agreement of his mother, Mary Collyn. The court then allocated portions of the estate to various members of the family: Agnes Moore, *alias* Barton, the 'Aunt Barton' to whom Dorothy Arthur left nothing in 1596, was to receive £6 10s.; Sara Moore, daughter of the blacksmith, received £8 10s.; John Moore, son of the blacksmith and the probable husband of Jane Marlowe, £8 10s.; William Moore, the blacksmith's eldest son, £5; and Richard Moore, George Aunsell's ward, received £9. The matters were not yet entirely settled, however, for on 15 January 1584 Thomas and Ursula Arthur were obliged in court to disgorge the £9 due to the young Richard when it was made over to George Aunsell on Richard's behalf. As late as 1596, indeed, John Marlowe may have been involved with the residue of this estate when, following the death of Thomasina Moore, Ursula's mother, he seems to have been meddling with a deed of gift, executed by the same Thomasina, without waiting for probate.[53]

The often complex administration of modest estates reveals much of the intricate connections of family and kin as they struggled to profit from the division of the few possessions accumulated in their lifetimes. The Bartons and the Aunsells provide two examples from different levels of the urban hierarchy within the Marlowe circle. Christopher Marlowe must have known Solomon and Agnes Barton in the years of his two documented return visits to Canterbury in 1585 and 1592.[54] They had several children, all baptized at Ulcombe in the years between 1575 and 1585[55] apart from the last, christened at St Mary Northgate in March 1587, by which time they must have moved into Canterbury, following the Moores.[56] Solomon Barton was variously described as pailmaker and trugger, a manufacturer of flat chip baskets.[57] When his wife died in 1596 he became an 'intrant' or quasi-freeman, paying an annual fine to practise his trade on a year-to-year basis, and in the following year he was of sufficient standing to be nominated as a collector for the poor by the local justices.[58]

George Aunsell, the grocer, was of distinctly higher rank in Canterbury society and his household in Mercery Lane would have been well known to Christopher Marlowe. He came from Mersham, near Ashford in Kent, and had moved to Canterbury by 1569 when he purchased his freedom.[59] On 23 October 1570 he married Ann Potman at Ulcombe, she bringing, through her family, some tone of gentility to a circle of small craftsmen and tradesmen, bearing a coat of arms of considerable beauty, 'paly or and sable, in chief of the second, three cinqfoils pierced, of the first'.[60] Ann or Agnes was the daughter of Thomas Potman of Tunstall, Kent, who also had two sons, William and Richard, the latter of whom became a lawyer of Clifford's Inn and attorney of the common pleas and was knighted as one of the 400 dubbed before James's coronation at Whitehall on 23 July 1603.[61]

The Aunsells had a large brood of children, and by 1588 had also living with them Agnes's widowed sister Mildred, former wife of John Pledger of Mersham.[62] In 1597 the Aunsells' daughter Elizabeth, then nineteen years of age, having commissioned a new petticoat for Christmas of Colbrand the tailor, sued him for failure to deliver.[63] Her sister Ann, when already pregnant, made a runaway marriage with Joseph Buckley, the bookseller and stationer whom Christopher Marlowe may well have met in court in 1592 – Marlowe as the supposedly innocent victim of an assault by William Corkine, and Buckley on a charge of pushing a man into the river.[64] Later a sober and respected figure, Buckley became a city councillor.[65] No stranger to trouble himself, George Aunsell attracted the attention of the ecclesiastical courts as the result of several liaisons with married and unmarried women in Canterbury and the surrounding countryside, and on one occasion he quarrelled with Thomas Fyneux of Hougham in Kent, the likely father of Thomas Fyneux, the youth converted to atheism by Christopher Marlowe.[66] Christopher's father, John, was well acquainted with George Aunsell. They both marched together in the Canterbury trained band in 1588 when Marlowe carried a bow and Aunsell a caliver, and it was Aunsell who had then responsibility for negotiating supplies of gunpowder for his fellow warriors.[67] He was later to turn from grocery to tavern-keeping and in 1626 he died as a brother of Jesus Hospital, the almshouse outside the Northgate of Canterbury.[68]

For the Marlowe family in its early years friends, neighbours and acquaintances arose not only by way of marriage but through trade and craft connections as well as office-holding. As already suggested, John Marlowe's entry into the trading community of Canterbury probably came as assistant and later apprentice to Gerard Richardson.[69] Richardson was probably not English and may have been one of the many Germanic refugees who escaped to England from religious wars: there were many shoemakers in Canterbury with such origins. Other such immigrants had prospered – Harmon (Hermann) Verson, the glazier, for example, or Cornelius Gosson, the joiner – but Richardson seems to have been an unsuccessful businessman. Living in the Burgate ward, probably in St Andrew's parish near to the Canterbury Buttermarket, he appeared among the poorer citizens in a tax-assessment of 1558 when he was levied 3s. 4d., the lowest level of payment and in striking contrast to the £25 or £30 that might be paid by a wealthy alderman or gentleman. Earlier, when brought into court and fined in 1554 or 1555 for allowing his chimney to catch fire and opening his shop in church-service time on Sunday, the amount imposed for both offences was reduced by the borough to 8d., 'for that he is very poore'. Among other debts, that of 1557 may be indicative of his condition for, having difficulty in paying a fuel bill, he partly resolved his problem by supplying four pairs of shoes to his creditors.[70] When he died in March 1564, two weeks after the baptism of Christopher Marlowe, he was buried in St George's churchyard, his own parish having no ground of its own.[71] Richardson died intestate and administration of his modest property was granted to John Berverle and Robert Clerke. These two swiftly entered a plea of trespass against John Marlowe in May 1564, about a month after he had become a freeman, perhaps because he was known or thought to be in possession of leather or equipment belonging to his late master. Whatever the reason, the action seems to have been dropped.[72]

By 1564 or 1565 John Marlowe had his own shoemaker's shop for it was there that Laurence Applegate made his bawdy remarks about Godelif Hurte.[73] The trade company which Marlowe entered in 1564 comprised the shoemakers, tanners, tawyers, saddlers, glovers and indeed any craftsmen connected with the leather industry.[74] Of medieval origin, this craft association regarded the Blessed Virgin

Mary as its patron saint in the sixteenth century, though earlier it had claimed SS Crispin and Crispianus, the shoemakers of Soissons, martyred under the Emperor Diocletian. In a charter issued to all leatherworkers in the city on 1 December 1579, it was stated that they should all be united into one company embraced by the title of 'Fellowshippe companye crafte and mysterye of shoemakers'.[75] Entry could be secured by apprenticeship for seven years and payment of a fee of 3s. 4d. Those wishing to enter without apprenticeship might do so at the substantial fee of £5 (much more than a year's pay for a journeyman) or, if they were not English, on payment of £10. The feast-day was decreed as the Sunday after SS Simon and Jude (28 October), close to the medieval feast-day of SS Crispin and Crispianus, and on that day there was a dinner, each man paying 8d. for his meal. On this day the shoemakers may have carried their totem called 'the Pall', a velvet bier-cloth which John Marlowe may have seen, probably embroidered with images of patron saints, the Blessed Virgin with SS Crispin and Crispianus. Confiscated during the drive against superstitious images in Edward VI's reign, it was brought out again in the reign of Queen Mary and probably went out of use at the accession of Elizabeth, to be replaced later by a wooden board set in a frame bearing on one side a coat of arms and on the other a rambling record of its renewal in 1629.[76]

The officers of the company were specified as master, two wardens and four assistants or councillors, and it was these officers who were responsible for the welfare of members, assisting 'decayed' members with payments of at least 4d. a week and ensuring that when a craftsman died all the fellowship or mystery should attend the funeral under pain of fine set at 12d. The reissue of the charter of 1579 in 1601–2 with some amendments was similarly the responsiblity of these officers, and serving as one of the assistants at that time, now close to the end of his career, was John Marlowe.[77] His three colleagues were John Stockden, Thomas Free and Isaac Umberstone; the master was Leonard Doggerell, the currier; and the wardens were Leonard Ashenden and John Holland. Most of these men were closely involved in the story of John Marlowe's life.

According to a conspectus of wages paid to Canterbury craftsmen in the shape of an enactment printed by local magistrates in 1576, the shoemakers occupied a place far down the wage-scale, and John and Katherine Marlowe must have started married life on a very modest income.[78] By 1570, however, at the age of about thirty-four and some six years after gaining his freedom, John would seem to have risen considerably in the ranks of his company. A petition of about 1570 from shoemakers to the Justices of the Peace in quarter sessions requesting action against John Osberston, a troublesome member of the craft, was signed by seven men, Thomas Grenleff, John Marley, Fraunces Augar, James Benet, Leonard Ashenden, Christofer Ashenden and Christofer Graves (by means of a mark).[79] If these seven men are the officers of the company and their names are given in order of precedence, then Grenleff would be the master, Marley and Augar the wardens, and Bennet, the two Ashendens and Graves would be the assistants.

Between 1567 and 1593 John Marlowe is recorded as having taken five apprentices. The first was Richard Umberfield, enrolled in the financial year Michaelmas 1567–8, probably the son of the Canterbury blacksmith John Umberfield, a comparative newcomer to the city who had claimed his freedom in 1562 by right of marriage with the daughter of the Canterbury freeman John Watson, the draper.[80] Richard's father acted as cathedral clock-keeper, kept clocks in working order around the precincts and did maintenance work on the calivers in the corporation armoury, being a gunsmith as well as a blacksmith. His brother from Missenden helped him 'in boryng of gonnes'.[81] Of all his father's apprentices Richard may have been the best known to Christopher Marlowe for they were the longest in contact. Even so, his apprenticeship was cut short when he got into trouble and left the district, accused in April 1570 of having made pregnant Joan Hubbard of the parish of St George.[82] Early in 1590, however, a Richard Umberfield is found among a batch of prisoners held, because of their religious beliefs, in the Bridewell in London;[83] a fellow prisoner was named John Cranford – two prisoners bearing the names of former apprentices, one of them a future son-in-law, of John Marlowe. Perhaps this Umberfield did indeed have some connection with the apprentice.

On 21 April 1576 Lactantius Presson was enrolled as John Marlowe's apprentice.[84] He was probably the son of Thomas

Preston who was baptized at St George's, Canterbury, on 10 November 1551.[85] Aged a little under twenty-five years at the time of his apprenticeship, Presson may provide another example of fictitious apprenticeship, but whatever the case he did not complete his term of years. After a major domestic and workshop crisis which the thirteen-year-old Christopher Marlowe must have learnt all about, when master and apprentice came to blows and John Marlowe was fined for drawing blood, Lactantius Presson soon left.[86] On 5 August 1577 he married Marian Garrete at Fordwich, two miles downriver from Canterbury, and is next found ten miles further on at Sandwich when he brought his son John for baptism at St Peter's church on 14 June 1579.[87] Several other children were born to the family, but at the age of only forty-four 'Lacktenchyous Pressonne a poore man' was buried at St Peter's, Sandwich, in July 1595.[88]

Shortly before Christopher Marlowe left home to go to Cambridge in 1580, John Marlowe enrolled Elias Martin and William Hewes as apprentices on 23 July.[89] Martin did not become a freeman of Canterbury until July 1593 and it seems likely that he worked out his full term with John Marlowe.[90] By 1589, however, the evidence of the church courts would suggest that he was acting as a master, with his own shoemaker's shop, for he was cited with Thomas Ofspringe, the needlemaker, as one who refused to give his staff time off to join in churchgoing and merrymaking on May Day in that year, continuing to work and disturbing the service in St Andrew's church with their noise.[91] William Hewes was only admitted to the freedom on 26 April 1594 and by then had left his master's workshop.[92] Within eight months, however, he was involved in an assault upon John Marlowe, close by the Canterbury Buttermarket, for which he was subsequently fined 3s. 4d. having thrown himself upon the mercy of the court.[93] Hewes is present in many court cases of the period. He successfully took Cheyney Hales to law for non-payment of a debt of over £11 contracted in September 1595.[94] More than once he is named as a witness to an incident or transaction effected in a local public house. He was present in the Windmill, run by Christopher Marlowe's sister Anne and her husband, when a tangle of debts was being sorted out, and he was sitting in the Black Boy in the Buttermarket early in 1606 when the regulars were debating the Gunpowder Plot of two months before.[95] In 1593 he married Christian Bishop, the couple producing numerous offspring and losing several children when young.[96] At no great age he was buried, according to St Andrew's parish register, on 21 July 1609.[97]

Thomas and Edward Mychell were apprenticed to John Marlowe in the years following Christopher Marlowe's death. Thomas was enrolled in December 1593, though it would seem that he was a man already possessing some experience in the leather trade.[98] If he was yet another mature apprentice with an eye on cheap admission to the freedom, however, his admission is not recorded. The enrolment of Edward Mychell as apprentice has not survived, but a bastardy bond of 1598 discloses that the son of Robert Mychell, yeoman of St Bartholomew's Hospital, Sandwich, one Edward, now apprentice to John Marlowe of Canterbury, cordwainer, was the reputed father of one bastard child begotten upon Alice Alcocke, late servant with John Marlowe and probably his wife's maid. Unable to provide for the support of the child, he was committed to prison at the city's Westgate. However, his father and a friend came forward and entered into a bond for payment and by the end of August 1598 Mychell was once again working for John Marlowe, the maid-servant having departed from the Marlowe household.[99]

Evidence survives for only a few other members of John Marlowe's staff. An unnamed assistant was under suspicion in another paternity case involving a woman of bad character living close to the King's School, but the blame was shifted on to one of the senior pupils.[100] Sometime in the 1590s it would seem that William Saunders, the shoemaker 'servant to John Marlowe', was with others pressed in a body of 110 soldiers from the area and marched to Dover under the command of Captain Nethersole to join a contingent which served under the Earl of Essex in the great Cadiz raid of 1596.[101] And among the Canterbury muster papers is recorded Robert Coxee, 'John Marlowe his man', armed with a 'byll'.[102]

If John Marlowe was a good shoemaker he was probably a poor businessman. His career is punctuated by actions for debt launched against him by various claimants. He did not pay his rent, he did not pay his rates and he failed to meet his business obligations. He was even untrustworthy when acting as warden treasurer for his Company of Shoemakers. At no time in his life can he be found in a moderately satisfactory economic position.

In the 1570s and 1580s John Marlowe sought to take advantage of local sources of finance, as did a number of his contemporaries including more substantial citizens. He took up a loan of £2 from the Wilde Charity in about 1569 or 1570, and was still in debt to that institution in 1573.[103] Early in 1586, it would seem, he borrowed £5 from the so-called Streater legacy and paid back that sum on 2 February 1588 for it to be loaned to Henry Carre, the skinner, well known to John Marlowe as a member of his trade company and a fellow bowman in the same detachment of the Canterbury trained band of soldiers.[104]

The election of John Marlowe by the Shoemakers' Company as warden and treasurer in 1589 was perhaps, in the light of his record, doomed to failure. At the end of his year of office he was unable to produce the balance of the 40s. 10d., and after some months the company took him to law though they did not enter the case until 27 January 1592.[105] His pledges were John Den, apparently a member of the legal family of that name, and his son-in-law John Jordan, husband of Margaret Marlowe. His only defence was to protest vigorously that he had paid. When the case came to jury on 3 April 1592 the case was found against him. He must have faced a substantial bill for costs plus the obligation to find the sum claimed by the company. On 18 December 1592 he seems to have paid up but it is difficult to know how he found the money to do so.

Throughout his life John Marlowe would seem to have been one of the gregarious people hanging about in central Canterbury, ever ready to mind someone else's business, and one of those who hover about the edge of greater men's affairs. He was present when Alderman Rose headed a group of aldermen conducting negotiations in 1578 about a piece of corporation property called 'the Timberyard' in St Margaret's Street, and was employed by them as a witness.[106] When Alderman Rose died in 1591 John Marlowe, who owed him 10s., was one of those who helped draw up his inventory.[107] Able to sign his name and write a few words, he was frequently called in as a witness. At the house of a dying neighbour, William Newton the weaver, on 14 August 1575, he even received a legacy of 6s. 8d. for his trouble.[108] Naturally called upon to act as a bondsman, his signature is frequently found in this capacity, especially when he stood as bondsman for couples about to marry.[109] It was not that he stood to make any significant profit from such activity; more often it was the price of a drink and the gratification of intruding himself into someone else's affairs.

A string of cases in the Canterbury borough plea books record John Marlowe's conflicts with his fellow citizens. In 1570 or 1571 he was at grips with John Osberston the shoemaker.[110] In 1572 he took action against one Leonard Browne and against Hugh Jones, landlord of the Chequers;[111] in 1572–3 he was again in conflict with Osberston;[112] and in 1578 he took out proceedings against David Cheyney, gentleman, kinsman and servant to Sir Thomas Cheyney of Sheppey,[113] while at the same time squabbling with a man named Johnson and another named Henry Harwarde.[114] Augustine Saere and Richard Allen were separately prosecuted for debt in 1580–1 and in 1582–3 he was at odds with Richard Easton.[115] The words of his accusation against the basketmaker Michael Shawe were reported when he declared: 'Michaell Shawe thou art a thiefe and so I wyll prove thee to be.'[116]

John and Katherine Marlowe moved frequently with their family within the city and John quarrelled with a number of his landlords. The Marlowes entered into the tenancy of Alderman Nutt's house in St Andrew's parish in 1584 and within a year had defaulted on their rent payments. William Nutt, a lawyer by profession and mayor of Canterbury in 1582–3, took John Marlowe to court in a case which dragged on into 1586 with no recorded resolution.[117] When the Marlowes lived in the parish of St Mary Breadman they occupied a property belonging to Alexander Norwood, a young lawyer in the church courts, which must have stood on the frontage near and opposite Guildhall Street in Canterbury.[118] Once again the landlord brought John to court in a case which began in 1594 and then dragged on to no recorded conclusion as Norwood tried to evict his tenants.[119] From about 1594 George Powell leased to John Marlowe a property standing below Mercery Lane in Canterbury, next door

2

but one to the Chequers inn.[120] Towards 1600, it would seem, the same Powell made another lease of the same property to John Williams, ignoring the Marlowes, and the case against John Marlowe was brought by Elizabeth Williams, John Williams's widow, in 1602. This time however the case was settled by jury in favour of Marlowe.

Other cases in the 1590s illustrate a variety of John Marlowe's activities. In 1592 he was involved with a quarrel with one William Swaine over a gelding.[121] After the death of his brother-in-law, Thomas Arthur, in the following year, Marlowe was involved as defendant and plaintiff in a series of actions over bonds and other assets relating to Arthur's estate.[122] John Bedle brought a case against John Marlowe in 1594 for detention of goods which was apparently unresolved.[123] On 12 November 1595 the churchwardens and *parochiani* of St Mary Breadman parish complained of 'John Marley . . . for that he denieth to paye the clarkes wages as he himself hath always payd viz. vjd a quarter and is nowe behynd for three quarters of a yere at midsomer last past which commeth to xviijd'. Eventually he scraped together the money. Undaunted he even ventured into the market for bonds in 1599 dealing with John Archer, citizen and merchant tailor of London, who sold John Marlowe his bond of a debt owed by Jeremiah Country, the Canterbury innkeeper. Marlowe however burnt his fingers when Country failed to pay and he was successfully prosecuted by Archer.[124]

From the wealth of evidence it might seem that Christopher Marlowe's father was rowdy, quarrelsome, awkward, improvident, busy, self-assertive and too clever by half. None the less he served as inspector of leather, called a searcher, with Christofer Ashenden in 1581–2.[125] He was assistant in his company as well as warden and treasurer and probably also acted as beadle or secretary. Respected among his fellow tradesmen and craftsmen, though never prosperous, John Marlowe also held other minor offices in the community. In 1573 he seems to have been a sidesman for the parish church of St George, one of four *parochiani*, and in 1578 occupied the same post in his new parish of St Andrew.[126] Between 1591 and 1594, then living in St Mary Breadman parish, he held the more demanding office of churchwarden, serving successively with John Jemmett the tailor, John Samon the shoemaker and his neighbour Joseph Golfe the apothecary.[127] He was out of office by April 1595. Late in 1582 John Marlowe had attended the audit of his then ward of Newingate and at a city council meeting in November 1591 he was nominated to attend the audit on behalf of his ward of Westgate.[128] In 1591–2 he was chosen as constable of Westgate and would have been on duty when his son Christopher was involved in a breach of the peace there.[129] As constable he was himself in trouble in July 1592 for failing to ensure that the Westgate butts were properly maintained and was censured for not conducting a review of small arms in the ward.[130] Finally it should be recognized that for all his numerous appearances in court as a litigant John Marlowe also did frequent service as a juryman, perhaps especially busy in this way in the 1590s, occasionally serving with his friends Laurence Applegate and Thomas Plessington.[131]

However difficult a man he might have been, John Marlowe attracted loyal friendship. A special friend, Thomas Plessington the Canterbury baker, declared himself to have been born in Chester, though in various depositions he gave birthdates ranging from 1542 to 1552.[132] He had reached Canterbury by 1574 when he married Mary Elvyn, daughter of a saddler, who brought her husband the valuable dowry of the city's freedom.[133] By the early 1580s Thomas and Mary were living in St Margaret's parish, established in a baker's business on the corner of an alleyway almost opposite the church. Plessington seems to have been a more stable character than John Marlowe and, as a contributor to national taxation, was probably more prosperous, paying at the average rate of £3 while his friend seems never to have been liable for such payments.[134] Plessington too became a churchwarden and by 1593 was considered sufficiently well established to be asked to sign the return of Members of Parliament.[135]

John Marlowe's other close friend was Laurence Applegate, the Canterbury tailor, whose shop stood in the High Street some distance below St George's church, next to the Vernicle alehouse, which stood on the corner of Iron Bar Lane.[136] The defamation case of *Hurte v. Applegate* reveals Laurence and John setting forth on the

Dover Road one summer day in 1564 to go to Barham eight miles away, with Applegate boasting of his sexual prowess with Godelif Hurte.[137] Marlowe it seems had then known Applegate for four years, probably having become acquainted when he moved into St George's parish at about the time of his marriage with Katherine Arthur in 1561. Lora Atkinson, wife of Thomas the barber, described in her deposition a scene in the Vernicle which must have taken place before November 1565. The company in the public house consisted of Lora herself, Goodman Harmon (Harmon Verson, the German glazier), Goodman Shawe the basketmaker and his wife, and Goodman Marley and his wife. Though the lawsuit petered out inconclusively, Applegate was made to perform public penance. Laurence Applegate survived his friend John Marlowe by several years, but by 1609 his tailor's business had collapsed, the justices excusing him from payment of poor rate on account of his poverty.[138] On 4 January 1613 he was buried at St George's.[139] The two friends Laurence and John each had a son named Christopher and both sons had a tendency towards violence. Christopher Applegate (born 1572) channelled his energies into the military profession and was later named as lieutenant to the company of Captain Orrell, deceased. If Captain Orrell is George Orrell, identified among insurgents in the Essex rebellion of 1601, then he and Lieutenant Applegate probably had a mutual acquaintance in Christopher Marlowe, for Orrell was mixed up in the feuds leading to the death of William Bradley in Hog Lane in 1589 in which Marlowe was also involved.[140] When Christopher Applegate returned to live in Canterbury after forty years of military service he was known as Christopher Applegate, gentleman, or even esquire.[141]

The survival of two nominal rolls for the company of 200 men raised in 1588 under the title of the 'Selected and Enrolled Band' provides further evidence for the acquaintances of John Marlowe who served, as ever, as a private soldier.[142] At this time of crisis moreover a review of arms available in private hands showed John Marlowe's house to contain a bow, a skull or headpiece, a sword and a dagger as well as a brown bill or halberd.[143] John and his companions camped at Northbourne, building themselves cabins of sticks and leaves while the sound of gunnery came in from the sea. The only excitement for the Canterbury company was the seizure of a 'trayterous spye' named Field who was taken to the great camp at Tilbury across the Thames and then hanged.[144] At a muster in 1591, however, when deficiencies of equipment were noted, John Marlowe was noted to be without any equipment.[145] Perhaps during one of his periodic bouts of indigence he had sold his arms.

But if the experience of military crisis produced new kinds of relationship, more significant for the Marlowe family was the marriage of four daughters during the 1580s and 1590s. The marriage of Jane Marlowe in 1582 brought the Moores and the Marlowes closer together.[146] John Moore claimed to have been born about 1559 at Ulcombe in Kent and, at the age of fifteen, to have left for Faversham and then after seven years, perhaps of apprenticeship as a shoemaker, he came to settle in Canterbury in about 1580.[147] Marriage to Jane brought with it the freedom of Canterbury for her husband and their children, but because of her death in childbirth in 1583 there was some confusion over the status of John Moore and he was twice enrolled as a freeman in the city records: on 18 January 1583 he was called upon to pay the usual fee of 11½d. due from the husband of the freeborn daughter of a freeman, but a corporation minute of 31 August 1585 declared that John Moore should be admitted freeman, this time at the vastly greater fee of 40s., the actual admission taking place on 14 September following.[148] It would seem that the death of Jane tested the principle of the female conveyance of liberty to the limit. John Moore's second wife, curiously enough, was named Jane Moore and may well have been a bride drawn once more from his own family circle, though this time she was twenty-three years old when she married and about the same age as her husband.

The next of the Marlowe daughters to marry was Margaret, in 1590.[149] Her husband was John Jordan, a tailor currently servant with the Lord of Dover, Richard Rogers, Suffragan Bishop of Dover and Dean of Canterbury. On 21 April 1590 the Canterbury Burghmoot agreed that Jordan should become freeman by virtue of the freedom conveyed by his wife and on payment of a fine of 10s. They were married in June and John was admitted to the freedom in

2

August. The normal fine in such circumstances was of 11½d. and the reason for Jordan having to pay 10s. is not clear unless his allegiance to the Dean of Canterbury told against him.[150] If Jordan was active in his business, evidence of that activity has not survived in the Woollen-Drapers' and Tailors' Company account book. First mentioned in 1598, he is only noted as an absentee from the annual audit in that year.[151] In 1603, however, he was elected beadle of the company, the officer responsible for most of the administration, though he may have been hampered by an inability to write which lasted at least until 1616 when he came to serve as sidesman in his parish of St Mary Breadman, his mark of 'J Jo' being the nearest he ever came to a signature.[152]

John and Margaret produced a number of children, but the name of Jordan was locally very common and identification is difficult. John, Elizabeth and William occur in 1606 in the will of Katherine Marlowe, Margaret's mother.[153] A Mabel Jordan was baptized at St Margaret's, Canterbury, in 1601 and she may well be the woman of that name aged about thirty-three and described as of Elmstead who married a tailor of Wye in 1635, and whose father, John the tailor, stood as bondsman for the marriage licence.[154] Margaret Jordan, christened at St Margaret's, Canterbury, on 22 July 1604, may also have belonged to the family, but like Mabel she was not to be found in Katherine Marlowe's will.[155] After Katherine's death James Jordan was recorded as baptized at St Mary Breadman, Canterbury, on 13 December 1607, and Philemon Jordan was christened at All Saints' on 1 January 1612, probably taking his name from the Revd Philemon Pownall, rector there and one-time schoolfellow of Christopher Marlowe, the child's dead uncle.[156] John and Margaret, husband and wife, may have died within a year of each other, being buried in All Saints' in 1643 and 1642.[157]

Mention has already been made of Anne Marlowe's hurried marriage to the shoemaker John Cranford.[158] A little more than two weeks after the arrival of his daughter on 6 January 1594, John was formally admitted to the freedom of the city at the customary token fee of 11½d. for the husband of a freeborn daughter of a Canterbury freeman.[159] Giving testimony in 1598 and 1602, Cranford gave his age as thirty-eight and about forty years respectively, and his place of birth as Henley-on-Thames in Oxfordshire.[160] The parish register there shows him baptized on 13 January 1564, and he was probably related to one James Cranford, prominent in local affairs in the reign of Henry VIII.[161] When about twenty years old he went to live in Cambridge, arriving there in 1584 at a time when his future wife's brother was taking his degree of BA.[162] Leaving the university town he made his way south to Rye in Sussex, possibly appearing as a prisoner among Puritans in custody in London's Bridewell early in 1590.[163] He stayed in Rye for six months before moving to Ashford in Kent, and then after a year came on to Canterbury in 1592, married Anne in 1593 and settled in the city.[164]

Literate and able, John Cranford was nominated as sealer and examiner of leather in Canterbury in 1597–8 and also secured himself the ill-rewarded post of apparitor to the church courts with special responsibility for the deanery of Westbere, a windswept tract of ground some twenty miles long in north-east Kent.[165] On 26 June 1609 he was made one of the four serjeants-at-mace of the city of Canterbury and henceforth went around the town with one of the stubby silver maces which still survive, making arrests and serving writs.[166] His bond for good behaviour in office was countersigned by Valentine Everard, gentleman of Thanet, and by the illiterate Thomas Graddell, the innkeeper, landlord of the George and husband to Anne Cranford's sister Dorothy, who simply made his mark. Two years before he died in October 1615, Cranford added a final occupation to his varied list, acting as parish clerk of St Mary Breadman as his father-in-law John Marlowe had done before him.[167] Indeed there were other similarities between the two men. Like John Marlowe, Cranford was frequently to be found in civil and criminal courts in Canterbury. He took on all sorts of small jobs which might fall to anyone hanging about the courts, such as collecting petty debts, standing in as a witness or helping out executors with their duties.[168] John and Anne Cranford lived in a dwelling known as the Windmill, located on the western side of White Horse Lane in central Canterbury, and appear to have run their house as an alehouse.[169] Like other members of the Marlowe family group, the Cranfords were litigious and their quarrels were even extended to their own relations. On 6 November 1604, for example, John Cranford went to law with Thomas Graddell the innkeeper. The very same day Cranford began another action, this time naming Dorothy as co-defendant.[170] In conflicts over the estates of John and Katherine Marlowe, who both died in 1605, Cranford went for Graddell and Graddell went for Cranford while John and Margaret Jordan attacked the Cranfords.[171] Anne Cranford, mother to a dozen children, may have been particularly bad-tempered, sharing some of her brother Christopher's capacity for quarrelling and like him being a blasphemer. In an ecclesiastical Visitation of the City of Canterbury held in 1603, the church-wardens of St Mary Breadman presented Anne 'for a malicious contencious uncharitable person, seeking the uniust vexacion of her neighbours as the fame goeth in our saide parishe', and they went on to present her 'for a scowlde, comon swearer, a blasphemer of the name of god'.[172] Even after the death of her husband in 1615, at the age of fifty-five, she was to be found in conflict, involved in a skirmish with William Prowde in her own parish in 1626 armed with staff and dagger, and in May of the following year assaulted the same William with sword and knife.[173]

The Cranford children, born between 1594 and the 1620s, comprised eight girls and four boys. John, Anthony and Elizabeth were mentioned in Katherine Marlowe's will, Anthony having been baptized at St Margaret's, Canterbury, on 27 July 1595, Elizabeth being baptized at the same church on 30 March 1600, and John's baptism remaining untraced. Anne Cranford, the baby who occa-sioned the rushed marriage in 1593, is not mentioned in the will and may have died before it was made in 1605. Similarly Alice Cranford, baptized at St Margaret's on 8 January 1598, was not mentioned and may have died young.[174] The baptisms of Margaret, Elizabeth and Katherine Cranford have not been traced but they were probably born in the first decade of the seventeenth century. Collimore Cranford, who died in 1608, was baptized on 24 June 1606 at St Mary Breadman, probably taking his Christian name from Sir John Collimore who dwelt near by.[175] In 1611 Owen Cranford was baptized at St Mary Breadman and he died in 1638.[176] Rebecca Cranford was probably born in the 1620s and Sarah Cranford probably belongs to the family group though nothing has been traced of her origins. Margaret Cranford was to marry Richard Maple, the bricklayer, at All Saints' in 1622, Maple entering the freedom by right of his wife.[177] Katherine married John Anthony of London, a saddler, in 1628, when she was said to be twenty-one years old,[178] Rebecca married John Paine, the maltster, who in 1644 took out the city freedom by right of his wife,[179] and Elizabeth (II) married Thomas Smither who similarly acquired his freedom in 1633.[180]

If the widening of the family circle brought with it trouble and strife for the Marlowes, then it never led to more than in the case of Dorothy Marlowe's marriage to Thomas Graddell in 1594. Graddell, who was a glover by trade but was soon to change to become vintner, innkeeper and hackneyman, entered the freedom of Canterbury by right of his wife in the same year as his marriage.[181] Giving evidence later in 1605 he claimed that he had lived in Canterbury for twenty years and was now forty years of age. He had come from Preston in Lancashire, coming south to Canterbury in 1585 and marrying Dorothy when he was about twenty-nine, possibly having been married before.[182]

His marriage to Dorothy, however, got off to a bad start. In the summer of 1596 John Browne of Bishopsbourne, close to Canterbury, brought an action of defamation against Thomas Graddell, claiming that in February, March and April of 1565 he had uttered divers opprobious words in the presence of various people.[183] Graddell, he said, had asserted that Browne 'hathe lyen with his the said Thomas Graddelles wife, and hathe had carnall knowledge of her body' and of the body of another woman besides. Browne followed these charges with others. Graddell, he complained, continued to go round making his offensive remarks, adding now that Browne had lain with Dorothy 'seven times in one nyght' and that 'she was burnt by him', and that Browne said 'he knew who dyd cure her thereof'. After many delays the court declared against Graddell on 10 March 1596 and decreed an act of penance whereby Graddell was to acknowledge his fault before the minister and two others in St Mary Breadman church on a Sunday after Evensong. At first Graddell would not submit and was excommunicated.[184] In August 1596 he offered to undertake the penance and on

16 September a certificate of performance was returned into the church court. But legal fees of £3 6s. 8d. remained to be paid and before long, once more excommunicated, he was clapped into prison at the city's Westgate by the sheriff of Canterbury for failure to pay.[185] On 16 February 1597 he sought release from excommunication and undertook to pay the fees. His release, however, was celebrated by an abortive action launched by his wife on her own account in the church court claiming defamation of character against John Browne.[186] The case was dismissed on 6 April but legal fees ensued and the Graddells had to find another 9s. by the next court.[187]

Graddell was involved in a variety of court cases throughout these early years of his marriage, which was quarrelsome even by the standards of the Marlowe family, and until he died in 1625 he was seldom out of trouble of one kind or another.[188] On 27 January 1594, Nicholas Colbrand, landlord of the Lion next to the Guildhall, claimed that Graddell had accused him of stealing five of his pots.[189] In 1595, Joseph Buckley, husband of George Aunsell's daughter Ann, stationer and bookseller, brought an action asserting that Graddell had hired out and made sick and tired a gelding which he had left in the innkeeper's stables at a charge of 2s. per week.[190] Both he and his wife were accused, in 1595 and 1596, of not attending church in St Mary Breadman's and All Saints' parish to receive Holy Communion,[191] and in November of 1596 Dorothy was accused by a local woman, Parnella Watson, of having stolen her miscellaneous collection of cloth.[192]

By now established in the George, the great inn in All Saints' parish, Graddell's career becomes punctuated by cases involving his occupation. There were frequent scuffles. One night in 1610 burglars stole £5 10s.[193] Customers stole his towels and bedroom linen.[194] He did illicit deals in grain, he dabbled in bonds, and many times failed to renew his innkeeper's licence.[195] He often tried to dodge paying his debts. He was sued over the price of six dozen trenchers and in 1611 owed 50s. for twenty-five loads of fuel.[196] Just before Christmas in 1617 he took delivery of 'twoe Turkey cockes' from a poultry farmer at Herne, six miles away, but tried to evade the bill of 6s.[197] He was prepared to engage in black-market transactions as when he was in receipt of a stolen lamb from

Goodwife Blye the butcher's wife.[198] As late as 1623, his capacity for rough-handling undiminished, he was bound over to keep the peace in respect of one Richard Hibberd.[199] Gambling on the rumoured death of Sir Francis Drake, early in 1596, he later brought an action to recover his winnings.[200] Sometimes he would let his tongue run away with him and was abused in return, called 'a knave a cusnyng fellowe and lyved onely by cusnyng shyftyng and connye catching'.[201]

Dorothy Graddell was involved in her own struggles. She claimed in 1601 that a young blacksmith, Thomas Peeling, had entered the inn and violently assaulted her, Thomas Graddell giving chase.[202] In 1602 Dorothy had brought an action of defamation against Anthony Howe, formerly of Dover, where he had been known as a retailer of scandalous gossip.[203] Howe was now landlord of the Saracen's Head, opposite the George, near Stour Street, and was accused of blackening Dorothy's character.[204] A long-drawn-out lawsuit around 1608 in an action brought by a man called Bridges resulted in a mounting, unpaid bill for legal fees of £4 and consequent temporary excommunication.[205] And in 1610 Dorothy brought another case of defamation, this time against one Margery White.[206]

No longer well, Thomas Graddell made his will early in 1624 at the age of about sixty years.[207] In the ill-drafted and rambling document Dorothy, the 'loving wife', was to have an annuity of £3 a year. Two sons are referred to with one name of John. The elder, John (I), was assigned £57 to be paid within six months. The other, John (II), had a wife, Ann, who was to have her jointure made up from £15 to £20 per annum. Thomas's grandchild, Rebecca, daughter of John (II) and Ann, was to have all Graddell's silver plate, though Dorothy was to have the keeping of it until the one-year-old child should reach the age of sixteen. Moveable goods were to be divided between Dorothy and John (II?) and Dorothy was to be executrix. The will was witnessed by William Skinner, William Blogg, the successor to Anthony Howe as landlord of the Saracen's Head, and Philemon Pownall, parson of All Saints' and former schoolfellow of Christopher Marlowe.

Thomas Graddell did not die until 1625, his will being proved on

17 November. An inventory of the George was drawn up by Thomas Hudson, who had written Katherine Marlowe's will twenty years before.[208] He was aided by Dorothy's kinsman John Jordan, William Blogg the innkeeper and one Roland Dixon. They worked their way through the George noting the various chambers and their contents, the stock of sea-coal and £8-worth of liquor in the cellar. Administration, as might have been expected, proved troublesome and on 25 November Dorothy launched an action against John (I) Graddell.[209] The court pronounced for the authenticity of the will on 14 February 1626 and the last traces of the widow Dorothy are to be found on 26 December 1625 with suitors pressing their claims for her hand.[210]

With Moores, Jordans, Cranfords and Graddells, the rapid growth of a confused network of kin and connection brought little peace to John and Katherine Marlowe in the closing years of their lives. By 1603 they had made their last move within Canterbury and were living in All Saints' parish, perhaps in Best Lane, having left Powell's house in the parish of St Mary Breadman.[211] John Marlowe, now aged more than sixty years, may have begun to withdraw from the craft of shoemaking, being licensed in 1604 'to kepe comon victualing in his nowe dwelling howse'. He may also have taken on the office of parish clerk to St Mary Breadman at the same time, tolling the bells, writing out the banns of marriage, attending baptisms, marriages and burials, digging the graves, leading the responses, and keeping order among the juvenile portion of the congregation.[212] In the new year of 1605, however, John Marlowe was failing in health and on 25 January decided to make his will, calling in the experienced professional scribe, the Revd James Bissell, parson of St Mary Breadman and his close aquaintance. John's faithful friend, Thomas Plessington the baker, came as one witness and the other was the Revd Vincent Huffam. Huffam's presence is difficult to explain though he may have known Christopher Marlowe during his days in Cambridge and become a family friend.[213] He does however seem to have been temporarily resident in the neighbourhood and may have agreed, as a neighbour, to act as a witness.

John Marlowe's will was short and simple. He wished to be buried in the churchyard of St George's and he left his worldly goods, after the payment of debts and expenses, entirely to his wife who was to act as sole executrix. No longer able to make anything more than a blotched mark at the end of the document, he was happy to leave Katherine to manage his affairs. The cortege which carried him back to the parish where he had spent his early years in Canterbury made its way on 26 January, doubtless with a crowd of old friends and old contestants as well as the formal procession of the Shoemakers and Leatherworkers, perhaps carrying the company pall.

Within a month of John Marlowe's funeral a group of friends, including the ever-faithful Thomas Plessington, met together in the house in All Saints' parish to compile an inventory of his goods and chattels for purposes of probate. Assisting Plessington were Thomas Crispe (probably the tailor of that name) and Robert Lyon (with little doubt the blacksmith), making a good cross-section of tradesmen with a sound idea of prices.[214] They worked through the rooms in the small house and valued the contents at £21 14s. 2d., describing them in a list drawn up and dated on 21 February 1604. On the following day Katherine Marlowe and her daughters, Margaret Jordan, Anne Cranford and Dorothy Graddell, took will and inventory to St Margaret's church and the Archdeaconry Court to acquire probate.

The surviving inventory provides a precious word-picture of a household which must have been similar to that in which Christopher Marlowe grew up. Some of the items listed indeed may themselves have been familiar to him. It is tempting to imagine that the painted cloth, the most interesting item, though by this date thought to be worth no more than 1s., may have been present during Christopher's childhood. But the picture is above all a modest one. A 'little parlour', next to the street, contained a small table-top on its frame, with three joined stools, a 'court cupboard', a big cushion with five others and a carpet, probably used on the table rather than the floor. The main room downstairs was the hall where there was another little table with its frame, a chest, three chairs and a glass 'cage' (perhaps a kind of cabinet) with apparently nothing inside it; there was a collection of fire-irons, comprising tongs, brand-irons and a fire-shovel; and a pair of pot-hangers and the bellows. Katherine Marlowe's kitchen is plain to see, with spit, gridiron, skimmer, basting ladle, trivet, toasting iron and frying pan. She probably worked on the dressing board with the old cup left on it. She had a little table with a cupboard in it, and perched on a stool with a cushion, these last items shabby and old and worth only 2s. There was plenty of tableware: three basins, ten great platters, two small dishes, five pottingers, seven spoons, ten saucers, two pewter cups and two saltcellars. And finally there were two chamberpots. Upstairs the 'Great Chamber' contained the four-poster bed, the most valuable item of furniture in the house, worth 40s. with its bedclothes and fittings – perhaps the same bed in which Katherine bore her children. On its mat and rope net were a flock mattress, a blanket and a 'ruggle' with two bolsters, while around hung curtains from rods. In the same chamber were three chests and a press for their clothes. A cupboard contained some of Katherine's household treasures: eighteen pairs of sheets, some perhaps from Katherine Arthur's bottom drawer in 1561, four fine tableclothes and four coarse ones, a dozen fine napkins and a dozen coarse ones, four pairs of pillowslips and three pairs of coarse ones, and a dozen coarse handtowels. There was also another bed in the great chamber, a truckle bed and a bolster with a bag of feathers, worth only 2s., and a wicker chair. In another bedroom called the 'Little Chamber' there were blankets and rugs, pillows and cushions as well as John Marlowe's wearing apparel, valued at the respectable sum of 40s., and there were no less than four pairs of boots, said to be worth 20s. Out in the yard there were more odds and ends and especially three 'loads' of wood worth 15s., along with various items of 'old lumber'.

Notably the inventory discloses no silver standing cups or silver-rimmed stone pots such as existed in other Canterbury homes of the period, but there was a collection of ten spoons, six great and four others, as they reappear in Katherine's will.[215] There is, however, no mention of any cash. Only one book was listed and that was John Marlowe's Bible. Above all there are no shoemaker's tools. It would seem that John Marlowe had retired from business and had sold up 'St Hugh's bones', his last, his awls, his needles, his hammers, shears, paring knives and his stock of hides.

On Sunday 17 March 1605 Katherine Marlowe too lay dying. Still thinking of her noisy and improvident husband who had led her a wild dance, with ups and downs, unpaid bills, unpaid rent and long-standing debts, she asked to be buried in the churchyard of St George's 'neare where as my husbande John Marlowe was buryed'. Thomas Hudson wrote her will and the literate John Cranford was chosen as executor, Sarah Morrice and Mary Maye acting as witnesses. She was buried the following day though probate was not granted until 22 July. Her will was mostly concerned with bequests to her daughters, her maid Mary Maye and Goodwife Sarah Morrice, a poor woman already in receipt of charity. John Moore may have been a favourite with Katherine, receiving 40s. as well as 'the ioyne presse that standeth in the greate chamber where I lye'. One instruction in particular provokes the imagination: 'unto my daughter An Cranforde a golde ringe which my daughter Gradwell hath which I would have her to surrender up unto her sister An.' It would have been worth watching as the two termagants strove for possession. Dorothy Graddell was to receive the 'ringe with the double posye' instead, and Margaret Jordan, perhaps the most favoured daughter, was left the 'greatest gold ringe'. The silver spoons and the eighteen pairs of sheets, previously mentioned in John Marlowe's inventory, appear again, distributed among the daughters and their families. But there seems to have been a sheet missing, and she 'which hath the odde sheete may have the [fourth] table cloathe'. Perhaps the missing sheet had been designated as Katherine's own winding sheet. If so it may not have found its way to St George's as Katherine had hoped. John Marlowe's patient and long-suffering wife and widow, of whom so little is heard in the records which contain so much about her family, may not have had her final wish, for as her children were about to attack each other over the meagre remains of the Marlowe estate, it was in the register of All Saints' and not that of St George that was written 'Catheren Marlowe was buryed the xviij° daye of Marche'.[216]

CHAPTER THREE

From King's School to Cambridge

Christopher Marlowe became a scholar at the King's School, in the shadow of Canterbury Cathedral, at Christmas in 1578.[1] He was then aged fourteen years and ten months and probably already had some schooling behind him. His preliminary education may have taken place at one of the small privately run schools in Canterbury, perhaps even in his own parish of St George, where a schoolmaster can be traced in 1558 and again in 1586.[2] Possibly it was there that he was taught the secretary hand or perhaps, with many of his contemporaries, he was instructed in handwriting by some peripatetic scrivener. It seems likely that he spent a few years at a private school before coming to the King's School as a fee-paying pupil and then concluded his schooldays with no more than twenty-one months as a scholar.

How his fees would have been paid is a mystery, if it is assumed that his indigent father is unlikely to have found the necessary money. Charity or patronage may provide the answer, as it seems to have done for other local boys at this time – Christopher Pashley, the poor tailor's son, Samuel Bedle, the carpenter's son, Leonard Sweeting, son to the penniless rector's widow, not to mention other clergymen's children around the diocese. The intention of the cathedral statutes was clearly to provide scholars' places for poor boys: 'fifty poor boys, both destitute of the help of friends, and

42

For notes see p 162

endowed with minds apt for learning'.[3] From the start there was pressure from affluent families to put their sons in the places. This pressure was strongly resisted by Archbishop Cranmer and, at least in Marlowe's days, the rule seems to have been largely maintained, for many of his contemporaries were poor enough.[4] But how such poor children reached the standard necessary to enter the ranks of scholars remains problematic.

Founded by Henry VIII in 1541, the King's School as Marlowe knew it was located in the great range of cathedral priory buildings called the Almonry, flanking the Mint Yard in a corner of the cathedral precincts. Originally a vast chapel served by priests and almost a separate institution from the cathedral itself, it incorporated some domestic buildings. When it became the school, floors were inserted into the chapel to make classrooms, while the domestic buildings (at the west end and in the Mint Yard) became residences for the headmaster and the usher, or second master. The dean and chapter were responsible for the salaries and expenses, the headmaster being paid £20 and the usher £10 per annum plus accommodation. They supplemented their income by admitting fee-paying pupils, the commoners, over and above the fifty scholars whom they were bound to teach by the terms of the cathedral statutes. It appears that extra staff were employed to cope with the numbers of students, paid, and probably badly paid, out of the fees. Scholars and commoners might also be taken in as boarders by members of staff to provide a supplementary source of income.

In order to foster a communal spirit, the school shared a dining hall with lower and junior members of the cathedral foundation, with everyone except the senior canons, who had their own houses, eating together. During the reign of Elizabeth, however, the prevalence of clerical marriage led to the minor canons eating at home, leaving the dining hall to choristers, scholars and a few vergers. One near-contemporary kitchen account has survived to show the kind of food for which the boys had to pay from their allowances: neck or breast of mutton, peas and prunes, with fish every Friday and quantities of salt fish, red herring and white herring though Lent.[5]

Surviving cathedral accounts for 1578–9 and for 1580–1 indicate that scholars were provided with an allowance of £4 per annum, well above the amount which some families of poor workmen lived upon.[6] Christopher Marlowe received his first quarterly payment at Lady Day 1579 and received his £1 at Midsummer 1580 and at the following Michaelmas.[7] By the time the surviving accounts provide further evidence of payment in Michaelmas 1580, Marlowe had already left for Cambridge and his name is no longer recorded on the clerk's list.[8] For such an allowance, however, Christopher Marlowe and his contemporaries endured a long, hard day's work at school. Under the guidance of the usher they started in the morning at six o'clock and only left off thirteen hours later. The headmaster was allowed by the regulations to start an hour after the usher and entered the schoolroom at seven. Prayers were at six and were almost certainly conducted in Latin. The sleepy boys prayed for the queen and recited Psalm 21. Verses and responses followed, with the Lord's Prayer. Towards the end of the long day's work came Evening Prayer as the cathedral clock struck five and the boys stood up to recite the little psalm *Ecce nunc benedicte*. Then came more versicles and responses, with the lovely 'Collect for aid against all perils', *Illumina quaesumus*. Even after this the boys could not disperse. There was an interval until six o'clock during which a meal was probably served in hall, and between six and seven the boys had to recite their lessons to seniors who had become 'ripe in learning'. Masters were to be on duty. Finally, the dayboys left through the brick arch in the Mint Yard out into the city, while the boarders were bedded down between 'coarse sheets for boys'.[9]

Attendance at the cathedral services was an integral part of school life. It was not only required on Sundays but on saints' days and other festivals.[10] Repeatedly Christopher Marlowe must have found himself changing from the purple gown he wore in class into a surplice to go and troop with other scholars into the great church. Services must seriously have diminished lesson time, for the Church of England commemorates a large number of saints and confessors, and the boys might have been obliged to sit through services, often in conditions of severe cold, as many as eighty times in a year.

The influence of the King's School upon Marlowe's development is difficult to assess but the influence of schoolmaster and fellow schoolboys may have been important. Christopher Marlowe knew three schoolmasters during his career at the school and probably also knew some of the supernumary junior masters engaged privately by the headmaster. His first headmaster had been John Gresshop, MA, a man of scholarly attainments who had been a 'Student', or don, at Christ Church, Oxford. He had come to Canterbury in 1566 and died about the beginning of 1580 when Marlowe had been a scholar for one year.[11] Gresshop was succeeded by Nicholas Goldsborough, MA, chaplain of Corpus Christi College, Oxford, though originally from Cambridge, some time between March and Michaelmas 1580.[12] Throughout Marlowe's period at the King's School the usher was John Rose, MA, a former student at the school and a native of Canterbury. In 1562 Rose had gone to St John's College, Cambridge, but by 1572 had returned to Canterbury where he remained for about twenty years, finally settling at Bishopsbourne, close to the city, during the time that Richard Hooker was rector there.[13] In discussing the staff a word might be said of the school cook, one James Felle(s), a figure who might have loomed as large as the teachers themselves in the eyes of the schoolboys. Coming from Bolton in Lancashire, Felle now lived near the school in the area known as Staplegate. Acting also as part-time court attendant, gaoler and prisoners' escort, Felle seems to have been an unattractive character of questionable piety and disreputable acquaintances, charged in 1580 of stealing a ring from the purse of Esther Kemp, a woman of ill repute.[14]

But Christopher Marlowe seems to have been fortunate in growing up under the tutelage of scholarly men at the King's School. John Rose was a man who was interested in his school and profession. He had private means and, later, under the terms of a deed of gift dated 1618, he established four exhibitions at the universities for members of the King's School. Little is known of Nicholas Goldsborough's studious activities, though there is evidence that he borrowed the *Golden Epistles* of the Spanish bishop Antonio de Guevara from Minor Canon William Browne.[15] But the most learned among the masters was undoubtedly John Gresshop, who owned a remarkable library.[16]

Gresshop seems to have been unmarried at his death and evidently had no kinsfolk in Canterbury, for Henry Parvishe of Guildford and his wife Anne were named as his administrators. Since Henry and Anne Parvishe lived a long way from Canterbury, Canon John Hill of the cathedral acted on their behalf, and it was he who headed a group of members of the cathedral foundation which met on 23 February 1580 at the late headmaster's house to make an inventory of his goods. Canon Hill, Minor Canon William Browne and two lay clerks, John Marden and William Faunt, found little of note in the way of furniture, noting 'iij coarse sheets for boys' which may have been used for boarders. The list of Gresshop's clothing tells us what he looked like to his boys. There were two pairs of kersey hose, two old doublets, one of smooth fabric called 'rash' and the other of 'mockadew' (a cloth much worn by the middle classes). He had an old Spanish leather jerkin, a cap and a hat, with an old mockadew cassock. There were old cloaks and old gowns. There was a jacket of old damask probably surviving from younger days at Oxford, with a girdle of changeable silk. When the weather was cold he appeared in a round cloak with clasps worth 30s. Everything is 'old' apart from his best doublet of rash and best hose of the same, worth 13s. 4d.

The valuers made a round of other chambers noting feather-beds, blankets, pewter candlesticks, glass lanterns, pewter chamberpots and a washbasin on an iron hooped stand. Two of the bedrooms were styled 'Bul's chamber' and 'Darrell's chamber' – perhaps the rooms of supernumerary teachers employed by the headmaster and resident with him. Gresshop also possessed some plate, including a silver gilt pot worth 44s. 8d.; he had some spoons and trinkets among which was a silver whistle; and he had over £12 in ready money. He left, however, several unpaid debts mostly owed to Canterbury and other local tradesmen. Their size suggests that they were school debts accumulated in the course of running a boarding establishment on a private basis. On 6 July 1580 Canon Hill met fifteen of Gresshop's creditors at the probate court held in the cathedral nave under the north-west tower. William Potter the butcher recovered 24s. 8d.; Thomas Beane the linen-draper was paid 34s. 6d.; William Symes the apothecary received 27s. 6d. for goods supplied to the school; and John Aylesbury the bookbinder from the parish of St Dunstan's in Canterbury had a bill for only 6s. 8d. Two shoemakers put in claims: Thomas Durkyn recovered 36s. and John Marlowe wrote 'reserved by me Jon Marlowe' beside the sum of 16s. 4d.[17]

Perhaps the most remarkable aspect of Gresshop's inventory was what it reveals of his extensive library. The compilers at first contented themselves with noting the number of volumes. There was a window in the house flanked on the eastern side by a shelf bearing 114 books and on the other western side by two shelves, one above the other, the upper bearing twenty-eight books and the lower thirty-six. In the window embrasure there were likewise thirty-six. Now assisted by the usher, John Rose, and Mr Francis Aldrich, Canon Hill supervised the compilation of a detailed catalogue giving authors, titles and sizes. They began with a list of books 'in the upper study by the schoole door' and recorded the details of 217 volumes, probably the same volumes previously merely counted. The valuers then descended to a 'lower study' where they found a further collection of 125 volumes, making a total collection of more than 350 volumes. Christopher Marlowe's headmaster had a larger private library than almost anyone outside of the circles of bishops and noblemen, far greater than the private collections of university dons.[18]

The classics were strongly represented: Plato (in Latin), Cicero, Virgil, Theophrastus, Thucydides, Aristophanes (the Greek authors in that language, it may be supposed, unless otherwise stated). Plautus and Terence are there, and perhaps the boys acted their plays. Sophocles, Isocrates, Claudian, Juvenal, Caesar, Aulus Gellius and Boethius are all present. There was a mass of polemical Reformation literature including works of Luther, Bishop Fisher, 'Against Luther', Bucer, Melancthon, Beza and so forth. John Knox is evident in more than one item. And writers like Boccaccio, Petrarch, Laurentius Valla, Ficino and Vives, with of course More's *Utopia* and also the works of Palingenius. The headmaster had plenty of Bibles. He had a 'Latin Bible' (evidently Jerome's Vulgate), a Geneva Bible, a couple of Greek Testaments, another Latin Bible in the version of Sante Pagnino and yet another in the rendering of Sebastian Castallio. Medical works were represented

by Galen and Fabritius (with fearsome diagrams of surgeons'
instruments and engravings of dissections). Gresshop liked his
history books and had Languett's *Chronicle*, Fabian's *Chronicles*,
Ascham's *Discourse of the Affairs of Germany*, Solinus's *Polyhistoria*
and Munster's *Cosmographia*. As a schoolmaster Gresshop was also
interested in the professional literature of his calling. He had
Sadolet's *De Pueris Instituendis*, a volume called *De Ratione Studii
Puerilis*, Sebastian Castallio's *Dialogi* and the celebrated English
educational classic of the day, Roger Ascham's *Scholemaster* with its
advanced and humane theories of teaching methods. There were
also a whole group of school textbooks such as Aesop's *Fables*, and a
whole clutch of Nowel's *Catechisms*. Ovid's *Metamorphoses* 'with the
pictures' was, however, with its hundred or more woodcuts
depicting heady riots, incests, rapes, a book which might astonish
and shock and would probably have been kept well away from the
schoolroom door in the lower study. English poetry was also one of
Gresshop's interests. He possessed a copy of Chaucer, the *Tragicall
Discourses of the Lord Buckhurst*, 'A book of Songes and Sonnettes,
English'. Books which were later to influence Marlowe's own
writings were to be found among the headmaster's library, including Fenton's *Discourse of the Warres in France*, the *Fal of the Late
Arrian*, Lonicerus's *Historia Turcorum*, and Munster's previously
mentioned *Cosmographia*.

The influence of Gresshop upon Christopher Marlowe is impossible to determine but remains a tantalizing possibility. Had the
headmaster been prepared to allow his boys near his books then
Marlowe would not have been compelled to wait until his arrival at
Cambridge before having the chance to browse through a learned
library. The mere proximity of books to the schoolroom may, of
course, have acted as a stimulus to inquiring minds. Indeed,
Gresshop may have conveyed something of his books and his
interest in them to his pupils. Perhaps in one way or another
Gresshop and his library were crucial to Marlowe's development.

Christopher Marlowe's schoolfellows may be readily identified
and it is possible to trace something of their background and
subsequent careers. Of the eighty or so pupils who may have shared
the same school benches with him, many became Anglican clergy

(as Marlowe might have done) and were growing old in country parishes in the reigns of James I and Charles I. Some spent their lives as Kentish yeomen, some as country gentlemen and one appears to have become Justice of the Peace. Two became lawyers (one serving as town clerk of Canterbury). Three schoolfellows became schoolmasters and one a cathedral choirmaster. One boy became a village tailor.[19]

Samuel Kennett was one of the more remarkable boys at school with Marlowe. He was baptized at Selling in Kent on 8 June 1563, being the son of William Kennett of that place, described as servant of Henry VIII, Edward VI, Mary and Elizabeth. Samuel's mother was Sybil Raynolds who had property of her own, and his great-great-grandfather served as standard-bearer to Henry V at Agincourt.[20] Samuel became a scholar at or before Michaelmas 1578 and had left by Michaelmas 1580. Perhaps through his father's influence he was appointed as yeoman warder in the Tower of London at a time when Christopher Marlowe and others were going off to university. Kennett, 'a most terrible puritan', was given charge of Roman Catholic prisoners, one of whom, John Hart, a priest, succeeded in converting him, forcing Kennett to flee to the seminary at Rheims. He arrived at Rheims on 23 June 1582, and was described in the records as '*elegans juvenis*' and as 'late warden of inmates in the Tower'. On 13 August 1583 Samuel Kennett set out for Rome, arriving on 1 October. He was ordained priest at the Lateran on 27 May 1589 at a time when Marlowe was deep in theatre life in London and dabbling in atheism. Kennett was in Rheims again on 31 July 1591, having returned by way of Paris, and he was then sent on the mission to England under the alias of William Carter. By 1600 he was back in Rome and in 1603 this one-time classmate of Marlowe on the one hand and of Henry Jacob, father of English Congregationalism on the other, was professed a monk of the Order of St Benedict. In 1611 he was back in England, part of the English mission to the north, and on 23 January, perhaps in 1612, the Benedictine obituary records his death.

A quite different career was followed by Leonard Sweeting, a boy who probably knew Christopher Marlowe as well as or as long as any. He was the son of the rector of St George's, Canterbury, and was baptized there on 16 May 1563 about eight months before Christopher's birth. Leonard's father, a former tailor, had been promoted in Archbishop Parker's mass ordinations after the accession of Elizabeth. Following the death of the rector in 1575 Leonard's mother was left in desperate straits, the family at one stage living in the dark and cheerless casemates of St George's Gate. On leaving school Leonard Sweeting was apprenticed to Francis Aldrich, registrar of the church courts, and lived with him in his big house beside St Margaret's church, Canterbury. By the age of twenty-three Sweeting was admitted to the grade of Notary Public and masses of papers in the church court records survive in his excellent secretary hand. He married twice, firstly in 1590 to Ann Berry of St George's parish, and secondly to Ann Gaunt, daughter of Richard Gaunt, the leading local lawyer, on 19 June 1594. Like his old headmaster, Leonard Sweeting, in a small way, was a book collector. The list of his books drawn up in 1608 included Lambarde's *Justice of the Peace*, Rastall's *Abridgement* and the *Statutes at Large*, as might have been expected. But again, like his old schoolmaster, he enjoyed poetry and had a copy of *The Garden of Muses* and the *Mirror for Magistrates*; and, perhaps the most interesting among his poetry books, there is *Hero and Leander*.[21]

Henry Jacob was the son of John Jacob, a yeoman from near Folkestone in Kent, and was born in 1563.[22] He probably left school in the autumn of 1581, turning up at St Mary Hall, Oxford, where he matriculated in November of that year. For some time he was sufficiently conformist to serve as precentor of Corpus Christi College, Oxford. But he leaned towards the sect of Brownists and with them went into banishment in Holland. After his return and further troubles he went again to Holland where he made contact with John Robinson at Leyden (one of the group known eventually as the Pilgrim Fathers). Jacob adopted Robinson's views and, in time, became a Congregationalist, establishing what has been called the first Congregational church in England. Later he carried his views to Virginia, where he founded a settlement called Jacobophilis before returning to England and dying in London in 1624.

William Potter, son of a Canterbury butcher, pursued a more orthodox career. He was admitted scholar of Caius College,

3

Cambridge, when aged seventeen, in March 1580.[23] He was BA by 1584 and may be the William Potter admitted MA in 1607. He took orders in 1588, becoming curate of St Dunstan's-in-the-East, London. In later years he held several successive livings in Kent. He was dead by January 1620. His father was clearly the same Potter, the butcher, who made claims against Gresshop's estate for unpaid bills in 1580, and Christopher Marlowe probably knew William well before becoming his schoolfellow at the King's School, for Potter senior kept a butcher's stall in Iron Bar Lane quite close to John Marlowe's shop. Another local boy, Roper Blundell, son to the Revd Edward Blundell, vicar of St Dunstan's, Canterbury, was presumably named after the great man of the parish, William Roper, prothonotary of the Queen's Bench and husband of Margaret More, favourite child of Sir Thomas More. Roper Blundell had been a choirboy of Canterbury cathedral for many years before becoming a scholar of the King's School. He disappeared from the list of scholars at Christmas 1580 and at the same time reappeared as a *substitutus* in the choir, as one of the singers and instrumentalists standing between minor canons and lay clerks.[24] Blundell eventually left Canterbury but did not leave cathedral music, for within a short while he became choirmaster of Rochester Cathedral, returning to Canterbury in 1587 to marry a girl from St Alphege parish named Elizabeth Elam.

Philemon and Barnabas Pownall could have retailed stories of the English Reformation to their schoolfellows. Their father, Robert Pownall was born in Dorset in 1520 and, by the reign of Edward VI, was a married priest dwelling at Calais. On Mary's accession he fled to Switzerland and it was probably he who wrote the *Admonition of the Towne of Calais* (1557). He was prominent among exiles living at Aarau. On Mary's death in 1558 Robert Pownall joined the stream of returning refugees and settled for some while at Dover where his son Philemon was born in 1562. In 1561 he had become one of the 'Six Preachers' of Canterbury Cathedral and by 1563 he was a minor canon.[25] Israel Pownall, one of Robert's sons brought back from exile, became a scholar at Canterbury, went on to Christ Church, Oxford, and was MA by 1578. Nathaniel Pownall, similarly brought back from exile, also became a Canterbury scholar. Of Robert's four sons born back in England – Philemon, Abdias, Barnabas and Jonas – Philemon and Barnabas became scholars at the King's School and Jonas became a cathedral chorister. Robert was buried in the cathedral nave near his fellow exile, Bishop John Bale, and they were later to be joined by another former exile, Minor Canon Richard Beseley. Ample provision was made by the dean and chapter for Robert's wife down to her death in 1604. Barnabas has not been traced to a university but he took orders, becoming incumbent of Charlton next to Dover, and acquiring the living of West Hythe, Romney Marsh, which he resigned in 1629. Philemon was to become a non-graduate teacher in Canterbury and on 4 April 1583, when about twenty-one years old, he was granted a licence to teach boys in the city, perhaps in his mother's house in the cathedral precincts. Later he took orders and was admitted minor canon at the cathedral. In 1609 he became rector of All Saints', Canterbury, with the Graddells as rowdy parishioners, and in 1626 he was rector of St Margaret's, Canterbury, three years before his death.

A final example of Christopher Marlowe's contemporaries at school was one Benjamin Carrier, son of the Revd Anthony Carrier, vicar of Boughton Monchelsea, Kent, who had become a scholar at Canterbury by Michaelmas 1580.[26] In February 1582 he was admitted sizar, or student-servant, at Corpus Christi College, Cambridge, at a time when Marlowe was a member of the *convictus secundus* or middle grade, and would therefore have been waited on at table by Carrier. In due course Carrier took the degree of BD. He was Fellow of Corpus Christi from 1589 until 1602 while he occupied the living of Paddlesworth, Kent, for a short period (1598–9). He was vicar of Thurnham, Kent, from 1600–13 and was rector of the valuable sinecure of West Tarring, Sussex, in 1602. In 1603 he became chaplain to James I and was Fellow of the abortive college at Chelsea before becoming a cathedral canon at Canterbury in 1608. Later, under cover of visiting a spa for his health, he defected to Rome and died in France in 1614, having published works justifying his defection. Henry Oxinden, the Kentish gentleman who also set down notes about Marlowe, recorded that Carrier was but a shallow man.

Of the many young men who were to find their way from

Canterbury to Cambridge in the sixteenth century, a good number were to benefit from the generosity of Matthew Parker, Archbishop of Canterbury, which enabled many a poor man's son to be sent to Corpus Christi College.[27] As master of the institution then known as Bennet College, Parker and the college Fellows founded six scholarships in 1548 which provided 8d. each a week for commons and a small allowance 'for Landress and Barber, together with a Chamber and his Reading in Hall free'.[28] The allowance was subsequently increased to 10d. and then to 1s. per week to meet rises in the cost of living. In about 1565 Matthew Parker founded another scholarship, partly from his own funds and partly from those left by John Mere, once bedel and registrar to the university. In 1567 Parker established the three 'Norwich' scholarships for the benefit of his native city. The 'Canterbury' scholarships were founded in 1569, deriving their income from Westminster rents, youths being nominated by the dean and chapter of the cathedral from pupils attending the King's School in Canterbury. To supplement the income for these scholarships Parker transferred £6 13s. 4d. per annum from the revenues of Canterbury's Eastbridge Hospital to support two more scholars at Corpus Christi College, Cambridge. In all more than £40 per annum had been provided by Parker for the scholarships and, when he died in 1575, three more scholarships were founded by the terms of his will. The archbishop determined that a chamber of the college called the 'storehouse' should be prepared for these scholars who were to be brought from Canterbury in Kent and from Aylesham and Wymondham Schools in Norfolk. Each scholar was to have £3 6s. 8d. annually for his allowance and was to be a native of the community in which his school was to be found. After 1575, and at the time of Christopher Marlowe's appointment, John Parker, son and executor of the archbishop, retained control of nominations to places under the terms of the 1575 arrangements.

Exactly how Christopher Marlowe's application for a scholarship came to the attention of John Parker is unknown, but he succeeded one Christopher Pashley whose name first appears in the list of scholars at Canterbury in 1572 and who seems to have been about eight years older than Marlowe.[29] Pashley had been given financial support at Cambridge by the dean and chapter to the sum of 20s. in each of the years 1577–8 and 1578–9. He was probably the son of John Pashley, called both weaver and tailor, who at one time worked for Bathurst, a large-scale weaver established in the Canterbury Blackfriars. In old age John Pashley was admitted as a bedesman of Canterbury Cathedral, walking in processions bearing a white rod and dressed in a gown emblazoned on the shoulder with a Tudor rose. Christopher Pashley became BA within the year 1578–9 and stayed on in college, applying for admission to holy orders at the ordinations to be held on 21 December 1580. On 14 April 1581 he secured a mandate for his induction to the church of St Margaret at Cliffe near Dover. In 1582 he returned to Cambridge to take the degree of MA and in 1589 he moved to Linstead in Kent where, among reluctant parishioners, he knew the Catholic Ropers, still with their memories of Sir Thomas More and his circle. Pashley was to take up the post of 'Six Preacher' of Canterbury Cathedral, delivering sermons periodically either in the cathedral itself or in churches around the diocese, at the generous stipend of £20 per annum. He held other incumbencies and died in 1612 when aged about fifty-six.

The Cambridge of Marlowe's day was a community of over 1,800 teachers and students, set in a flourishing town of almost 5,000 men, women and children.[30] There was a wide variety of academic buildings, some descending from the Middle Ages, while building and rebuilding were going on. Christopher Marlowe's quarters were probably in the old quadrangle at Corpus Christi College. The living quarters of Parker's Norwich scholars were equipped with a small but useful collection of fundamental texts and reference books such as Greek and Latin Bibles, Erasmus's New Testament, a Latin Bible concordance, classical lexicons and *thesauri*, and, for slightly lighter reading, a history of Cambridge. No doubt Marlowe had access to these volumes. But there were other collections of books accessible in the college and outside, and Marlowe's extensive learning, displayed in his plays, shows that he ranged far beyond the demands of any officially necessary reading.

It is very difficult indeed to assess the way in which contemporary students passed their working time. Statutory regulations survive but seem to have borne little relation to reality.[31] To obtain the degree of BA students were to be in residence for sixteen terms or four years according to the statutes, though in practice this was reduced to little more than three years. In his first year at Cambridge a young man, or teenage boy, was supposed to hear lectures in rhetoric, while the second and third years were to be devoted to logic. Finally in the fourth year full time was given to the study of philosophy. The statutes prescribed that the lecturer in rhetoric was to read either the works of Quintilian, those of Hermogenes or the *Orationes* of Cicero. Furthermore, the lecturer in logic should explain Aristotle's dialectical works and Cicero's *Topics*, while the lecturer in philosophy should treat 'the problems, ethics, or politics of Aristotle, Pliny, or Plato'. Whether Marlowe or anyone else, however, went to lectures with any great regularity is a debatable point. This medieval method of instruction was going out of fashion. Christopher Marlowe's name was entered on a list of students due to attend lectures of Mr Johnes, professor of dialectic, but neglect of statutory lectures was a subject of complaint in that age. Much of Marlowe's learning must have been acquired at the hands of an individual tutor or from textbooks, side by side with maintaining an interest in theology, reading his Bible and attending chapel sermons. Drama performed in Cambridge would have provided another dimension of his education.

The Corpus Christi buttery books and college accounts provide more information about his finances than survives for his education.[32] Marlowe reached the college at some time early in December 1580. The meals laid on in hall had to be paid for and were accounted for week by week at the kitchen. The first entry for Christopher Marlowe records the expenditure of 1d. in the buttery book, perhaps made on Saturday 10 December. His expected income was only 12p. per week and can have barely met the demands upon him. At his entry the college gatekeeper exercised his right to demand a fee of 4d. due from each new arrival.[33] There was another fee of 4d. exacted when a young man was admitted scholar, and the college itself charged the substantial sum of 3s. 4d. for entry into the ranks of scholar. As with other new arrivals, Marlowe must have frequently been in contact with Mr Kett, the college steward, the same man later to meet a dreadful death at the stake in the castle ditch at Norwich in 1589 for heresy. 'Marlin', as the accounts call him, entered the second rank of the university and college community, the *convictus secundus*, above the poor sizars doing their menial jobs and below the Fellows and the Fellow-commoners whose families paid their fees and expenses. In March 1581 'Christoferus Marlen' was entered in the university register of matriculations, possibily a formal registration of an arrangement effected verbally at an earlier ceremony.[34]

Marlowe's expenditure in his second week amounted to the extravagant sum of 3s. 1½d. The buttery books and account books henceforth provide evidence of his income and outgoings and, thereby, about his presence in Cambridge.[35] He was paid 12s. for the spring quarter of 1581 and the same sum (or, as it happened in some quarters, 13s.) to the end of his undergraduate career just before Easter 1584, except for two quarters. One was the quarter ending at Michaelmas 1582, when a payment of only 7s. suggests that the young man had absented himself for five weeks in the previous three months, and the other was the quarter ending at Midsummer 1583, when he must have been absent for at least six weeks, to judge from the payment of half his allowance. After Marlowe's graduation in the spring of 1584, his regularity of attendance seems to have been broken. He seems to have been in full attendance in the quarters ending at Midsummer and Michaelmas of 1584, and may only have lost half of one week in the quarter ending at Christmas in the same year. In the autumn of 1584 he drew only 3s., indicating the absence of nine weeks, yet there are entries against his name in the buttery book in the second, third, fourth, seventh, eleventh and twelfth weeks. In the spring term of 1585 Marlowe draws 7s. allowance but the buttery book records entries in nine weeks. In the term ending at Midsummer in 1585 the allowance was only 4s., disclosing an absence of some eight weeks, roughly confirmed by a lack of entries in the buttery book from the fifth to the twelfth weeks inclusive. Before Michaelmas 1585 Marlowe was paid only 5s. for three months and the buttery book agrees, with a lack of entries from the fourth until the twelfth weeks inclusive.

The sole surviving evidence of the buttery book for the year beginning at Michaelmas 1585 indicates an absence of two weeks, and this is confirmed by evidence from the Canterbury archives which shows that Marlowe had gone home. On either 7 or 14 November 1585 Christopher Marlowe was in the house of the widow Katherine Benchkin in Canterbury, and read, according to his brother-in-law John Moore, 'plainely and distincktly' the new version of the widow's will.[36] Her husband James had been lay clerk in the choir of Canterbury Cathedral and had served the dean and chapter for many years as bedel, or general agent on their manor of Monkton in the Isle of Thanet where he collected rents and other dues.[37] In 1585 Katherine lived in St Mildred's parish in a house which stood near the southern end of Stour Street, adjacent to a blocked alleyway called Ballock Lane.[38] She had invited John Marlowe, his son Christopher, his son-in-law John Moore and Thomas Arthur (invited by Katherine's son John) to witness the will. Katherine went upstairs and brought back two wills, one of which 'she tooke . . . to Christofer Marlye to rede'. Once read Katherine made her mark, an ill-drawn cross. John Marlowe signed first, as 'Jhan Marley'; then Thomas Arthur; then 'Christofer Marley'; and finally John Moore. Why Christopher Marlowe was in Canterbury at this time is unknown. Perhaps he simply came to visit his family. He did, however, have a possible connection with Katherine's son John, who had entered Corpus Christi College as *convictus secundus* in the quarter running from St John Baptist 1585, apparently on or after 30 June and before 8 September, though Christopher and John do not appear to have left Cambridge at the same time to travel down together.[39]

Back in Cambridge, in the spring of 1586 there are three weeks without entries for Marlowe.[40] His attendance seems to have been slight in the quarter ending at Midsummer with entries in the last two weeks and only one entry before those. In the term ending at Michaelmas, surprisingly enough, Marlowe, who had appeared to be fading from the Cambridge scene, seems to have come back into full residence, as demonstrated in the buttery book for a few weeks following Michaelmas after which the volume gives out, not to be renewed until the eighteenth century. In his last year (from Michaelmas 1586) Marlowe seems to have put in most of a full term down to Christmas since he was assigned 9s., and in the spring he received 5s. 6d., seemingly indicating residence for nearly half a term.

Marlowe successfully passed the formidable series of tests for BA and submitted his formal application for the degree. His *supplicat*, backed by college tutor Thomas Harris, MA, Fellow of Corpus, stands in the university register.[41] Graduates were styled '*dominus*' and Marlowe's name appears with this title in the buttery book in the seventh week after Christmas 1583, having successfully undergone his examinations by the week ending 14 February 1584. He was probably not admitted formally and ceremonially to the degree of BA until Palm Sunday following.

The period during which Christopher Marlowe was an aspirant for the degree of MA is clouded by obscurity. As before, the college records disclose frequent absences. Marlowe may have become a confidential agent or messenger working for the government.[42] He was perhaps suspected of Catholicism as, in due course, he was suspected of atheism. There were clearly rumours that the absentee, atheistic, Catholic theatre-haunting post-graduate student had slipped overseas. The existence of Catholic seminaries at Douai and Rheims, filled with clever young Englishmen supposedly plotting treason, fostered such suspicions. Every so often some young man would defect and next be heard of across the water. Marlowe's own school produced a crop of such defectors.[43]

Marlowe submitted a formal application for admission to the degree of MA by March 1587, but the Cambridge authorities were unwilling to oblige him.[44] He then took the remarkable step of securing the intervention of the Privy Council on his behalf in this matter. Quite why he received the support of the Privy Council is unknown. What remains is the provocative and tantalizing passage in the Privy Council register which records that Christopher 'Morley' was reported to have a determination to go beyond the seas to Rheims. The council certified to Cambridge University (under date 29 June 1587) that he had behaved himself orderly and discreetly and had done Her Majesty good service. Christopher 'Morley', said the Lords of the Council, should be furthered in that degree which he was to take at the next commencement because 'it was not Her Majesty's pleasure that anyone employed as he had been in matters touching the benefit of his country should be defamed by those that are ignorant of the affairs he went about'. The Cambridge dons knew better than to gainsay the Privy Council, especially when they were quoting the views of the Queen. Moreover, the university chancellor was Burghley, himself a member of the Privy Council. So Christopher Marlowe was admitted to the degree of Master of Arts some time between July and Michaelmas 1587. The Cambridge Grace Book shows that within the year there were seven Corpus men admitted as Master of Arts.[45] Of these Thomas Lewgar, Christopher 'Marley', Edward Elwyn, John Burman and Abraham Tylman had been admitted BA at the 1584 graduations and the names of Lewgar and Marlowe stand still together in the graduation lists known as *Ordines Senioritatis*.[46] By the late summer of 1587 Christopher Marlowe, MA, has (as far as we can tell) forsaken his college and university for ever.

Friends and acquaintances at Cambridge may have proved as influential as any aspect of formal education. Thomas Lewgar who appeared as a Parker scholar at Corpus by Easter in 1580, may well have been a friend. On more than one occasion they were absent from Cambridge at the same time though it is difficult to draw conclusions from such evidence.[47] Lewgar's name stood in the same group with Marlowe's in the *Ordines Senioritatis* for 1583–4. He was MA by 1587, and was ordained priest of the diocese of Norwich, becoming vicar of Norton Subcorse and Raveningham, both in Norfolk, in 1590. In 1616 he was to be rector of Stokesby near Yarmouth. Another Corpus man, probably well known to Marlowe, was John Benchkin, who seems to have still been in Cambridge in 1592 though he did not take his degree, returning to Canterbury in 1594, calling himself gentleman and marrying locally.[48]

In 1581 one William Peeters, during Marlowe's absence, was granted Marlowe's food which was charged against him in his absence, but little is known of Peeters that can explain his connection with Marlowe.[49] Much more is known, however, about another contemporary, one Greenwood, who matriculated as sizar of Corpus in March 1578 and was admitted as BA within the year

1580–1.[50] At an early stage Greenwood read prayers in the house of the Puritan Lord Riche at Rochford in Essex, and in August 1582 he was ordained deacon in the Church of England (as one of the diocese of London) and priest (in the diocese of Lincoln). He held livings at Wyham, Lincolnshire (1582–3) and perhaps at Rackheath, Norfolk, but grew discontented with the church. In 1586 he was arrested for holding conventicles and he was thrown into the Clink prison. Released from the Clink, Greenwood was later rearrested and imprisoned along with Francis Johnson, a like-minded thinker, and later with John Penry, an author of Marprelate tracts.[51] While in prison Greenwood and Johnson wrote subversive books which were smuggled to Middleburg in Holland to be printed. From the association of Greenwood and Johnson have been traced the origins of English Congregationalism. Johnson was a Fellow of Peterhouse at Cambridge University while Marlowe was a scholar across the road at Corpus Christi College. Among other contemporaries Marlowe may well have known Thomas Nashe of St John's College, whose name was one day to appear with his on the title page of *Dido, Queene of Carthage*; and he surely saw in the streets Edmund Spenser's friend, Gabriel Harvey, who would abuse Marlowe sneeringly after his death in 1593.

In the earlier months of 1587 there had appeared at Corpus Christi College another youth from Kent, Thomas Fyneux. It was reported in country-house gossip half a century later that Christopher Marlowe converted this young man to atheism, and it is possible that the conversion took place in the few months in 1587 when Marlowe and Fyneux overlapped at Cambridge, Marlowe's views being already developed, though this is far from clear.[52] The episode was recorded by Henry Oxinden, a gentleman and minor man of letters living in Barham in Kent.[53] Oxinden, an early collector of plays with an interest in Marlowe's work, derived his information about Marlowe from Simon Aldrich, MA, Fellow of Trinity College, Cambridge.[54] Simon Aldrich probably gained his information about Marlowe from his father, Francis Aldrich, whose close acquaintance with Leonard Sweeting and the Marlowe household in Canterbury probably gave him special information, as did his association with Roger Raven, headmaster at the King's

X Harvey queried Marly's death in the Newe Letter

School.[55] Oxinden reported that Fyneux would go into a wood at midnight and pray heartily on his knees that the Devil would come to him and that he might see him, though he did not believe that there was a Devil.[56] He was a very good scholar and got all Marlowe by heart and other books too. Fyneux rejected his own disbelief and when he came to take his degree he made a speech on the text 'The fool hath said in his heart, there is no God'. Fyneux would say, as Galen said, that man was of a more excellent composition than a beast and could speak, but he affirmed that his soul died with his body and, as we remember nothing before we were born, so shall we remember nothing after we are dead.

One last young man whose appearance Christopher Marlowe certainly knew was the twenty-one-year-old character who sat in 1585 for his portrait, clad in a splendid jacket, slashed and gilt-buttoned. The portrait was found at Corpus Christi College in 1953.[57] There is no known portrait of Marlowe and this new-found painting was readily seized upon and has now for many years passed as that of Christopher Marlowe. The dates agree with his and the motto on the portrait seems made for him – '*Quod me nutrit me destruit*'. A splendid young man, born in 1564, has been destroyed by that which sustained him. But there were other young men in Cambridge of those years at that moment and the gilded youth who stares from the portrait does not look like a hard-up shoemaker's son, still (nominally) an aspirant for holy orders.

CHAPTER FOUR

London and beyond

The first evidence of Marlowe's residence in London comes from his involvement in an affray in 1589.[1] In the early afternoon of Thursday 18 September he was set upon by William Bradley in Hog Lane on the way up from Moorgate to the theatre district. Bradley, the son of William Bradley, landlord of the Bishop inn at the corner of Gray's Inn Road and Holborn, had been involved earlier in a quarrel with Marlowe's friend Thomas Watson over a debt of £14 owed by Bradley to John Allen, innkeeper, and possibly brother of the actor Edward Alleyn. Bradley may have recognized Marlowe as Watson's acquaintance and attacked him for that reason. Shouts were raised by onlookers and Thomas Watson appeared on the scene, appeals being made to him to separate the combatants. Bradley turned upon Watson with the words 'Arte thou now come? Then I will have a boute with thee.' Bradley then wounded Watson slightly with his sword and his dagger, forcing him back to the brink of one of the water-filled ditches bordering the lane. Watson lunged at Bradley to defend himself and ran his blade into the right side of Bradley's chest. The wound was fatal.

Marlowe and Watson submitted to arrest and were detained until the arrival of Sir Owen Hopton, Lieutenant of the Tower of London, acting as Justice of the Peace. Both were committed to the gloomy recesses of Newgate prison under the conduct of the

For notes see p. 167

constable, Stephen Wyld the tailor. Watson is described as 'gentleman' and Marlowe as 'yeoman', both being residents of Norton Folgate.

The liberty of the City of London extended up Bishopsgate, beyond the hospital known as 'Bedlam', for the reception of mentally deranged people, for a few hundred yards before giving way to the district known as Norton Folgate or Shoreditch, exempt from control by the city corporation and belonging to St Paul's Cathedral.[2] A dramatic industry had grown up, centred on the yards of great inns such as the Red Lion in Stepney, the Bull in Bishopsgate Street, the Bell and the Cross Keys in Gracechurch Street and the Belle Savage near Ludgate. Out beyond the liberty Norton Folgate was an attractive place of residence for players and others frowned upon by the city government. Bounded on its south by Hog Lane, there was in this area a tract of ground called 'the Curtain', signifying an enclosure. This ground was delimited to the north by another alley known as Holywell Lane which took its name from the ancient dissolved nunnery of Holywell to which it served as a southern boundary. The Curtain field and the Holywell precinct were far outside the jurisdiction of the London authority and here James Burbage, actor, organizer and joiner by trade was safe in setting to work his carpenters in 1576 to build the first theatre exclusively for dramatic presentations to be erected since Roman times.[3]

Marlowe's companion in confinement was a man of considerable reputation.[4] His Latin and English verses earned him distinction and it was William Shakespeare who was known as 'Watson's heir'. He was born in 1557, studied abroad and visited Paris where he knew the then ambassador, Sir Francis Walsingham. He studied also at Douai and probably went to Italy and read civil law. Back in England he chose a literary rather than a legal career, and in 1582 produced his *Hekatompathia or Passionate Centurie of Love*, his most important work, embodying eighteen-line English poems called 'sonnets'. He maintained his neo-classical studies and in 1586 translated out of Greek into Latin Colothus's *Rape of Helen*, reputedly transposed out of Latin into English by Christopher Marlowe in a version now lost. Watson's interests included music

4

and he counted among his friends leading composers like William Byrd, who supplied airs to Watson's madrigals. When Watson's *Amintae Gaudia* was eventually published in 1592, some time after the poet's death in 1592, its flowery dedication to the Countess of Pembroke, goddess of literary men – 'Sidney's sister, Pembroke's mother', is signed 'C.M.', in all probability Christopher Marlowe.

Incarcerated on 18 September 1589, Marlowe and Watson faced inquest before the Middlesex coroner Ivo Chalkhill, gentleman, on the following day. The narrative of events was recited and a verdict of self-defence was set down.[5] However, the prisoners could not yet go free. Marlowe may have spent his time listening attentively to John Poole, a long-term prisoner accused of coining. Marlowe collected from him information on the skill of mixing metals which he was later so effectively to employ. On 1 October Marlowe and Watson were brought before William Fleetwood, esquire, Recorder of London at the Old Bailey, adjacent to Newgate, himself a collector of early dramatic quartos. Watson was sent back to prison but Marlowe was released on bail, two sureties for his subsequent appearance having been found, each standing under bond for £20 – Richard Kitchen, gentleman, and Humphrey Rowland. Kitchen was a lawyer from Yorkshire, then at Clifford's inn, and Rowland was a horner of East Smithfield. There is nothing to show why they were prepared to stand for Marlowe.

At Newgate Sessions on 3 November 1589 Marlowe surrendered to bail and presented himself before a formidable and crowded bench comprising William Fleetwood the Recorder, with the Master of the Rolls, the Lord Mayor, a couple of aldermen and some Middlesex justices.[6] Not least upon the bench was Sir Roger Manwood, Chief Baron of the Exchequer, well known to Marlowe and possibly his former benefactor.[7] At all events Marlowe was finally set at liberty though Watson did not emerge from Newgate until the following February.

✗ By May 1592, however, 'kind Kit Marlowe' was again in trouble.[8] On 9 May Allen Nichols and Nicholas Helliott, constable and beadle of the Holywell area, presented themselves before Sir Owen Hopton, Knight and JP. The two officers brought into court one Christopher 'Marle' of London, 'gentleman'. Doubtless recalling

✗ "kind Kit Marloe," in the M.S.

the Hog Lane episode, Hopton obliged the constables by binding over Marlowe ('Marle') in the sum of £20 to be raised in case of trouble 'from his goods, chattels, lands and tenements', following the normal legal formula and not implying that Marlowe necessarily held any property. Marlowe was also to appear at the next general Session of the Peace for the County of Middlesex, to be held in the first week after Michaelmas of 1592. But he failed to appear at Finsbury Court. At that very time he was indeed entangled with the law yet again far away in Canterbury.[9]

On Friday 15 September 1592 Marlowe came to grips with one William Corkine, somewhere close to the corner of Mercery Lane and possibly in the great inn known as the Chequers where the city aldermen would often sit in the galleries watching dramatic entertainments in the yard below.[10] Here, just below the central crossroads of Canterbury, Christopher Marlowe was affirmed to have attacked Corkine with a stick and dagger.

William Corkine was a tailor of musical accomplishments who daily left his stitching to sing in the cathedral choir.[11] Excused in 1585 from making a contribution of ½d. per week towards the support of the poor, this indigent tailor lived in the Northgate area around 1586, a married man whose child John died within a few days of his baptism on 13 February in that year.[12] By 1589 he had managed to accumulate the substantial fee of 40s. to enable him to be admitted to the freedom of the city but not until 1595 is record of him made in the company records of the Woollen-Drapers and Tailors, when the unusually heavy entry fine of 40s. for admission to the freedom of the company is noted as due. Only in the 1590s does he appear to have gained any prominence, and then in 1595 he was nominated as one of the citizen auditors and had moved out of Northgate into the central parish of St Andrew, his daughter Elizabeth being baptized there in that year. At the same time he seems to have taken up the trade of innkeeping, by 1597 at least supplying provisions from the Mitre, a tavern close to St Mary Breadman church, opposite the Chequers. Curiously, another William Corkine, possibly the tailor's son, who appears as a choirboy in the cathedral lists, also had a connection with Christopher Marlowe.[13] It was William Corkine (II) who first published the air to Marlowe's poem 'Come live with me and be my love' in 1612.[14]

William Corkine senior soon filed a suit for assault, selecting as his attorney the unpleasant Giles Winston. The case survives entered in the plea book of Town Serjeant James Nower:

City of Canterbury	William Corkyn sues Christopher Marlowe, gentleman, on plea of transgression. And pledges to prosecute viz. John Doo and Richard Roo. And the plaintiff by Giles Winston his attorney makes plaint that the said defendant on the fifteenth [this figure has been inserted in a space left originally blank] day of September, in the thirty-fourth year of the reign of Our Lady Elizabeth by the Grace of God, of England, France and Ireland, Queen, Defender of the Faith here in the City of Canterbury aforesaid, in the Parish of St Andrew, and in the Ward of Westgate of the aforesaid city, did by force of arms [vi et armis], viz., with staff and dagger, make an assault upon the aforesaid plaintiff, and against the Peace of the said Lady the Queen. Wherefore the said plaintiff says he has suffered loss, and has incurred damages to the extent of £5, and hence produces his suit.[15]

In a state of open arrest Marlowe had to find surety for his appearance in court. His father came forward and paid the 12d. exacted by the court for the mainprise which was probably effected in court on 25 September. Unusually, Christopher Marlowe does not seem to have proceeded to submit any counterplea proving his innocence and laying the blame on his opponent. Instead he and his attorney, John Smith, chose a different course of action. The autumn quarter sessions were now imminent. The court met on the very next day, Tuesday 26 September. John Smith now prepared an indictment for the quarter sessions:

City of Canterbury	The Grand Jury present for Our Lady the Queen that William Corkyn of the City of Canterbury 'taylor', on the tenth [sic] day of September in the thirty-

fourth year of Our Lady Elizabeth by the Grace of God, of England, France, and Ireland, Defender of the Faith, here in the City of Canterbury aforesaid, in the parish of St Andrew and in the Ward of Westgate in the aforesaid city, did make an assault upon a certain Christopher Marlowe, gentleman, and the same Christopher Marlowe did there and then beat, wound and maltreat, and other atrocities [enormia] did there and then inflict upon the said Christopher Marlowe, to the grave damage of the aforesaid Christopher and against the Peace of Our present Lady the Queen, etc.

In the absence of the mayor, Alderman Richard Gaunt, JP, acted as Chairman of Sessions, and also present would be the town clerk and Clerk of the Peace, Robert Railton, son of Alderman Richard Railton, JP. Gaunt was himself a lawyer and brother-in-law of Marlowe's attorney. Railton was related by marriage to both Gaunt and John Smith.

The tables were now turned. William Corkine, who had launched a civil case against Christopher Marlowe for assault, now found himself up in court on a charge of attacking his adversary. Despite the apparent difference in the dates of the two incidents reported it would seem that they refer to the same episode. The Grand Jury, assembled on 26 September, soon made up their minds as to the alleged assault upon Marlowe. They threw out the indictment and the clerk slashed the parchment with his penknife in the customary way. William Corkine was free to leave the court.

The civil case *Corkine v. Marlowe* came up on 2 October, the following Monday, and Winston submitted his narrative of Marlowe's assault upon Corkine. With the defendant given leave to answer the charge the case was adjourned until Monday 9 October. By now tempers had cooled and by mutual assent the case was dropped. Christopher Marlowe's dismissal from court on 9 October 1592 marks his last recorded appearance at Canterbury and indeed is the last precisely dated evidence for his whereabouts until his arrest and death the following May. Town Serjeant Nower started a new plea book on 28 September, still entering matter concerned with last year's cases. Shortly after Marlowe quitted the court, close to entries for cases heard in court on 12 October, a rosebud was dropped into the new plea book where it was recently found, its shape pressed into the pages.[16] This bud, a strange irrelevance among all this legalism, was about to blossom into a late rose of the summer of 1592. When the next year's roses were beginning Christopher Marlowe lay dead at the other end of Kent.

At the same time that Marlowe was involved in the brawl with Corkine, the notorious Robert Poley was in or close to Canterbury. It seems an improbable coincidence that two men connected with the world of secret service should have been in the same place at the same time unless their visits were connected and that they knew each other; all the more so since a third man, also associated with undercover work, Paul Ive the engineer, was also around, supervising work on the Canterbury canal scheme.[17]

All through the 1580s and 1590s Poley comes and goes, dimly seen but constantly sensed, like an evil spirit. He forges letters, dabbles in ciphers, intercepts correspondence, snaps up fees and bribes. He was the very genius of the Elizabethan underworld, as much the outstanding man of his own chosen sphere of activity as any of the dramatists, poets or men of action in that age. For some time he had worked for the government. Wherever he goes there is an evil odour of fraud, crime and double dealing. Utterly deceiving Anthony Babington, he was a principal agent in sending that youth to the scaffold, enabling the government to strike on 2 August 1586 just as the conspirators were about to assemble for supper in Poley's garden. Despite his assistance, Poley was imprisoned in the Tower of London, only securing release through his influence with Sir Francis Walsingham. Often employed as a special messenger, he went off to Scotland, the Low Countries and to France. One such journey was undertaken in 1592, payment being made

To Robert Poley upon a warrant signed by Mr Vicechamberlain dated at the Court of Oxford 25th September 1592 for his charges and pains in carrying of letters of post concerning Her Highness' special affairs from the Court at 'Swedley' [Sudeley, Gloucester-

shire] Castle to Dover and for his return with like letters of answer
to the Court at Oxford the 24th September 1592.

The court had moved to Sudeley by 10 September but moved on to
Sherborne in Dorset by 14 September. Poley therefore left the court
within a day or two of 12 September to go to Dover and was back at
court, now established at Oxford, by 23 September. Now if Poley
went to Dover he must have passed twice through Canterbury
somewhere around the middle of the month of September in 1592,
and probably stayed there one or two nights, a day or two at the
most from the moment we find Christopher Marlowe fighting
William Corkine.

Whether Marlowe was still living in Norton Folgate in 1592 is
unknown, but around 1591 he seems to have been sharing a room
for writing purposes with the scrivener–turned–dramatist Thomas
Kyd.[18] If Kyd is to be believed, it was at this time that their papers
became mixed together in a way which was to have disastrous
consequences for Kyd. Born in 1557, Kyd was some six years older
than Marlowe, but by 1592, when his room-mate had put several
successes on to the stage, Kyd seems only to have brought out his
Spanish Tragedy. By this time Marlowe's mind was already turning
into dangerous channels. He cannot have presented a flagrantly
unorthodox figure before 1587 for he retained his scholar's place at
Cambridge, and hesitations about giving him his MA degree do not
seem to have been based upon misgivings regarding his religious
orthodoxy. His conversion of the young undergraduate Thomas
Fyneux to atheism is none the less suggestive. By 1588 there is the
further suggestion of atheism in the epistle to Robert Greene's
Perimedes the Blacke-Smith, published in that year: 'I could not', says
Greene, 'make my verses iet upon the stage in tragicall buskins . . .
daring God out of heaven with that Atheist Tamburlan'; and he goes
on to talk of 'mad and scoffing poets that have propheticall spirits as
bred of Merlin's race'. The final phrase is an unmistakable play upon
Marlowe's name.[19]

Commenting upon severe edicts directed against the Catholics,
Father Parsons speaks of a popular school of atheism ('*schola frequens
de atheismo*') of Sir Walter Ralegh, frequented by 'no small crowds of

noble youth', and if there was no compact group, freethinking was certainly current among the scholars associated with him.[20] A certain 'necromantic astronomer', whom Parsons referred to as a tutor in this school, may be identified with the brilliant mathematician Thomas Harriot, and Walter Warner and Robert Hues, two other outstanding mathematicians, were also members of this doubting circle.[21] The poets George Chapman and Matthew Royden were also involved, and both of them were known to Marlowe. Chapman discloses his relationship in the dedication to his continuation of Marlowe's *Hero and Leander*, and Thomas Kyd spoke of Royden and Marlowe in terms which suggest acquaintanceship.

Harriot's mathematical inquiries extended over astronomy, navigation, ballistics, optics and, in fact, into almost every quarter of the sciences. It was he who went as scientific observer on a voyage to the New World financed by Ralegh, and by 1609 he was scanning the heavens with his telescope – the earliest known map of the moon was drawn by him. John Aubrey in his *Brief Lives* remarked upon Harriot that he valued not the story of the creation of the world: '. . . he would say *ex nihilo nihil fit*' and made 'a philosophical theology wherein he cast off the Old Testament and then the New One would consequently have no foundation'. He was a deist.[22]

Rumours of atheistic activities among members of this circle were substantial enough to prompt an inquiry in 1594 at Cerne Abbas close to Ralegh's house at Sherborne.[23] Loose speech and irreligious remarks there certainly were, ranging from blasphemous ejaculations to discussions on the nature of the soul. But no official action was taken. Ralegh was far from being an out-and-out disbeliever. He stood apart as a man with the political power to make a stand against persecution and an inclination to do so. It was he who secured a reprieve for the Puritan John Udall even though that unfortunate died in the Tower of London as a result of ill-treatment. Ralegh held out against the Bill proposing to put to death the whole sect of Brownists. He was the enlightened and generous patron of Giordano Bruno during that freethinker's sojourn in this country from 1583 to 1585.

Ralegh's friendship in the later 1580s with the young Earl of

Northumberland, Henry Percy, the ninth earl, brought Ralegh's clients into the circle of the young earl's patronage.[24] Securing a lease from the Crown on the former nunnery of Syon at Isleworth, the ninth earl established himself here in the south, close to London and the court. By 1591 Harriot was living as a member of his household and from 1593 was probably in receipt of a pension. A building at Isleworth was long known as Mr Harriot's lodging, and Warner and Hues were also taken up by Northumberland, who called the three his *'tres magi'*. Through his patronage of scientists and his own interests in scientific subjects, Percy acquired the name of 'the Wizard Earl'.

Still friendly with Ralegh, Harriot was named as a beneficiary in Ralegh's will in 1597 and was probably among those present at Ralegh's execution on 29 October 1618, a note among Harriot's papers being apparently a record, taken down at the time, of Ralegh's departing speech. Ralegh's name is linked in legend with the introduction of tobacco into England, and the Northumberland–Ralegh circle certainly used it, Harriot being credited with the actual first introduction and reports on its usage by the Indians, and the earl himself moving about enveloped in clouds of smoke. In two notorious remarks Marlowe also mentions the weed. Known to Harriot and certainly to Ralegh, Marlowe would also be likely to be known to Northumberland. A letter from Sir Robert Sidney to Lord Burghley written on 26 January 1592 indicates that Marlowe was prepared indeed to claim acquaintance of the earl.[25]

In return for financial aid to the Dutch in their struggle against Spain in the 1580s and 1590s, Queen Elizabeth had demanded pledges in the form of 'cautionary towns'. One of these towns was Flushing in the Isle of Walcheren, and it was as governor of Flushing that Sidney wrote to Burghley. He said that he had three prisoners who were returning to England in the charge of an ancient. One was called Evan Flud or Lloyd, possibly the nephew of Lord Lumley who had served traitorously in Sir William Stanley's regiment against the Anglo-Dutch forces before Nijmegen in the summer of 1591. The other two were a goldsmith named Gifford Gilbert and a scholar named Christopher 'Marly', both of whom had been taken at Flushing for coining and were being sent over with their

71

incriminating false money. Gilbert and 'Marly' had been accused by 'one Richard Baines', their chamber-fellow. Examined separately, both 'Marly' and the goldsmith did not deny the charges but protested that they did it only to see the goldsmith's cunning, and Sidney generously conceded that whatever the intent of the other two the 'poor man', as he thought, had been brought in only for that purpose. 'Marly' and Baines accused each other, said Sidney, of being inducers of the goldsmith and of intending later to practise counterfeiting. They had, however, produced only one Dutch shilling and were unlikely to have put many into circulation, for the metal was only plain pewter and might have been discovered at a glance. 'Marly' claimed to be well known both to the Earl of Northumberland and to Lord Strange. He and Baines accused one another of intending to go over to the enemy or to Rome. Since some of the false coin manufactured was Her Majesty's, Sidney decided that the best way to deal with the difficult case was to send them to be dealt with in England.

The Christopher 'Marly' in question, with the acquaintance of Strange and Northumberland and appearing in the proximity of Richard Baines, can only point to Christopher Marlowe, the poet and dramatist. Baines was soon to be once more closely associated with Marlowe.[26] The connection with Lord Strange lends support to suggestions about their involvement. It has been suggested that the 'Lord' who fell out with Marlowe over his atheistic tendencies was the Catholic Lord Strange, patron of the company which put Marlowe's works on the stage, and 'Marly's' claim perhaps gives weight to this argument though Northumberland now must be added to the shortlist.

The outcome of Marlowe's arrest and transfer, however, though it was noted that they had been 'taken for coynage, to be tryed here for that fact', was that Marlowe seems to have completely escaped trouble in the early months of 1592. Nothing seems to have come of the charges levelled by Baines and Marlowe of intent to go to the enemy or to Rome. Marlowe may have had a sneaking regard for Catholicism: in 1586, when he was taking his MA degree, he was under suspicion of going beyond the seas. Baines actually went to Rheims. But by May of the same year Marlowe was free to torment the local police of Shoreditch. Perhaps by now, however, he was a marked man.

In addition to Lord Strange, Ralegh and the Earl of Northumberland, Marlowe seems to have enjoyed the friendship of Mr Thomas Walsingham of Scadbury in Chislehurst, seven miles from Greenwich.[27] He was the grandson of Sir Edmund Walsingham, Lieutenant of the Tower, and one who had profited from the sale of monastic lands under Henry VIII. Sir Edmund's nephew was Sir Francis Walsingham, Principal Secretary of Queen Elizabeth. Thomas was probably born in 1568 and was consequently about four years younger than his friend Christopher Marlowe. He was probably still a bachelor and was not yet a knight when Marlowe was frequenting his house at Scadbury. His marriage to Audrey Shelton, a Lady of the Bedchamber to Queen Elizabeth, seems to have taken place some years after Marlowe's death. The relationship between Marlowe and Thomas Walsingham senior is tantalizing. That it was more than the casual contact between a patron who gave a donation in exchange for a dedication of some occasional verses published or unpublished is made clear in the address to Walsingham prefixed by Edward Blunt, the publisher, to the extended version of *Hero and Leander*: 'in his lifetime you bestowed many kind favours entertaining the parts of reckoning and worth which you found in him with good countenance and liberal affection'.

1596

When the Privy Council decided in May 1593 to summon Marlowe before them they instructed their agent, Mr Henry Maunder, to go and seek him in the first instance at the house of Mr Thomas Walsingham in Kent.[28] Perhaps after this summons Scadbury was not quite so ready to open its doors to Christopher Marlowe. Twelve days after the summons we shall find him at Deptford, in sight of Greenwich Palace and only five miles from Scadbury.

A picture can be assembled from chance remarks by men who knew Marlowe of a young man with an unbridled tongue looking for every occasion to lash out at religion, not only by jeering in bibulous table-talk but by reasoned exposition of the weaknesses of religion as publicly and traditionally presented. If Marlowe had a god it was probably the being described in *Tamburlaine*:

. . . He that sits on high and never sleeps,
Nor in one place is circumscriptable,
But everywhere fills every continent
With strange infusion of his sacred vigour . . .

Reformers thought they had come a long distance, but to a man like Marlowe they had hardly moved away from the superstitions of the medieval church. Indeed they had no more than shed the outward, liturgical attractions of religion for which Marlowe admitted a sneaking regard.

Institutional religion was in any case fair game. Marlowe knew his Bible with its enjoinment of self-denial and consideration for others, yet at Canterbury, Cambridge and London there were wealthy clerics wallowing in accumulated wealth inherited from the medieval church flaunting itself side by side with utter poverty. Biblical chronology was a very weak point indeed but it was rank heresy to question it. Christopher Marlowe was in contact with one of the greatest mathematical intelligences of the age, who comprehended that the official timespan allotted to the earth of a mere 6,000 years was infinitely too narrow.[29] The Indians (no doubt those encountered by Harriot in America) had traditions, so Marlowe said, of events going back 16,000 years.[30]

Marlowe threw all prudence to the winds. To make his irreligious, homosexual and subversive remarks was bad enough in an intolerant age, but he made them in front of men wholly dedicated to the destruction of others. Before the informer and double agent Richard Cholmley such remarks were tantamount to suicide.[31] Cholmley actually confessed that he was persuaded 'by Marlowe's reasons' to become an atheist. But he was a government spy, used for the apprehension of papists and other suspects. He was prepared to take bribes and let them go or ignore them. He betrayed his own accomplices. Cholmley had his own gang, some sixty strong. They said that as soon as the Queen were dead they would choose a king among themselves and live according to their own laws. Anxious to lay Cholmley by the heels as early as March 1593, the government hesitated to join battle with his gang. He was arrested, however, on Monday 29 June and when questioned revealed that 'one Marlowe was able to shew more sound reason for atheism than any divine in England is able to give to prove divinity, and that Marlowe told him that he had read the atheist lecture to Sir Walter Ralegh and others'.[32] Whatever his service to the government, whatever his popularity with the theatre-going public, his views would very soon have provoked official action. Before his death in May of 1593, a report was being compiled by an informer and submitted for examination in government circles perhaps the weekend before Marlowe died. The informant was Richard Baines.

Like Marlowe's acquaintances Robert Poley and Richard Cholmley, Baines was yet another member of an underworld of conspiracy, spying and accusation. It accords with what we know of him that he should be the apostate seminary priest who had been at the English College at Rheims, where he concocted a scheme for betraying his former co-religionists and for slaying them by poisoning the college well in true Marlovian fashion. He may well have been the Richard Baines who was hanged at Tyburn on 6 December 1594, just eighteen months after Marlowe's death. The historians of Chislehurst, when discussing the Walsingham circle at Scadbury, remark that Baines was hanged for a degrading offence but supply no further detail nor any source for such information.

Even Christopher Marlowe's casual remarks might have been enough to warrant execution, but there is evidence sufficient to show that he went far beyond the casual. Simon Aldrich reported to Henry Oxinden that Marlowe wrote a great book against the Trinity (or against the Bible) but it could not be printed, and there is Cholmley's statement that Marlowe had delivered the atheist lecture. Baines's report may indeed not be a mere gathering of chance observations but a précis of the lecture requiring only a little rearrangement to arrive at its author's intended order. It has been noted that the accusations against Marlowe fall under four main topics: (1) Attacks upon the Old Testament, especially in connection with chronology; (2) Jeering at Christ in regard to the Virgin Birth, his divinity, and alleging homosexuality; (3) Criticism of the *methode* of the Christian religion; (4) Statements of Marlowe's efforts to secure converts to atheism.[33]

Some of Marlowe's remarks as reported by Baines retain an

impact even today, and their affect upon an Elizabethan audience can scarcely be imagined!

– Moses was but a juggler and one Heriots being Sir W. Ralegh's man can do more than he.

– That the first beginning of religion was only to keep men in awe.

– That if there be any god or good religion then it is the Papists' because the service of God is performed with more ceremonies, as elevation of mass, organs, singing men, shaven crowns, etc. That all Protestants are hypocritical asses.

– . . . to write a new religion he would undertake a more excellent and admirable methode and that all the New Testament is filthily written. [Marlowe is not the only student who had first encountered unpolished New Testament Greek with surprise and shock.]

– That all they that love not tobacco and boys were fools.

– He [Marlowe] has as good a right to coin as the Queen of England and that he was acquainted with one Poole a prisoner in Newgate who hath great skill in mixture of metals, and having learned some things of him he meant through the 'help of a cunning stamp maker to coin French crowns, pistolets and English shillings'.

– Holy Communion would have been much better being administered in a tobacco pipe.

And Baines adds that Cholmley had been made an atheist by Marlowe and that almost into every company where Marlowe came he persuaded men not to be 'afeared of bugbears and hobgoblins'.

An equally dangerous document was prepared in May of 1593 but was submitted and in part compiled after Marlowe's death.[34] Early in May 1593 there were disorders in London directed principally against Dutch immigrants. On 11 May the Privy Council empowered a body of commissioners headed by the Lord Mayor to arrest and examine any persons suspected of setting up 'divers lewd and mutinous libels' around London. Their quarters were to be searched for writings and papers and if a confession were wanting to put them to torture in the Bridewell house of correction. Probably because of this order the playwright Thomas Kyd was seized within twenty-four hours. His rooms were searched and among his papers came to light a manuscript rendering of a treatise entitled *The Fal of the Late Arrian*, a work in which an orthodox cleric, John Proctor, set out and refuted the anti-Trinitarian views of an obscure heretic named John Asseton who recanted his views before Archbishop Cranmer.

The surviving manuscript corresponds fairly closely to passages in Proctor's printed book of 1549. It is no impassioned polemic but more a quiet, reasoned approach to the question. As a whole the book was not forbidden literature and was included indeed in the library of John Gresshop, the King's School headmaster of Marlowe's day. But the manuscript version was endorsed with the date 12 May 1593 and the memorandum 'vile hereticall conceiptes denyinge the deity of Jhesus Christe our Saviour found emgst the papers of Thomas Kydd prisoner'. A note was added in a different ink: 'which he affirmeth that he had from Marlowe'. In panic and anxious to exculpate himself, Kyd claimed that the manuscript had become shuffled in with his own papers when, two years before, he had shared a room with Marlowe.

Later Kyd made further attacks upon Marlowe in two letters, both probably intended for Sir John Puckering, Lord Keeper of the Great Seal, and both probably dating from after Kyd's release from prison. He is anxious to reinstate himself in favour and service with the unknown 'my Lorde' who had repudiated Marlowe. Any doubts that Baines had merely been inventing charges against Marlowe in order to ingratiate himself with the government or to obtain reward are dispelled by these letters. By the time of their writing Marlowe had been killed. Kyd refers to him regularly in the past tense. Marlowe *was* 'intemperate and of a cruel heart', while Kyd excuses himself for taxing and upbraiding the dead who cannot retaliate.

Kyd made it clear that he was not of Marlowe's vile opinion and suggested that inquiry be made of those with whom the dramatist had talked: Harriot, Royden and Warner, and the printer-publishers in St Paul's churchyard. After these statements in his first letter, Kyd was evidently pressed to enlarge upon what he had revealed. In his second letter he spoke more openly of what he called 'Marlowe's monstruous opinions'. When Kyd first knew him, at least as early as 1591, it was Marlowe's custom to jest at the Scriptures and jibe at prayers and he continued his mockings and blasphemous remarks in table-talk. Marlowe said St John was Christ's Alexis. When Kyd proposed to write a book on St Paul's conversion it prompted Marlowe to esteem Paul a juggler (possibly a conflation by Kyd of Marlowe's evaluation of Moses and St Paul). One of Marlowe's jeers now seems harmless: he said, it seems, that the prodigal child's portion was but four nobles; he held his purse, said Marlowe, so near the bottom in all pictures that either it was a jest or four nobles was thought a great patrimony in those days (Marlowe and Kyd lived in an inflationary age). Marlowe said, furthermore, that things esteemed to be done by divine power might as well have been by observation of men. He was accused of bringing 'soden pryvie iniuries to men', and Kyd concludes by claiming that Marlowe 'would persuade men of qualiti to go unto the King of Scots, whether I heare Royden is gon and where if he had lived he told me when I saw him last he meant to be'.

A letter written on 1 August 1593 by Thomas Drury to Anthony Bacon (brother of Francis) sheds an obscure light on Marlowe's last weeks.[35] Drury, another member of the band of agents, double agents and spies, had recently returned from an intelligence-gathering tour on the continent and was about to enter the service of the Earl of Essex. He was angered at lack of recognition and payment for his services. He said that there was a command lately laid on him to stay 'one Mr. Bayns'. He had located 'Bayns' (clearly Baines the informant) and got the 'desired secret' at his hands, for which the City of London had promised 100 crowns, but Drury had received no cash.

He went on to say that there was a libel found by his means and a 'vile book' taken, and a notable villain or two, now close prisoners. By his means there had been 'set down unto the Lord Keeper' (Puckering) and the Lord Buckhurst (Thomas Sackville) the 'notablest and vilest articles of atheism . . . the like was never known and read in any age'. He says they were shown to the queen and command given by her to prosecute the matter in full. But he had never received a penny in reward. He rambled on about 'a book that doth maintain this damnable sect', and says that great sums would be given for it. A merchant he knows could tell who wrote the book, to whom it was delivered, and who read the lecture and where.

It is difficult to know what to make of Drury's tirade. Doubtless it is related to the proclamation and offer of 100 crowns reward made in the City of London on 10 May 1593 for information about the authors of mutinous libels. Which was the 'vile book' is hard to say. Marlowe's opinions as set out in Baines's 'libel', in the hands of the government since probably late May, would certainly qualify. Drury appears to claim that they were set down at his procurement. As to the name of the lecturer, Drury may not have known in August that he had been positively identified. Whatever the case, on the 18 May 1593, by virtue of orders issued by the Privy Council, a messenger of Her Majesty's Chamber was commissioned to arrest Christopher Marlowe and bring him to Court.[36]

CHAPTER FIVE

'Tell Kent from me she hath lost her best man'
Henry VI, Part 2, Act 24, Scene 10

By 30 May 1593 Christopher Marlowe lay dead in the house of Mrs Eleanor Bull of Deptford. At the time only Parts I and II of *Tamburlaine* had appeared in print, and even these texts were anonymous. After his death Marlowe was not blessed with faithful friends with an urge to assemble his plays and poems. Their survival depended upon a few manuscript copies, tattered from use in the theatres, or upon the memories of actors who had learned various parts. Few celebrated authors depend for a reputation upon such a collection of bad texts – fragmentary, interpolated and generally unreliable. After generations of argument a list of the major works may be presented as follows, in a probable or approximate chronological order:

Ovid's *Elegies* (translations)
Lucan's *First Book* (translations)
The Tragedie of Dido, Queene of Carthage
Tamburlaine the Great, Part I
Tamburlaine the Great, Part II
The Jew of Malta
The Massacre at Paris
Edward the Second
Doctor Faustus

80

For notes see p 170

'Tell Kent from me she hath lost her best man'

The Passionate Shepherd
Hero and Leander[1]

The Latin epitaph of Sir Roger Manwood is attributed to Marlowe; a Latin prose dedication to Thomas Watson's *Amintae Gaudia* (1592), signed 'C.M.', is his without question; and there is some evidence to suggest works now lost. Controversy has also surrounded claims for Marlowe's participation in, or authorship of, certain plays such as *Henry VI*, Part II, and *Arden of Feversham*. From the earliest works begun in Cambridge to the unfinished *Hero and Leander*, his surviving writings, whatever their themes, were repeatedly enriched by the experiences of youth in his native city.[2]

By the middle of May 1593, Marlowe must have felt fate closing in upon him; he was not to see Canterbury again. Henry Maunder, acting upon the commission of the Privy Council as he had done many times before, acted speedily and successfully and on Sunday 20 May, according to the Privy Council register, Christopher Marley, 'gentleman', had entered his appearance and had been commanded to give daily attendance upon their Lordships until licence should be issued to the contrary.[3] The court itself, centering around the Queen, was at Greenwich Palace, about four and a half miles down the Thames from Westminster. The Privy Council seems to have met in its own quarters and minutes of meetings on 23, 25 and 29 May are dated from the Star Chamber.[4] There is, however, no record in the Privy Council register of Marlowe's daily appearances, and we may suppose that he was laid under obligation to report to some official resident at either Westminster or Greenwich.

Marlowe was probably arrested for reasons of religion during Archbishop Whitgift's fierce campaign to eradicate religious dissidents.[5] Robert Greene's pamphlet *A Groat's worth of Wit bought with a Million of Repentance*, circulating in London in the autumn of 1592, contained a virtual charge of atheism against Marlowe, as had the same author's *Perimedes* back in 1588.[6] In April 1593 John Greenwood, previously allowed by Marlowe to occupy his scholar's place and have his commons when he left Cambridge in 1581, was hanged at Tyburn in company with Henry Barrow.[7] And

Marlowe must have known that the government sought to arrest Richard Cholmley, whom he was said to have converted to atheism and who was, indeed, apprehended less than three weeks after Marlowe's death. Yet it was probably the disclosures of Thomas Kyd that resulted in Marlowe being placed under surveillance.

It was at such a time, besieged by anxieties, that Marlowe was to be found with Robert Poley, Ingram Frizer and Nicholas Skeres in Deptford.[8] A map drawn originally in 1623 gives a picture of the manor of Sayes Court and Deptford no more than a generation away from Marlowe's day.[9] The principle buildings were the church, the manor house known as Sayes Court, Trinity House with its almshouses established by Henry VIII, and the royal storehouses around the dock close to Sayes Court. The area of Deptford between the church and the river, bounded on two sides by the Thames and the Ravensbourne Creek, was known as Deptford Strand. The London Road ran some distance away to the south, crossing the creek just above the tide-mill by a wooden bridge rebuilt in 1576.[10] Lying at Deptford was one of the famous ships of the age, Francis Drake's *Golden Hind*, at rest after its adventures and now the victim of souvenir hunters who would cut from it chips of wood. Running from the church towards the Thames was a wide street called Deptford Green or the Common Green. Trinity House stood away to the right. There were houses intermittently on either side of the Common Green. This wide street turned sharply westward at a distance short of the river into another street, this one narrow and very crooked, which ran parallel with the Thames. This street was called in later centuries Butcher Street or Butcher Row (now Borthwick Street) and was connected with the waterfront by three alleys known as the Upper, Middle and Lower Watergates. Between the Middle and Lower Watergates (to east and west), and lying between Butcher Street and the River Thames (to south and north), was a narrow lane flanked by small houses, one side of which backed on to the Thames. Butcher Street met another street at a right-angle, the modern Watergate Street, itself a continuation of the Upper Watergate. Close by lay Henry VIII's great dock and a little further off the map of 1623 depicts Sayes Court, a tall gabled building. Here there were twenty-eight ox-stalls

and slaughteryards, for the occupant of Sayes Court had the special
duty of providing meat for the royal household when in residence
across the river at Greenwich.

A water-colour painting of the eighteenth century shows a town
of considerable beauty.[11] In the foreground runs the high road
coming up from Kent, flanked by trees, some four miles yet to go to
London Bridge. Between the road and the Thames is an area of
tumbling rough pasture intersected by shallow dry ditches and
broken fences with an isolated tree standing here and there. Beyond
the pasture lies the town of Deptford, a cluster of red roofs
dominated by the handsome new church in classical style, erected in
1730. The old church of St Nicholas, as seen by Marlowe, stands
nearer the river and is shown with a grey embattled tower of the
common Kentish type. The body of the church had been rebuilt in
brick in 1697. Above the roofs at the waterside stands a line of masts
and yards, dipping gently, as we can imagine, in the running tide
and breeze. As a backdrop rises a line of green hills which would
appear to be the heights of Essex around Brentford. To the right is a
clump of trees through which the towers of Greenwich Palace can
be seen, and at the extreme right looms the height of Shooter's Hill
and Blackheath, thick with foliage. On the morning of 30 May
1593, the district around Deptford must have offered a spectacle of
fresh green fields and hedges and of stretches of sparkling water.

The widow Mrs Eleanor Bull lived in Deptford Strand, probably
not very far from the line of Butcher (or Borthwick) Street, between
Deptford Green and Sayes Court. Mrs Bull's house, and by
implication Mrs Bull herself, have been given a bad name.[12] It may
have been a place of public refreshment and, although probably not
a large establishment, it does seem that she served meals and charged
for them and, therefore, may have been licensed for that purpose.
Equally she may have been no more than a landlady whose lodger
brought in some friends for the day and to whom she served food
for which she expected payment. Whatever the truth, she served at
least eight meals on 30 May, dinner and supper to each of four men,
and the bill must have been considerable. Though there is nothing to
substantiate it, there has been a long-standing conviction that
Marlowe was 'killed in a tavern brawl'. Certainly in Deptford there

was no want of taverns: the survey of 1609–10 describes the Maiden Head, the George, the White Hart, the Christopher and one formerly known as the Bell, though not every building with a sign was necessarily an inn or tavern.[13]

Tradition, indeed, has assigned some unpleasant frequenters to the widow's house: 'bawdy serving men', 'lewd loves', 'harlots'. Her residence has become a brothel and bawdy house or, at the least (and as late as 1938), 'half brothel half public house'. If this were so then its activities would have come under the scrutiny of the officials of the Bishop of Rochester. A certain Richard Thakerie was accused of keeping a bawdy house to which resorted both day and night suspicious men and women.[14] The same courts which recorded this are also concerned with local accusations of fornication and witch-craft, Deptford women being accused of keeping familiars in the form of toads. But the Rochester act books reveal nothing of Eleanor Bull's supposed house of ill-fame and it may be inferred that both Mrs Bull and her house were quite respectable.

It seems, indeed, that Eleanor, whose family name was Whitney, had married Richard Bull (later called 'gentleman') at St Mary's le Bow church in the City of London on 14 October 1571.[15] She had probably been born at the latest at the end of the 1550s and the parish register records that 'M^{ris} Bull was buryed the 19 day of March [1596]'.[16] Action taken in connection with the administration of her property confirms that this is, indeed, Eleanor Bull, who from the description 'Mrs' may be understood to be a woman of some social standing. Though Richard Bull, who died in 1590, curiously finds no place in the Rochester probate records, the act book does record for 20 March (the day after Eleanor's burial) that a certain John Whitney of Lambeth, claiming to be Eleanor's uncle, sent a messenger or servant to enter a caution designed to delay action regarding her estate until he should have been called in.[17] When on 12 June 1596 administration of the widow's goods was granted, however, it was to George Bull, next of kin, described as of the parish of Harlow in Essex. His bondsmen may indicate the social standing of his family, and perhaps also of Eleanor: wealthy London friends, George Hanger, clothworker, and Robert Savage, iron-monger.[18] George Bull himself may well have been a prominent member of his community of Harlow and, though no will or administration survives in Essex probate records, he may be the George Bull who died at Deptford no more than about five months after Mrs Bull, being buried at Deptford parish church on 20 August 1596. In his nuncupative will he describes himself as a 'yeoman' and he made his heir and executor his son-in-law William Wright.[19]

Eleanor's husband, Richard, held the rank of sub-bailiff of the manor of Deptford, being responsible for its administration to the lord of the manor, Christopher Browne, Clerk of the Green Cloth, the financial department of the royal household which paid wages, settled bills and collected rents and dues.[20] The bailiff of the manor was Sir George Howard, probably brother of Katherine Howard. Howard presumably delegated administrative responsibility to Richard Bull. Bull may later have been promoted to the office of bailiff but he is strongly absent from surviving records, including the lay Subsidy Roll for 18 Elizabeth I.[21]

Richard Bull may possibly have been a lawyer, but, whatever the case, the vision of Mrs Bull as a poor ale-house keeper, eking out a squalid existence at Deptford docks, is utterly now dissipated. The mention of Eleanor Bull in the will of Blanche Parry, gentlewoman to Queen Elizabeth, has opened up new possibilities of the discovery of Eleanor's identity and family background.[22] Blanche Parry (ap Harry) was born about 1508 to a family of Welsh border gentry. She was brought to court and became attendant upon the infant Princess Elizabeth. The close relationship was terminated only in 1591 when Blanche died, aged and blind. In a draft of her will set out by William Cecil, Lord Burghley himself, he refers to Blanche as 'cousin' and it seems likely that the Burghleys and the Parrys were related. A long and distinguished list of beneficiaries includes the Whitney family which can be identified with the very ancient Whitneys of Whitney in Herefordshire, who dated from at least the thirteenth century and numbered a line of county knights and sheriffs.[23] They had been connected with the court back in the days of Henry VIII when one James Whitney was Server of the Chamber. Blanche Parry names her god-daughter Blanche Whitney in her will and goes on to mention her cousin Anne Whitney and a Eustace Whitney. After Anne's name in Burghley's draft comes that of Mrs

Bull, called 'cousin', and in the prerogative court version this is expanded to 'my cousin Elinor Bull' who is to have £100 in the form of a debt recoverable from a third party. What can be concluded is that the supposed ale-wife or bawdy-house keeper of Deptford dockside came of an ancient armorial family with members close about the queen and a distinguished ancestry going far back into the Middle Ages.

On the morning of Wednesday 30 May 1593 Christopher Marlowe, Ingram Frizer, Nicholas Skeres and Robert Poley had come together in Mrs Bull's house by ten o'clock. All but Marlowe were designated 'gentlemen' in the coroner's record. Poley was said to be of London, Frizer and Skeres late of London, and Marlowe was given no place of abode. Nerves on that morning were probably very bad. The chief subject of conversation might well have been the execution at five o'clock the previous afternoon of Robert Penry, an author of the Martin Marprelate tracts, run to earth at last. The execution had taken place at St Thomas Waterings, less than three miles up the road towards London and standing half a mile away from the Tower of London across the marshes and the river.

Robert Poley, 'gentleman', we have met already. Currently in the service of the Crown he had departed on a journey to the Hague on 8 May and had, as is likely, reported back to the court. On 8 June he drew his wages and expenses on returning to court, established by then at Nonesuch in Surrey.[24] Since he was certainly back in England on 30 May it may be that he had made two journeys in the period.

Ingram Frizer has been revealed as another unpleasant personality with a career of sharp dealing.[25] In 1589 he is known to have bought the Angel inn at Basingstoke and resold it less than two months later. One of the vendors of the Angel imprudently entered into a bond with Frizer for £240, but failed to discharge his obligation by the stated term, whereupon Frizer seized the golden opportunity and secured judgement against him at Easter term, 1592. In or soon after 1593 he managed to get into his toils a young man named Drew Woodleff, the son of Robert Woodleff, gentleman, and Ann, his wife, of Great Missenden in Buckinghamshire. The father had died 7 January 1593 and the widow and her young son between them badly mismanaged their affairs. Foolish, and possessing landed property, they formed an extremely attractive proposition for a rogue like Frizer and his associates. Drew Woodleff, who was badly in need of money, tried first to raise a loan from Nicholas Skeres. Unable or unwilling to oblige, Skeres turned to Frizer. Frizer was not ready to lend cash but offered a 'commodity' in the solid form of iron guns lying at Tower Hill. Woodleff signed a bond for £60, the supposed value of the guns. Frizer then offered to sell the guns on behalf of Woodleff but came back with only £30, claiming it was all he could get, though there was the strongest suspicion that he had made no effort to sell the guns at all. Further frauds followed. Frizer was scheming with Skeres to mulct Drew Woodleff of 20 marks. In the course of the case Ingram Frizer claimed as 'master' 'a gentleman of good worship', none other than Mr Thomas Walsingham.

There may also have been a link between the Woodleff group and the Pooley family.[26] Away in Whitechapel stood the Boar's Head inn (one of many houses of that name), and here a scheme was set afoot by 1595 to adapt the building as a playhouse. The owners of the copyhold under the manor of Stepney were a Jane Pooley and her son Henry. The husband may have been Edmund Pooley (steward-cum-secretary and nephew-in-law to the second Lord Wentworth). The Pooleys leased the whole place except for some upper quarters to Oliver Woodliffe, a haberdasher in the City of London. The various engagements were risky, the plans for conversion were changed, and Woodliffe found himself in want of capital. A whole maze of actions at law entangled the participants. Robert Poley, Ann Woodleff and her credulous son do not enter this story, but though their connection with the parties involved at the Boar's Head in Whitechapel is nowhere stated, the conjunction of their surnames is striking, suggesting complexities of relationship in the circles of Marlowe's acquaintanceship of which we have only the faintest notion.

Nicholas Skeres has not been satisfactorily identified. A Nicholas Skeeres is named in 1589 as one of a group of masterless men and cut-purses who robbed gentlemen's chambers and artificers' shops in and around London.[27] An individual called 'Skyrres' was involved, like Poley, in the Babington plot, and both of these may be the same man concerned with Ingram Frizer in the swindling of young Woodleff. There is less confidence in claiming him to be a member of the family of Nicholas Skeres of Furnival's Inn, son of Nicholas Skeres senior. In its various forms the name Skeres appears at different points in Kent, especially in the Isle of Sheppey and the adjacent mainland. There was an armorial family settled at Newn-ham near Ospringe.[28] They bore arms 'Or, on a band azure, between a lion rampant in chief, sable, and three oakleaves in base, as many escallops of the first'. There was also an armorial family at Alderthwaite, Wentworth, Yorkshire, named Skeres. No positive connection between them and the family at Newnham has been demonstrated, but each line bore the same coat of arms.

There are two near-contemporary accounts of the tragedy which befell Poley, Frizer, Skeres and Marlowe at Deptford that day: one by Thomas Beard in *The Theatre of God's Judgements* of 1597 and one in William Vaughan's *The Golden-grove*, published in 1600.[29] Beard produced a tremendous collection of moral stories recounting God's immediate and dreadful vengeance upon blasphemers, liars and other offenders. It satisfied its public not only in providing sen-sational stories but in connecting such stories with familiar places. Marlowe, of course, richly qualified for inclusion. Beard's account found a place in Edmund Rudierde's *The Thunderbolt of God's Wrath* (1618), the work of a like-minded author.[30] Francis Meres printed his *Palladis Tamia* in 1598 and used Beard's story while adding some colourful details of his own, recounting how Marlowe was stabbed to death by a bawdy serving man, a rival of his in lewd love.[31]

Beard's version in his *Theatre* runs as follows:

Not inferiour to any of the former in Atheisme and impiety, and equall to all in maner of punishment was one of our own nation, of fresh and late memory, called *Marlin* [marginal note: Marlow], by profession a scholler, brought vp from his youth in the Vniuersitie of Cambridge, but by practice a playmaker, and a Poet of scurrilitie, who by giuing too large a swinge to his owne wit, and suffering his lust to haue the full raines, fell (not without iust desert) to that outrage and extremitie, that hee denied God and his sonne Christ, and not only in word blasphemed the trinitie, but also (as it is credibly reported) wrote books against it, affirming our Sauiour to be but a deceiuer, and *Moses* to be but a coniurer and seducer of the people, and the holy Bible to be but vaine and idle stories, and all religion but a deuice of pollicie. But see what a hooke the Lord put in the nosthrils of this barking dogge: It so fell out, that in London strets as he purposed to stab one whome hee ought a grudge vnto with his dagger, the other party perceiuing so auoided the stroke, that withall catching hold of his wrest, he stabbed his owne dagger into his owne head, in such sort, that nothwithstanding all the meanes of surgerie that could be wrought, hee shortly after died thereof. The manner of his death being so terrible (for hee euen cursed and blasphemed to his last gaspe, and togither with his breath an oth flew out of his mouth) that it was not only a manifest signe of Gods judgement, but also an horrible and fearefull terrour to all that beheld him. But herein did the justice of God most notably appeare, in that hee compelled his owne hand which had written those blasphemies to be the instrument to punish him, and that in his braine, which had deuised the same. I would to God (and I pray it from my heart) that all Atheists in this realme, and in all the world beside, would by the remembrance and consideration of this example, either forsake their horrible impietie, or that they might in like manner come to destruction: and so that abominable sinne which so flourisheth amongst men of greatest name, might either be quite extinguished and rooted out, or at least smothered and kept vnder, that it durst not shew it head any more in the worlds eye. [32]

Vaughan's version in *The Golden-grove* embodies some details unknown to or unrecorded by Thomas Beard:

Not inferiour to these was one Christopher Marlow by profession a playmaker, who, as it is reported, about 7. yeeres a-goe wrote a booke against the Trinitie: but see the effects of Gods iustice; it so hapned, that at Detford, a little village about three miles distant from London, as he meant to stab with his ponyard one named Ingram, that had inuited him thither to a feast, and was then playing at tables, he quickly perceyuing it, so auoyded the thrust, that withall drawing out his dagger for his defence, hee stabd this Marlow into the eye, in such sort, that his braines comming out at the daggers point, hee shortlie after dyed. Thus did God, the true executioner of diuine iustice, worke the ende of impious Atheists. [33]

There survives, however, an official and quite unassailable document to depend upon for a record of Marlowe's last day – the famous record of the coroner's inquest. [34] This record sets out the story in Latin with some English phrases inserted for clarification. It tells as follows: 'About the tenth hour before noon' on 30 May in the thirty-fifth year of Her Majesty Queen Elizabeth (1593), there were met together in a chamber in the house of a certain Eleanor Bull, widow, Ingram 'Frysar', late of London, gentleman; Christopher 'Morley'; a certain Nicholas Skeres, late of London, gentleman; and Robert Poley of London, gentleman. The group passed the time in the room and there they dined. After dinner they were quiet together and walked into the garden belonging to Mrs Bull's house. Here they spent the time until six o'clock and then moved back into the house where they had supper. A surviving description of the nearby garden of Sayes Court may help the imagination fill in details of that garden where Marlowe and his fellows spent some hours on that early summer's day: in the garden of Sayes Court was a summer house with 'a settle round about of turned pillars and back all of wainscot' and there were six apple trees, grafted, with three apricot trees and eight plum trees and cherry trees 'grafted and plashed againt the walls'. [35] Since the four men spent the hours before supper in the garden it was probably dry and warm. Perhaps they smoked as they talked and drank ale or sack.

The room to which they returned for supper is given some description in the record. There was a bed but this need not indicate an upstairs room. There was a table long enough to accommodate at least three men sitting on one side, perhaps a ponderous piece of Tudor furniture with a heavy frame with rails on which people rested their feet. Along the table on the side nearer the bed ran a bench and here sat Robert Poley, Ingram Frizer and Nicholas Skeres, in that order, as they ate their meal. Perhaps the table was

5

pushed against a wall or perhaps there was only one bench and all four sat in a row with Christopher Marlowe at one end.

When they had finished eating Marlowe got up, went across and threw himself upon the bed. Very soon bitter exchanges started between Marlowe and Frizer about paying for the food. Vaughan says that Frizer had invited Marlowe to a feast and perhaps Frizer demanded Marlowe's share of the expenses only to be refused. The argument between the two men continued, Marlowe lying on the bed and Frizer sitting with his back to him 'nere the bedd' while, if Vaughan is to be believed, playing at 'tables' (backgammon). No indication is given of Poley and Skeres participating in the quarrel.

Suddenly Christopher Marlowe got up from the bed where he was sprawling, leaped at Frizer in a rage and pulled Frizer's dagger from its sheath as it hung behind him from his belt. The next action is not specifically described, but Marlowe may have done what so many Elizabethans did in a brawl, which was to seize the dagger by the blade and beat his adversary's head with the pommel, in this case breaking the flesh twice and giving wounds each two inches long and a quarter of an inch deep. Trapped between Poley and Skeres, the table in front of him and the bench at his back, Frizer was unable to break away or defend himself from the attack coming from behind. Twisting round, he tried to get his weapon from Marlowe and, according to Thomas Beard, caught hold of Marlowe's wrist. In the struggle he must have pushed the dagger away from himself with some force just at the moment when it was level with a point above Marlowe's right eye. The blade went two inches into Marlowe's head and was evidently jerked about in the wound, which was more than an inch across (according to the record). Then and there Marlowe died. If Beard is to be believed, he cursed and blasphemed to his last gasp. Beard's further suggestion, that medical help was sought, though not impossible, may owe more to its author's sense of the dramatic in his moral story.

It seems likely that the dagger entered just above the eye but beneath the eyebrow. What might have happened is this: the dagger point slid over the upper side of the eyeball and entered the skull through the superior orbital fissure where the nerves from the eye and its muscles pass through to the brain, accompanied by a large blood vessel (the cavernous sinus) which drains into the jugular vein and hence into the heart. Pressure in the blood vessel is low and a puncture from the dagger point would enable air to enter, rapidly spreading throughout the circulation and resulting in unconsciousness within a minute or so. In such case Christopher Marlowe died from air embolism and would have had just enough time to voice curses and blasphemies.[36] Marlowe with a bloody face collapses cursing on to the rushes. Ingram Frizer, his legs still caught between bench and table, stands awkwardly in a daze, his hair dripping with blood from his scalp wounds. Perhaps Poley or Skeres goes rushing out crying for a surgeon.

By now, at around seven or eight o'clock at night, it was probably too late to notify authority. With the Royal Court in residence at Greenwich, just across the Ravensbourne Creek, the coroner of the Royal Household exercised jurisdiction over the 'Verge', a district extending to a radius of twelve miles from the Queen's person, and took precedence over the district coroner. The Coroner of the Verge at this time was William Danby, gentleman, a professional lawyer, probably identical with the William Danby who entered Lincoln's Inn on 1 August 1542.[37] He had been coroner for somewhat under four years at the time of Marlowe's death and may have been approaching seventy years of age in 1593. There was a William Danby living at Woolwich, possibly the coroner, so perhaps someone would have had to ride the four miles down-river to find him.

In any case, it was not until Friday 1 June that William Danby came to Deptford to 'sit upon the body' of Christopher 'Morley'. Meanwhile a jury had been empanelled, headed by Nicholas Draper, gentleman, his fifteen fellow jurors being Wolstan Randall, gentleman, William Curry, Adrian Walker, John Barber, Robert Baldwine, Giles Feld, George Halfpenny, Henry Anger, James Batte, Henry Bendin, Thomas Batte senior, John Baldwin, Alexander Burrage, Edmund Goodcheape and Henry Dabyns. There is everything to show, in the identification of these men, that the jurors were good, solid, middle-class Englishmen, a group utterly unlike any kind of jury which might be suborned into giving false verdict. They are the very opposite of slippery hangers-on at court, of devious men from the underworld, or of mere men of straw who could be induced, deceived or intimidated as the case required.

Of those that have been traced, Nicholas Draper, gentleman, may be the Mr Nicholas Draper who lived at Leigh, near Tonbridge in West Kent.[38] Wolstan Randall, gentleman, held a house and stable on lease from the Lord Admiral in Deptford which he left to his wife by his will dated 1603.[39] William Curry, George Halfpenny and Henry Dabyns all held tenements in Deptford. Curry, called 'gentleman' in his will in 1612, held a wharf and yard, living perhaps on the foreshore, not far from the alley between Borthwick Street and the water.[40] A George Halfpenny was a baker at Limehouse, across the Thames. Giles Feld was a grocer in Deptford. James Batte, a husbandman, came from Lewisham, two miles from Deptford. Robert Baldwine, called 'yeoman', came from Greenwich across the Ravensbourne Creek from Deptford. Henry Anger has been identified among the tenants of Sayes Court manor. Henry Dabyns appears to have been a baker.

Of three of these jurors, William Curry, Giles Feld and Robert Baldwine, a little more may be said. In March 1583 William Curry of Deptford Strand was in possession of sixteen acres of arable in 'Newdrossefeilde' together with eighteen acres in two 'closes' called Longlandes and Brookshottes, all held from Sayes Court manor.[41] He leased all this ground to Thomas Foxe for sixteen years for £11 13s. 4d. payable in two annual instalments, at St John Baptist (24 June) and at Christmas, in the north porch of Deptford church, together with six bushels of 'good and sweete uplande wheate' and the delivery at Christmas each year of 'one load of good and sweet rye strawe, ffrank and ffree', with a promise to lay 640 loads of dung upon the land. To this lease William Curry appends his signature. In December 1583 three acres of meadow in the tenure of William Curry, lying in Church Marsh at Deptford, was granted by Richard Willis, citizen and leatherseller of London, to John Hawkins and his wife Katherine. John Hawkins, the famous sailor, was involved in shipbuilding at Deptford at this period. And another document involving Hawkins reveals William Curry holding ground in Bromeclose, Deptford, close to the highway to Deptford Strand. A grant by Richard Higginson and his wife of Deptford dated 1592 shows another juror, Giles Feld, to be holding land from Trinity House, close to the highway from Lewisham to London.

A further grant by Richard Willis, the leatherseller, made on 11 April 1588, concerns the transmission of Brooke Myll at Deptford to one Henry Brooke at a sale price of £110, the mill being in the tenure of Robert Baldwine, miller, another juryman. In the following year the mill, newly built, with the accompanying dwelling and fifteen acres called Chalke Close, was sold by Willis for £620. The location of the mill, probably that which spanned the Ravens-bourne, may account for Vine Hall's description of Baldwine as residing in East Greenwich – he had a foot in both Deptford and East Greenwich. The same Robert Baldwine appears as a witness to another document concerning the mill, executed by Willis and dated 23 December 1589. Here his connection with another juryman, John Baldwin, seems to be explained, for along with the name of his wife Elizabeth and a certain Thomas Baldwyn, shoemaker, is that of John Baldwin, 'the sonne of Robert Baldin, Miler'. This would seem to be the same John Baldwin who lived in 'High Street East' in Greenwich.

The sixteen members of the jury debated upon the death of Christopher Marlowe. Poley and Skeres were brought forward as witnesses and the jurymen concluded that Ingram Frizer had killed Christopher Marlowe but in self-defence. The dagger was held forfeit to the value of 12d. Ingram Frizer was held in prison until pardon should be issued. Within the month he was released, his pardon being issued on 28 June 1593.[42]

Once the verdict of the coroner's inquest had been delivered and registered, Christopher Marlowe's mortal remains could be buried. The body was carried to St Nicholas churchyard at the end of Deptford Green and Mr Macander the vicar, known for his squabbles with his bishop and his parishioners, probably conducted the service, according Marlowe Christian burial on the first day of June 1593.[43] News of Marlowe's death may have brought acquaintances to the graveside, perhaps even Thomas Walsingham from Chislehurst. The language of Edward Blunt in the dedication of *Hero and Leander* sounds more than mere formality:

'Tell Kent from me she hath lost her best man'

. . . we have brought the breathless body to the earth . . . albeit the eye there taketh his ever farewell of that beloved object, yet the impression of the man, that hath been dear to us . . . lives in an after life in our memory . . .

An entry of interment was made in the parish register of St Nicholas, Deptford, perhaps by Mr Macander: 'Christopher Marlowe slaine by Francis Frezer: the. 1. of June', wrongly listing Ingram Frizer's Christian name.[44]

Christopher Marlowe's dramatic death was unquestionably the talk of the town. Some of the talk found its way into print. The envious Gabriel Harvey launched into a triumphant, sneering rodomontade, entitled 'Gorgon, or the wonderfull yeare', which was published in September 1593.[45] Recounting events taking place across Europe in that year, he was mainly concerned with Marlowe's death, 'Whose corps on Powles, whose mind triumphed on Kent', continuing 'Weep Powles, they Tamberlaine voutsafes to dye'. Marlowe, he said, never 'ought admired but his wondrous self'. Writing a month after Marlowe's death, Thomas Nashe inscribed a nobler epitaph in his *Unfortunate Traveller*:

It was one of the wittiest knaves that ever God made . . . His pen was sharp-pointed like a poniard; no leaf he wrote on but was like a burning-glass to set on fire all his readers. Learning he had, and a conceit exceeding all learning, to quintessence everything which he heard. His tongue and his invention . . . what they thought, the world confidently utter . . . His life he contemnedd in comparison of the liberty of speech.[46]

In which part of Deptford churchyard Christopher Marlowe was buried we shall never know. If there was a tradition that he was buried on the north side of Deptford church it can be of no great antiquity for Marlowe was forgotten for over a century and the rebuilding of the church a century after his death included the provision of a charnel-house for the bones lying thick in the graveyard soil. Some of Marlowe's bones could well have been deposited among these remains.

Something must be said of the three survivors of the affair in Mrs

Bull's house. Robert Poley, messenger, spy and double agent, was in the full flood of his career.[47] On 14 July 1593, he was paid again for carrying letters to France and returning with answers, within six weeks of Marlowe's death, and again and again he can be traced travelling backwards and forwards to the continent. He seems to have been in and out of prison, acting as *agent provocateur*, and it has been suggested that he could have been one of the 'two damm'd villans' who, as Ben Jonson told William Drummond, were jailed with him to catch him out, possibly when he was in the Marshalsea in 1597 for his part in the subversive play *Isle of Dogs*. Poley continued to be involved in plots and counterplots right up to 1602, at which time he seems to have been in low estimate with Robert Cecil, Secretary of State. In 1618 a Robert Poley, 'gentleman', in company with Robert Jermyn, Charles Bartlett and John Shelton, all styled 'gentlemen', was licensed to travel overseas for three years, taking four servants, on condition that none of them went to Rome. It is to be noted that Shelton was the maiden name of Lady Walsingham, wife of Sir Thomas. In 1624 Robert Pooley, esquire, appears with Roger Palmer, esquire, as Member of Parliament for Queenborough in the Isle of Sheppey.[48] The two men had been elected by the Jurats of Queenborough following recommendation from the Earl of Montgomery in a letter dated from Whitehall 6 January 1623–4. The first Parliament of the new reign met at Westminster on 17 May 1626. On the Queenborough return of 9 May, though Palmer's name is listed Poley's is not, and in his place is now Sir Edward Hales. Lord Montgomery's pressure had clearly been resisted by the electors of Queenborough, for he wrote them a furious letter objecting to their rejection of his candidate Mr Robert Pooley, 'a gent. every way able to discharge a greater trust than happily might betide him from that corporation'. At the next election for the Parliament meeting, 6 February 1626, Pooley was duly returned with Palmer, but at the next in 1628 Hales had once again replaced him. If this is the same Robert Pooley he would by now be in his early or middle sixties.

Ingram Frizer seems to have settled down to responsibility. By 1602 he was established at Eltham, a few miles from Deptford and Chislehurst.[49] In 1603 he acted as agent for Lady Walsingham, wife of Sir Thomas, in connection with a lease of ground belonging to the Duchy of Lancaster. As a leading inhabitant of Eltham he served as assessor for taxation purposes in his parish and was a member of a commission concerned with certain local charities in such distinguished company as that of Sir Thomas Walsingham and the Bishop of Rochester. Married with two daughters, serving as a churchwarden, he died in 1627 and was buried in the parish church of Eltham.[50]

Nicholas Skeres continued to be elusive. A Nicholas Kyrse *alias* Skeers, called servant to the Earl of Essex, was arrested on 13 March 1594 by Alderman Richard Martin of London and said to have been 'in very dangerous company' at the house of one Williamson.[51] He was imprisoned in the Counter in Wood Street to await examination, and on 31 July 1601 the Privy Council issued warrants to the keeper of Newgate prison for the removal of Nicholas 'Skiers' and another prisoner called Farmer to the Bridewell. Thereafter Skeres disappears into the shadows.

A considerable literature has grown up around the circumstances of Marlowe's murder. Was it the outcome of an ordinary affray or something more sinister.[52] One theory would have it that Lady Walsingham contrived the death of a man who knew too much about her scheme to secure the English throne for James VI of Scotland. But there is no evidence that Thomas Walsingham and his future wife were even betrothed as early as 1593. Her later use of the services of Ingram Frizer as her agent, given his connection with her husband, is hardly grounds for imagining a conspiracy. Another theory suggests that Ralegh engineered Marlowe's death because Marlowe knew too much about Ralegh's supposed atheistic tendencies. But if this were so the whole Ralegh circle might have been in danger and it does not explain why Marlowe alone should have been murdered. The suggestion that Marlowe did not die but was spirited away to live in secrecy is equally unconvincing. In the sixteenth century a coroner's jury would not sit discussing a sudden and violent death while the body was delicately kept out of sight in a hospital mortuary. The jurors went to view the corpse and inspected the wounds causing death, even to the extent of measuring them. Certainly sixteen men on oath saw the body of Christopher

X Williamson

Marlowe lying dead in the house of Eleanor Bull at Deptford, with a conspicuous wound above the right eye.

But what was he doing in the house of a woman closely connected with the court circles of the day and in the sinister company of men involved in spying or double dealing? Whatever the explanation, there is no need to invent a plot to put Marlowe out of the way. He was a victim of his own temperament. Four times at least he was involved in violent struggles with other men: at Hog Lane in September 1589 when William Bradley was slain; in May 1592 when he scuffled with the constable and sub-constable of Shoreditch; at Canterbury in September 1592 when he fought with William Corkine; and now at Deptford. For every case which came to the notice of the courts there may have been many times when Marlowe was involved in other incidents – 'sudden privy injuries to men'.

'Quod me nutrit me destruit.' The portrait at Cambridge may or may not be a likeness of Marlowe but the motto inscribed there is a likeness of his fate. That brilliant mind, tensed like a coiled spring, ready to soar into flights of genius, was equally ready to erupt in a fire of uncontrollable temper. Now, at the last, goaded by worry and prospect of disaster, he attacked a man who turned and killed him in self-defence. The surges of excitement generating his mighty verse were very close to the sudden rages which convulsed him. The same passion which sustained him as a poet destroyed him as a human being.

Contemporaries of
Christopher Marlowe at the King's School,
Michaelmas 1578–Michaelmas 1579

(List of names derived from Canterbury Cathedral Archives and Library, CAC, Accounts, New Foundation, Treasurer 9, and Miscellaneous Accounts 41)

1. THOMAS RUSSELL.
2. RICHARD BETHAM.
3. STEPHEN NEVINSON. He must certainly be a connection of Stephen Nevinson, DCL, chancellor of the diocese of Norwich and prebendary of Canterbury by c. 1570. Dr Nevinson had a cousin Christopher Nevinson (born in Cumberland), who was appointed for the diocese of Canterbury in 1538 by Cranmer. The family acquired entensive landed property in East Kent.
4. SAMUEL KENNETT. *See* p. 49.
5. SIDRAC KEMESLEY. He is almost certainly one of the five children of John Kemsley, styled 'yeoman', who was left property at Hamestall, at Stockbury, near Maidstone. There is no evidence for an academic or clerical career for Sidrac, and it may be imagined that he led the quiet life of a Kentish yeoman.
6. ROBERT GROVE(S). Possibly of the same family as Ralph Grove(s) (see no. 46, below).
7. WILLIAM PLAYFER.
8. RICHARD PARRETT (PEROTT). *See under* Clement Parrett, no. 31, below.

9. JOSIAS SNOW.

10. ISAAC CLERKE. It has been suggested (*The Times Literary Supplement*, Feb. 1964) that this boy was, in later years, the Canterbury builder and decorator, but the dates are not easy to reconcile.

11. CHRISTOPHER DUCKETT. Some ten years after he had left school he may be found trying his hand at teaching at an elementary level (*in literis alphabeticis*) at Wingham, some six miles east of Canterbury. He is quite certainly identical with Christopher Duckett, said to be aged thirty-three in December 1597 (and therefore of much the same age as Christopher Marlowe), who gave evidence in a case in the church courts. He was then the village tailor of Ickham, a mile or two from Wingham, and told an entertaining story about a local lady, Emblyn Sharsted, whose expensive clothing was inconsistent with the modest income of her husband and was probably paid for by an illicit admirer. Duckett might have combined his teaching activities with a trade but he had failed to fulfil the youthful promise which had gained him a scholar's place at Canterbury.

12. JOHN MARSHALL. There is a sizar or scholar-servant of Pembroke College, Cambridge, of the same name who matriculated within the year 1580–1.

13. EDWARD PARTRIDGE. There was a family of gentry called Partridge established at Bridge, three miles from Canterbury. An Edward Partridge of Bridge married in 1627 Katherine the daughter of Sir Arthur Throckmorton (and niece of Sir Walter Ralegh). This may have been a late marriage by Marlowe's contemporary but a generation probably lies in between. Edward Partridge the schoolboy might also be a son of a Partridge family settled at Greenway Court, Kent, and possibly father of Sir Edward Partridge, MP for Sandwich in 1640.

14. HENRY LOVELACE. He was probably a member of the distinguished Kentish family which included Richard Lovelace, the poet, and Francis Lovelace, second English Governor of New York, but it has not proved possible to fit Henry into the pedigree.

15. BARTHOLOMEW KETTELL. The cathedral clerk was careless in reproducing surnames. It is therefore possible that this boy is

identical with a Bartholomew 'Kevell' who was living in Dover in 1599. He had been there for seventeen years and was then aged thirty-three. He was classed as a yeoman.

16. REGINALD STAFFERTON.

17. THOMAS TAYLOR. There is a scholar of St John's, Cambridge, by Easter 1580 who might have been the same individual. There were two men of the same name who were clergymen in Kent. One died as parson of Leveland by 1604. Another was rector of St Mary's in Romney Marsh, from which living he resigned in 1630.

18. HENRY BROMERICK. He appears to be Henry Brownrigg, scholar of Corpus Christi College, Cambridge, in 1582, where he became BA in 1585–6. If so he would have known Marlowe both at school and at university.

19. WILLIAM BOLTON.

20. LEONARD SWEETING. See p. 49.

21. NICHOLAS ELMYSTON.

22. RICHARD LEWKNER. He may have been a member of a Kentish landowning family, and was possibly son of Edward Lewknor of Challock. Richard Lewkner (Lewknor) is mentioned in the will of his grandmother Agnes Lewknor in 1570.

23. RICHARD READER. He is called both Richard and Robert in the accounts. The boy, whatever his name, was probably kinsman to the Revd Robert Reader, instituted vicar of Wormshill, Kent, in 1580.

24. WILLIAM PLAYSE (PLACE). He is likely to be the young man of that name who matriculated as sizar of St John's, Cambridge, at Michaelmas 1582. He was BA in 1585–6. He served as vicar of Boughton-under-Blean, Kent, from 1590 until his death in 1637, almost a record even in that slow-moving age. He indicated, when giving evidence in a lawsuit, that he was born at Badlesmere (near Boughton) about 1564. This suggests that he was son to the Revd Peter Place, BA, admitted vicar there in 1559. Peter Place was dead by 1570 so William would have been an orphan while at school.

25. HENRY JACOB. See p. 50.

26. WILLIAM POTTER. See p. 50.

27. HENRY DREWRY (DRURY). There was a distinguished armorial family at this time with connections in Kent, headed by Sir Drew Drewry or Drury, gentleman usher of the Privy Chamber to Queen Elizabeth. Lady Drury was daughter of William Fynch of Linstead, Kent. But Henry Drury does not readily fit into a pedigree.

28. THOMAS WYN. He may be a member of the prosperous Canterbury family of the name.

29. JESSE GILBART (GILBERT).

30. RICHARD PUREFREY. This boy was probably son of Francis Purefrey, rector of Ruckinge, near Ashford, Kent, who in 1585 became vicar of Horncastle, Lincs., and earned a name as a Puritan.

31. CLEMENT PARRETT. He was probably connected with Richard Parrett (see no. 8, above), and with John Parette (see no. 80, below), and was probably a commoner at the school.

32. CALEB SMYTHE.

33. WILLIAM LYLLYE (LYLY). This boy's main distinction is as younger brother to John Lyly, author of *Euphues*. There were two Williams among the children, and this is clearly the younger, baptized in 1568. He was a scholar by Michaelmas 1578, when he was barely ten years old. Despite this early promise he left little mark of himself, and cannot be traced to a university.

34. PETER OLYVER.

35. CHRISTOPHER STRETESLEY.

36. THOMAS COLWELL (COLDWELL). He was scholar of Corpus Christi College, Cambridge, styled 'of Kent'. He matriculated at Michaelmas 1582. He was BA in 1585–6, MA in 1589 and Fellow of his college from 1588 to 1593. Clearly he knew Marlowe well, both at Canterbury and Cambridge, if slightly his junior. He incorporated under his degree at Oxford, and served as rector of Newbury, Berkshire, and of other livings. He was sub-dean of Salisbury from 1595 to 1599. He was probably son of John Coldwell who left school at Canterbury early in 1550 and, after holding livings in Kent, became Dean of Rochester and in 1591 Bishop of Salisbury, being the first in his

office to be married. It was he who alienated Sherborne manor to Sir Walter Ralegh.

37. THOMAS HAMMON. He might be a member of the land-owning Kentish family of Hammon (Hammond). But the name is common in Kent.

38. ROPER BLUNDELL. See p. 51.

39. JOHN WILFORD. He might be a member of the Kentish armorial family of Wilford or Wilsford, numbering Justices of the Peace, among whom was John Wilford who with his colleagues reported on the state of Dover Castle in 1627. It is possible that the scholar and the Justice may be identical.

40. NICHOLAS WILDER. He was scholar from 1578 to 1581, and could possibly be the youth who matriculated as commoner of Magdalen Hall, Oxford, in 1584. But this latter individual came from Berkshire, which reduces a likelihood of identification. Nicholas Wilder of Magdalen Hall was MA by 1592, and is likely to be the rector of Dunsfold, Surrey, of that name in 1606.

41. ALEXANDER CLIFFORD.

42. BARTHOLOMEW GODWYN. He is likely to be son to Thomas Godwin, Dean of Canterbury, 1567–84.

43. JOHN ELMLEY. This name appears under Christmas 1578 only.

44. THOMAS SCALES. He was scholar by 1576 but left by Lady Day 1579, having overlapped with Marlowe by one term. However, since Marlowe was probably a commoner before becoming a scholar, they undoubtedly knew each other rather longer. Scales is probably identical with the youth who matriculated as scholar of Queens' College, Cambridge, in 1579. He was MA by 1586, and incorporated at Oxford in 1588. He entered the church and became vicar of Hagnaby, Lincolnshire.

45. EDWARD BRADFORD.

46. RALPH GROVE(S). He had become scholar by Midsummer 1576. He left school at Midsummer 1579. The family came from Henley-on-Thames, Oxfordshire. Ralph Groves said in giving evidence in 1597 that he was about thirty-four, so providing a birth-date of 1563 or 1564. But the Henley parish register shows that he was baptized 31 April 1560, and was, therefore, sixteen when admitted scholar, well above the statutory limit. Was this

an honest error or a case of deliberate concealment? As a boy at Henley, Ralph Groves must have known John Cranford, who was later to marry Christopher Marlowe's sister. Ralph Groves left school at the advanced age of nineteen, late indeed in that age. He took up the law, and appears some years later as attorney in the Canterbury borough courts. He was admitted freeman of the city by purchase in 1592, and was soon elected city councillor, becoming in due course town clerk, an office which he held while councillor, as was customary. His residence was established in the precinct of the old dissolved priory of St Gregory, Canterbury. As a lawyer he left an enormous amount of his handwriting behind him, bad at first and becoming execrable by his death in 1635 when he was still in office as town clerk at the age of seventy-five. On December 1 in that year he wrote in the heading for council business on that day in the city minute book but collapsed before he had time to enter the minutes themselves. He was buried in the small graveyard at St John's Hospital, Northgate, opposite his house at St Gregory's.

47. NICHOLAS PARKER.

48. GEORGE HAWKES.

49. BARNABAS POWNALL. See p. 51.

50. CHRISTOPHER MARLEY. The boy appears at Lady Day 1579, and therefore had become a scholar by Christmas 1578. He continues until Michaelmas 1579, when a gap in the accounts occurs.

51. JOHN GWYN. This boy's surname is rendered Edwyn on occasion by the cathedral clerk, but the true form seems to be Gwyn. He may, like Pownall, have entered the ranks of non-graduate teachers, and may be identical with the John Gwyn, *literatus*, who on 12 January 1591, some ten years after he left school, was licensed to teach boys within the city of Canterbury *in arte grammatica*. When the licence was issued, note was made that the applicant had been licensed in other dioceses.

Nos. 52–6 below appear at Michaelmas 1579, having become scholars at Midsummer in that year.

52. BARTHOLOMEW BESELEY. He was probably the son of Richard Beseley (Beasely and variants), BD, the Marian exile who had known Henry VIII and Cromwell, of whom he is said to have been a favourite. He was Fellow of All Souls, Oxford, and rector of Cumnor near Oxford. By 1535 he had moved into Kent and was rector of Staplehurst, being presented by the patron, Thomas Cromwell, Principal Secretary. In 1547 Beseley was one of the 'Six Preachers' of Canterbury Cathedral. On Mary's succession he fled as a married priest and is found at Frankfurt in 1557 with a wife and two children. He returned with the majority of the *emigrés* in 1558 and was restored to his preachership at Canterbury in August 1560. He had livings in Kent at Sandhurst and at Chislet. In 1585 he made his will, desiring to be buried near Bishop Bale and Robert Pownall (see p. 51), companions in exile, in Canterbury Cathedral.

53. PHILEMON POWNALL. See p. 51.

54. JOHN REYNARD. He appears as a scholar at Michaelmas 1579 and was still at school at Michaelmas 1581, after which records are defective. He could be the sizar of Clare College, Cambridge, matriculating at Easter in 1583, who migrated to Corpus Christi College in 1584. He was MA by 1591, and became vicar of Headcorn, Kent, in 1602.

55. NATHANIEL BULL.

56. SAMUEL WHITE.

Nos. 1–56 above are names of boys appearing in the lists as scholars from Michaelmas 1578 until Michaelmas 1579, at which point the accounts are lost for one year. At Michaelmas 1580 they become available again, and though 'Christopher Marley' and several others have gone there are still those who knew him: Wyn, Bromerick, Drewry, Colwell, Olyver, Partridge, Wilder, Gwyn, Parrett, Reynard, Bolton, Place, Wilsford, Barnabas Pownall, Gilbart, Bull, Lyllye, White, Beseley, Blundell, Nevinson and Hammon. There are fresh names and some of these boys certainly overlapped with Christopher Marlowe as it is very unlikely that he left in 1579 when the accounts stop. In any case, most of them were probably commoners before becoming scholars and could have been in school with him for a few years.

57. THOMAS GOOGE (GOUGE).

58. THOMAS PRATT.

59. SAMUEL PLAYER.

60. ROBERT WARDE.

61. BENJAMIN CARRIER. See p. 52.

62. CHRISTOPHER DIGGES. This boy was a member of the ancient Kentish family, and a kinsman of Leonard Digges, senior, and Thomas Digges, the mathematicians, with Leonard Digges, junior, who wrote the prefatory poem to Shakespeare's First Folio. Christopher Digges was an improvident young man, and is more than once found in court for debt.

63. WILLIAM HEWETT.

64. MATTHEW PARKER. He was son to John Parker, son of Archbishop Matthew Parker. He was the recipient of 1,100 books from his grandfather's library. He was born 19 May 1570 at Canterbury, and matriculated as fellow-commoner at Corpus Christi College, Cambridge, at Michaelmas 1588. No subsequent academic career is recorded.

65. LAURENCE GARDINER.

66. EDWARD GEST.

67. JOHN DOBSON.

68. BEVELL LEWES.

69. WILLIAM DALTON (DAWTON).

70. FRANCIS WALLEYS.

71. FRANCIS MUNDAY.

72. RICHARD CONSANT. This boy is probably connected with Thomas Consant, usher of the King's School in 1588. Richard might be the scholar of Corpus Christi College, Cambridge, who matriculated in 1584. There is no evidence that he took a degree. Richard Consant at the King's School and his namesake at Cambridge are likely to be identical with Richard Consant (not specified as a graduate), accorded licence on 12 March 1588 to teach children at the tiny village of Preston near Wingham, Kent. As there were few village children to be taught, it is likely that Consant was to act as tutor in a private house.

73. STEPHEN CHURCH.

74. EDWARD WILLIAMS.

75. CHARLES TURNER.

76. THOMAS WALSALL. He was undoubtedly connected with the Revd John Walsall, one of the 'Six Preachers' of Canterbury Cathedral at this time, and with the Revd William Walsall, who acted as minister at St George's church, Canterbury, for a short while from 1582, and was vicar of the neighbouring parish of St Paul from 1586.

77. RICHARD SHELLEY. He might conceivably have been a connection of the poet who had Sussex origins. The Canterbury scholar could have been kin to the William Shelley who held Patching manor, Sussex, from the dean and chapter of Canterbury. But there were humbler families about of the same name, such as the group in St George's, Canterbury (though no Richard is recorded among them).

78. JOHN PENDLETON.

79. —— MUNGEY. John Marlowe the shoemaker made claims for footwear and board for 'Mungey' and John Parette at the settlement of the headmaster's (Gresshop's) estate in 1580. He was probably a commoner at the school, and known to Marlowe. The name Mungey occurs as such, but may be a form of 'Mounjoy'.

80. JOHN PARETTE. See no. 79, above.

The inventory of John Gresshop, 1580

(Kent Archives Office PRC 21/4, fos. 169–75.)

[*fo. 169*]

Greshop

The apprisement of suche goodes as were late Mr John Greshops schoolemaister at Caunterburie deceased made the xxiij[th] [xxviij[th]?] of february 1579 R.R. Eliz. 22. By Mr Thomas Swifte Mr Will. Browne ministers of the saide churche, Mr John Marden singinge man, and [——] Faunt singing man.

Goodes in the great chamber where he died.
A ioined bedstedell wth head and tester of wainescot wth a rope and a mat – xij s.
A fetherbed, a Boulster, and a pillowe – xxx s.
An oulde matteris there prised at – ij s. vj d.
A paire of old blankets – iij s. iiij d.
A couerlet of greene dornix – viij s.
A white rug blanket – vj s. viij d.
Three olde curtins of say Red and greene wth iiij curtin Rods – iiij s.
An olde presse cubberd wise of wainscot – xvj s.

A ioyned cheste – v s.
A plated cofer – x s.
An olde cubberd – ij s. vj d.
A table upon a frame and a forme – ij s. vj d.
An olde courte cubberd – xij d.
A paire of Andirons, fireshouell, tounges, and gridiron – v s.
A paire of olde bellowes – ij d.
Two olde turned chaires – xij d.
An ould Curtin in the windowe wth a rod – viij d.
A hoope for a Basan, and a hooke for a towell – viij d.
The painted clothes there – xvj s.
apparell
Two paire of olde carsey hose – iij s. iiij d.
His best dublet of rashe, and best hose of the same – xiij s. iiij d.
Two old dublets one of rashe, and thother of mockadow –
 iij s. iiij d.
An olde spanishe lether Jerkin – ij s.
A cap, and a hat – ij s.
An olde peese of course serge – xij d.
An olde mockadowe cassok – xij d.

[*fo. 169v*]

A black cloth cote – viij s.
A cloke w^t sleeves – xiij s. iiij d.
A rounde cloke with silver clapses – xxx s.
An olde gowne of buffin faced w^t budge – x s.
The beste gowne – liij s. iiij d.
An olde cloth gowne faced w^t budge – x s.

In the plated chest
A surplace and a hood – vj s. viij d.
five olde shirtes – xij s.
fiue iij cornerd kirchers – ij s. vj d.
Three handetowells – xij d.
Three short table clothes – iij s.
Foure olde pillowberes – iij s.

xj table napkins – iiij s.
An olde wallet – iij d.
Certaine new cloth and Remnantes – iij s. iiij d.
vj paire of sheetes – xxx s.
iij course sheetes for boyes – v s.
v sheetes in a bag – xx s.
ij good shirtes wth ij peeses of shirtes in a bag – x s.
v pillowe cotes – vj s. viij d.
An olde corner kircher and vj handkerchers – xx d.
foure tynne spoones – ij d.
A pot, and a glasse – xij d.
A dagger – vj d.
A girdle – j d.
A girdle of chaungeable silke – xij d.
An olde crowne of a velvet hat – ij d.
A Jacket of olde damaske – iij s. iiij d.
Sixe bookes in the cofer – ij s.

In the paved Chamber
A foldbedsteedell, coorde, and mat – xiij s. iiij d.
The tester of the same bed w^t iij curtins of unfrised cotton all greene
    – vj s. viij d.
A little fether bed, a boulster, a pillowe, and a mattrice – xxvj, s.
    viij d.

[*fo. 170*]

A course paire of blankets, whereof one is linse wolse – iij s. iiij d.
A coverlet of tapistrie course – xiij s. iiij d.
iij curtyn roddes – xij d.
5 olde ioinde stooles and a courte cubberd – iiij s.
A square table, and a ioined foorme – iiij s.
A little old cubberd, and an olde chaire – ij s.
Two pewter Basons, and one pewter dishe – ij s.
A glasse lanterne – xij d.
Two tyn candlestickes and a pewter pot – xvj d.
A rapiar, and a skene – iiij s.

Two stone pots – iiij d.
A table of praedestination – iiij d.
The hanginges – x s.
A curtin rod in the windowe – vj d.
viij cushins – viij s.
A longe cushin – xvj d.
A cubberd clothe partie coloured wᵗ rowse – ij s.
A peece of penniston greene – vj d.
A deske – iiij d.
ij chaires – xij d.
A lattin candelsticke – viij d.
An olde ches boarde and men – xij d.
A cofer wᵗ a locke upon it for Wilder – xx d.
A couering of rowed worke and coloures much like to churche
    worke – x s.
A flocke bed and a strawe bed, and a flocke boulster – v s.
An olde fethered boulster – ij s.
A matterice, a mat, and a flocke boulster in the chamber underneath
    Mr Dorrels chamber ad lavam – xvj d.

In the chamber of W.D.
A bedsteedell – xx s.
A rounde table wᵗ a seat very olde – xij d.
A ioyned stoole – vj d.
Two olde courte cubberds – ij s.
Two olde peweter chamber pots – xvj d.
An old lattin candelstick –

[*fo. 170v*]

In Buls chamber
A little olde fetherbed and an olde flocke boulster – x s.
A truckle bed an a mat – ij s. vj d.
A table wᵗ trestells – vj d.
An olde foorme – iiij d.

Summa totalis – xxviijˡⁱ iiij s. v

Thomas Swyfte
William Browne

[*fo. 171*]

In the upper study by the schoole doare

(In primis in the windowe bookes – xxxvj
Item upon the east shelve bookes – Cxiiij
Item upon a hie shelve westward book – xxviij
Item upon a shelfe under that books – xxxvj)

Viz. Libri in folio
Brentius in Osea, una cum Buceri libro de regno christi – iij s. iiij d.
Concordantiae Zisti Graeca – ij s.
Hofman de paenitantia – iij s.
Tabulae locorum Philippi Melancthonis – ij s. vj d.
Roffensis contra Lutherum – ij s.
Philippus presbiter in Jobu – xij d.
Biblia pagnini – ij s. vj d.
Liber Charlaceus –
Tomus tertius et 4^{tus} et v^{tus} operum Melancthonis – iij s. iiij d.
Commentarius in rhetorica Ciceronis – iij s. iiij d.
Commentarii Doleti vol. 2 libri due – x s.
Urbani grammatica graeca – viij d.

quarto
Institutiones Juris Civilis graecae – xij d.
Demosthenis Epistolae, pars thucididis, Comaediae Aristophanis
    uno vol graeca – postilla peruetus –
Opuscula quaedam Lutheri, Calvini, Bullingeri, Gualteri uno
    volumine in quarto – x [—]
Claudius Sissellus de providentia – vj d.
Martis in Epistolam ad Corinthios – iij s.
Casninus in Galatas – viij d.
Victoria papatus – xij d.
Calvinus in psalmos – xx d.
Oeco Lampadius in Danielem – x d.
Retmanius de Justificatione – iij d.

An Answere to the Crosse Anglice – x d.

And Englishe booke for the governement of women alias the harborow etc. – iiij d.

Lanaeterus in Josnan – xij d.

octavo

Petrus Lombardus – vj d.

Liber Digestorum – viij d.

Opera quaedam minuta Augustini – iiij d.

Zodiacus vitae Anglice – vj d.

Bezae Epistolae –

Liber vetus hieromini vidae de poetica – j d.

Martir de Caelibatu et voti – 12 d.

Lutherus in Ecclesiasten – 4 d.

[*fo. 171v*]

Wolfgangus Capito de Missa et iure magistratus – 6 d.

Ecclesiasticae disciplinae liber – 4 d.

Sturmij prolegomena – 4 d.

Pij poetae uno volumine – 6 d.

Lutherus in 7 caput prioris ad Corinthios – 4 d.

Carmina phocilidis graeco latina – 2 d.

An Englishe booke of divinity Commen places – 4 d.

Catechesis Christiana – 2 d.

De linguae graecae pronunciatione liber – 3 d.

Ars loquendi et tacendi, Knanstino Autore – 2 d.

A viewe of mans estate englishe – 2 d.

A Catechisme Englishe – 1 d.

Nowels Catechismes two in Latin, one in Englishe –

Portius de ponderibus et mensuris – 1 d.

the Sickmans salve – 6 d.

Melancthon de renovatione Ecclesiasticae disciplinae cum caeteris – 6 d.

Liber de vitae et obitu Bucerj Carro authore – 6 d.

Prima pars Biblioni graece et Secunda graece, item at tertia – 3 s 4 d.

A faithfull admonicion made by Knokes – 2 d.

Varia poemata quorundam veteris de corrupto Ecclesiae statu – 6 d.
Liber psalmorum Davidis cum Annotationibus Stephanj –
Gregorius Nissenus de opificio hominis, cum opellis Ignatij – 12 d.
Boetij Consolatio – 14 d.
Epistolae Calvini duae – 6 d.
Beconus et Bertramus de Caena domini uno volumine – 8 d.
The Anatomie of the Masse – 4 d.
De religionis Conservatione, et de primatu magistratuum Laurentio
    humfrido autore –
Pandectae Scripturarum – 6d.
Oecolampadius in Mathaeu – 6d.
Oecolampadius in Joanni – 6d.
De compescendis animi affectibus Aloisius Luisinus – 3 d.
Oecolampadius in Genesiu – 5 d.
Opera Erasmi quadam uno volumine – 4 d.
Dionisius Carthusianus in Luca – 6 d.
Ecclesiastes Erasmi –
Sententia prosperj – 8 d.
Tirelus upon the Lordes Praier in Englishe – 6 d.
Liber de differentia Ecclesiasticae et regalis potestatis – 4 d.
Apologia Erasmi adversus quosdam Monachos –
Herman Archbushop of Colenia in Englishe – 6 d.
Peregrinatio Belgica – 6 d.

[*fo. 172*]

Oecolampadius in 4 minores prophetas – 6 d.
historia ecclesiastica Eusebij Latine – 3 d.
Silua Bibliorum Hominis – 6 d.
Oecolampadius in haebraeos – 4 d.
Trahern Upon the Apocalipse Englishe –
fabritius in Aba et prophetas minores – 12 d.
Artopaeus in Genesiu – 4 d.
Opera Cypriani aliquot 2 vol – 16 d.
ratio perveniendi ad veram theol. Erasmo autore – 6 d.
Loitherus de ferno arbitrio cum alijs – 6 d.
Pomeranus in Epistolas Paulj – 4 d.

The reliques of Rome –
Pandectes of the Evangelical Law made by pannel English – 6 d.
Colonienses adversus Melancthonem et aliorum – 5 d.
Anthologicon, id est florilegium graecorum aliquot – 6 d.
Synesij Epistolae – 6 d.
Bezae poemata – 6 d.
Lauaterus de spectris – 6 d.
Olaus magnus de gentibus Septentrionalibus – 8 d.
Catechismus ex decreto Concilij Tridentis – 6 d.
hemmingius de superstitionibus vitandis – 4 d.
Sermones aliquot Oecolampadij – 3 d.
Catechismus Carnutj –
A Sermon of Porders Englishe – 3 d.
Jewel ageinst Cole –
Peter Viret Englished by Shute –
Nowels Catechisme in Englishe 2 of them –
Doctor Smithes unwritten verities – 2 d.
Stephen Gardiners devels sophistry – o
Perrins sermons Englishe – 2 d.
Aliquot orationes demosthenis conversae a Carro Anglo – 6 d.
Whittingham of obedience to superior powers – 2 d.
A treatise for ministers apparrel Englishe – 4 d.
Marsilius ficinus de Christiana religione – 6 d.
Methodus Confessionis – 3 d.
Danaeus de beneficis –
Knoxe upon praedestinacion – 4 d.
Confessio Saxonicarum Ecclesiarum – 2 d.
Quaestiones pueriles Joannis Agricolae – 2 d.
Catechismus Anglicus autore Anonumo – 2 d.
Liber de Commuratione Scoticae reginae –
Cranmers Confutacion of unwritten verities – 4 d.

[*fo. 172v*]

Sillogisticon foxij – 3 d.
The Christian state of matrimonie Englishe – 1 d.

of obedience of Subiectes Englishe – 2 d.
An Englishe booke of the disclosing of the greate bull – 1 d.
A booke of Songes and Sonnettes Englishe – 1 d.
The philosopher of the Court in Englishe – 2 d.
Confession Ecclesiarum helneticarum – 4 d.
An Invective ageinst treason in Englishe – 1 d.
Epistola Lutherj contra Sabbatharios – 1 d.
The benefit of Christes death in Englishe – 1 d ob
Goughes answere ageinst fecknam –
Nortons admonicion to the Queenes subiects – 1 d.
An Admonicon in Scottishe –
Against the use of Popishe garments in the Church – 1 d.
A politicke discourse –
An Informacion to the parliament englishe – ob
Luciani dialogi aliquot – viij d.
Fentons discourse of the Warres in Fraunce – 2 d.
An Englishe Catechisme –
Bonners Dirige – j d.
A Sermon of Deringes – 1 d.
An Englishe Catechisme – 2 d.
Quaestiones Bezae – 3 d.
A Sermon D fulcke –
A warning ageinst papists – 1 d.
Calvinus de Praedestinatione – 3 d.
A Sermon of Bradfordes – 1 d.
Tragical discourses by the L Buckhurst –
The fall of the late Arrian – 2 d.
Vincentius Livinensis de Antiquitate fidej Cath. – 2 d.
Vives de Anima Libri tres – 16 d.
Macrobij opera – 8 d.
Aristoteles de mundo – 4 d.
Lexicon graecolatini Ciceronianis – 8 d.
Institutiones fricksij Medicinales – 10 d.
Gazae Grammatica graeca – 4 d.
Syntaxis linguae graecae Varennio authori – 4 d.
Demosthenis et Aeschinis orationes contrariae – 8 d.
Marcellus de proprietate linguae latinae – 12 d.

Marsilij ficinj opuscula – vj d.
Albertus magnus de formatione hominis – 2 d.

[*fo. 173*]

Luciani dialogi Latini factj – 8 d.
Digestorum liber secundus – 8 d.
Hesiodus Graecolatinus – 6 d.
Budaei Annotationes in Pandestas – 6 d.
Lingua Erasmj – 6 d.
Adrianus Cardinalis de Sermone Latino – 3 d.
Platinae dialogus de falso et vero bono – 2 d.
Some of Zenophon translated into Englishe – 4 d.
Vives de Lingua Latina – 2 d.
Polibius in Englishe – 4 d.
Vives de disciplinjs – 12 d.
De ratione studij puerilis – 6 d.
Erotemata rhetorica Jodoci – 8 d.
Sabellicus de moribus gentius –
Poema Alcimi – 2 d.
Balduinus de Constantino Magno – 20 d.
Caelius Secundus de Artificio disserendj – 4 d.
Sebastianus forius de historiae institutione – 4 d.
Aristoteles de arte rhetorica graece – 2 d.
Historia Sacrementaria de Caena – 8 d.
Phocilidis Poema ἐλληνικον – 2 d.
Nominis in Evangelium Joannis – 3 d.
Alcialtus de quinque pedum praescriptione – 3 d.
Aristophanis εἰρηνή graece – 2 d.
Item thre Paper bookes –
Demosthenes πρὸς Λεπτίνην 1 d.

books in decimo sexto
herodiamus graece – 4 d.
Cominej historia – 8 d.
Bellum grammaticale – 1 d.
Galenj de Compositione pharmacerum – 8 d.

Ilias homerij graece – 6 d.
Petrus Crinetus – 12 d.
Methodus medendi Galeno autore – 10 d. [20 d.?]
Biel de Canone Missae – 3 d.
Pentateuchus Moisis – 4 d.
Catechismus Calvinj Graecolatinus – 4 d.
Gribaldus de ratione studendi – 6 d.
Contemplationes Idiotae – 2 d.
Problemata Arist – 4 d.
Fenestella de Magis fratibus – 8 d.

[*fo. 173v*]

Knoxes Epistles – 1 d.
Compendium theologicae veritatis – 0
Ovid de tristibus Englishe – 2 d.
Nowels Catechismes in number 6 – 12 d.

Plate and other things of the said Mr Gressops

In primis a pot of silver and gilt with a covir waying ix ounz one
quarter at iij s ix d the ounce – xliiij s viij d.
Item iij silver spones waying iiij ounces and a quarter – xx s. vj d.
Item a bosse of a gyrdle and a whistle ij ounces almos – ix s. vj d.
Item two gold Rings half an ounce – 1 s.
Sum of the plat – vj li. iiij s. viij d.

[*fo. 174*]

In the lower study
in folio
Inprimis Plato Latini – ij s.
Opera Petrarchj – vj s.
Scotus in 4 ^um Sententiarum – viij d.
Officia Ciceronis cum Commentario –
Munsterj Cosmographia – iiij s.
Thesaurus Ciceronjs – vj s. viij d.
Annotationes Erasmj in novum testamentum – iiij s.

Fabians Chronicle – iij s.
Biblia Latine – iij s. iiij d.
Biblia Castalionis – iiij s.
Martir in Judicum, et Samuelem – vj s. viij d.
Concordantiae Bibliorum – xij d.
Martir in Rom. Anglici – iij s. iiij d.
Flores historiaris – iiij s.
Familiares Epistolae Ciceronis cum Commentario – ij s. vj d.
Chaucer – ij s.
Boccatius de genealogia Deoris – ij s.
Locj Communes Martiris – v s.
Galenus de temperamentis cum alijs – ij s.
A Geneva Bible – v s.
Virgilius cum Commentario – ij s.
Jewesl [*sic*] Defence of the Apologie – iiij s.
Ovidij Metamorphosis cum Commentario – viij d.

In quarto
Grammatica Clenardj cum annot. Antesignanj – xij d.
Lauaterus in proverbia – xx d.
Foxius in Osorium –
Aschams Schoolemaster – iiij d.
Camerarius et Alij in tusculanas quaest – xij d.
Dictionarium poeticum – xvj d.
Officia Ciceronis, cum diversorum Commentarijs – xvj d.
Philo Judaeus in Decalogum – vj d.
Martis in Ethicam Arist. – ij s.
Valla de summo bono – viij d.
Langnettes Chronicles – xvj d.
The Image of both Churches – iiij d.
Psalterum Latini – iiij d.

[*fo. 174v*]

Dionisius Carthusianus de orthodoxa fide – iiij d.
Bibliand. de fatis Monarchiae Romanae –

Rom'archijs contra de visibili Monarchia Saunderj – iij d.
Cartwrightes replie ageinst Whitegift – ij d.
Higini historia – iiij d.
Aristophanes Graec. – vj d.
Arist. Politica Strabaeo tralatore – iiij d.
Wilsons logick English – viij d.
Some bookes of Ovides Metam. English – ij d.
the praise of foly Englishe – ij d.
Haddoni Opellae – iiij d.
A discourse of the affaires in Germany by Ascham – ij d.
Liber Juris Canonicj prima pars – xij d.

In octavo
Institutiones Calvini – ij s vj d.
Plautus – xij d.
Grammatica Graeca Crusij – xx d.
Pij quida poetae uno vol. – x d.
Pars quarta Livij – vj d.
Diallacticon Sacramentarus Boquino autore – vj d.
Plutarchi quadam opuscula – viij d.
Terentius Cum Commentario – xij d.
Sophoclis Tragaediae Latini – viij d.
Confession Bezae, cum alijs – xij d.
Claudianus poeta – xij d.
Locij Communes Joannis Manlij – xij d.
Facetia Bebetij cum alijs – viij d.
Facetia Brusonij – viij d.
A praesident for a prince – ij d.
Valentinus Erithraeus de Conscribendis Epistolis – viij d.
Agrippa de vanitate Scientiaris – vj d.
Apollinarius graecus in psalmos – vj d.
Tusculanes Quaestions Englishe, wth the office – vj d.
Ovides Metamorphosis wth the pictures – viij d.
Syntaxis Linguae graecae – iiij d.
Linacri Grammatica – viij d.
Sophoclis Tragaediae graece – viij d.

[*fo. 175*]

Solinus polyhistor. – viij d.
A pretiouse perle, id est, and englishe booke so called – iij d.
Eliottes governor – vj d.
Erasmus Enchiridion englishe – iij d.
Castalionis Dialogj – xij d.
Catechismus Chytraes – iij d.
Physica, et Ethica valorij – iiij d.
De ratione discendae linguae Graecae – vj d.
Sadoletus de pueris instituendis – iiij d.
The new testament in Englishe – xij d.
Erotemata de Copia rerum et verborum, cum alijs – vj d.
Arithmetica Gemmae frisij – iiij d.
Processus Judiciarius Panormitanj – ij d.
Aesopij fabulae – ij d.
Juvenalis – iij d.
Orationes. 6. Isocratis, sex exiquis sed distinctis vol. – ij s.
Utopia Mori Latine – ij d.
Theophil in evangelia – xij d.
Theoph. in Epistolas – xij d.
Homiliae Bedae – viij d.
Grammerus de Transubs Cantiatione – iiij d.
Clauis theologiae – iii j d.
Sermones de tempore – iiij d.

In decimo sexto
Fabritius de poetica – vj d.
Flaminius in psalmos – viij d.
Novum testam. graece – viij d.
Epistolae ad Atticus – xij d.
Epistolae familiares – vj d.
Commentarij Caesaris – vj d.
Flaminij paraph. in 30 psalmos cum alijs – iiij d.
tres lib. de vitis Imperatoris Romanorum – ij s.
Preces Sacrae – iiij d.
Officia Ciceronis et Terentius uno vol – xij d.

Testamentum graecis in duabus partibus – x d.
Frutisius de medendj – viij d.
Sibillina Oracula cum alijs – vj d.

[*fo. 175v*]

Virgilius – viij d.
Manutij Epistolae – viij d.
Libri proph. omnis – vj d.
Palingenius – vj d.
Artus Gellius – xij d.
Concordantiae biblioni et Canonum perexignae – ij d.
Ephemerides Phialo – ij d.
A Dispraise of the Courtiers Life – ij d.
A praeparacion to the Lordes Supper – j d.
A touche stone for this praesent time – j d.
Symbola Joannis Laezij – j d.
Vassaeus de Judicio Trinarum – j d.
Summa totalis totius Inv^m – xlvj^li xij s. x d.

Priced by Mr John Hill Prebendarye in chists churche in Canterbury
  Frauncis Aldriche and [——] Rose the ij. Martij 1579.

Besides the bookes aboue named there are of old rustie bookes about
  xviij

Monye found after his deathe
In primis a spurre royall and a frenshe crowne of the value of – xxj s.
Item in mylle sixepences and Edward tweluepenns – xix s. vj d.
Item in pence and thre halfe pence – xl s.
Item in ready sylver in the tawnye purse – iiij^li ij s. xj d.
Item in an other purse – ij s. x d.
Summa Totalis – viij li. vj s. iij d.

The will of Katherine Benchkin of Stour Street,
Canterbury, widow of James Benchkin, read aloud
in her house by Christopher Marlowe on a Sunday in
November 1585; with evidence in a lawsuit
relating to the will decribing Christopher
Marlowe's part in the episode

A. *The Will*

(Kent Archives Office PRC 16/36.)
*Some inconsistent usage in punctuation and of capital letters has been regularized. Some
marks used as line fillers by the scribe have been ignored.*

In the name of god Amen. The xixth day of August in the xxvijth
yeare of the raigne of our Souereigne Lady Elizabeth by the grace
of god of England France and Ireland Quene Defender of the feith
etc. I Katherine Benchkyn of the parishe of St Myldred of the citie
of Canterbury widowe being in good and perfect remembrance
(god be praysed therfore) considering wth my self that all people
are mortall and vncertaine of the hower of the deathe, I do
therefore make my last will and Testament in manner and forme
following That is to say. First I commend my sowle to almightie
god my maker redemer and comforter most stedfastly trusting to
be saved and inherite eternall lief only by the death and passion of
my Lord and savio^r Jesus Christ, And my will is that after my
discease my body be decently buried in the churchyard of the
parishe of St Mildredes aforesayd as nere to the grave of my late
husband Jeames Benchkyn as may be: Item I will, there be made

att my buriall a sermon by some learned preacher, Item I give to the poore people of the parishe of St Mildred aforesayd xx^s, to be distributed amongest them within one weeke next after my buryall. Item I give to the poore people of the parishe of St Marie of Northgate of the same citie, xx^s to be distributed amongest them within one weeke next after my buryall. Item I will that my executors shall pay to the mayor and cominaltie of the said citie of Canterbury for the time being xx^l of good and lawfull monie of England within one [yere] next after my discease. And my will is that the sayd mayor and cominaltie of the same citie for the time being shall with the said monye within one yere next after the receit therof buy one Tenement within the sayd citie of Canterbury or within the liberties of the same And that the yearlie proffittes and revenewes of the said tenement shalbe and remaine to the vse of the brothers and sisters of the Hospitall commonly called Maynardes spittle Sett and being within the said parishe of St Myldred for ever, And my will that the said Mayor and cominaltie of the said citie of Canterbury for the time being shall vppon the receipt of the sayd xx^{li} be bounden in writing obligatory to my executor his heires or assignes in dowble the value therof, either to bestowe the same xx^l in manner and forme as is aforesayd and to the vse as is aforesaid, or ells to repay the same xx^l to my executor or to his assignes To the vse of my [said] executor his heires and assignes within one yeare and a quarter next after the said receipt therof. Item I give and bequethe to Jehan Ansted my mayd servant v^{li} of good and lawfull mony of England, a fetherbed, a bolster a blanckett a coverlett iiij^{or} payer of sheets ii^o pillowes two fine pillowe coates A spitt a dripping pan a brasse pott of ij^o gallons or therabouts, a cobyron a Stupnett a chafing-dishe & a chest To be payd and delivered her within one yere next after my discease, Item I constitute and appoint John Benchkyn the sonne of my late disceased husband Jeames Benchkyn to be the sole executor of this my last will and Testament and I desyer my kinsman Thomas [altered from 'Robert'] Greneleafe to be the overseer of the same. Also I will that the ccc^{li} that is now in my cosen Greneleafes handes to the vse of the sayd John Benchkyn yf he [sheet 2] dye before he comme to the age of xxj^{ty}

yeares shalbe payd to the major and cominaltie of the citie of
Canterbury for the time being to the vses and intentes herafter
following That is to say I will that the sayd ccc^{li} shall from time to
time herafter forever, by the mayor and cominaltie of the sayd
citie of Canterburie or the more part of them for the time being be
freely lent to suche persons as shall inhabite & dwell within the
sayd citie of Canterbury and liberties of the same, vsing the trade
of clothe making, that is to say in making of wollen clothe And
my will is that noe man shall have above l^l therof att one time But
a lesse portion therof as yt shall [seme] meete to the sayd mayor
and cominaltie of the sayd citie of Canterbury of the more part of
them for the time being during the space of fower yeres without
paying anie thing for the vse and occupieng therof, And that
every suche person which shall receive suche summe of mony or
lesse, (as to the ['sayd' cancelled] mayor and cominaltie or the
more part of them for tyme being shall seme good as aforesaid)
shalbe bound with two sufficient suerties to the mayor and
cominaltie of the said citie of Canterbury or the more part of them
in dowble the value therof for the repayment of the same to them,
att every suche iiij yeres end, and so from iiij yeres to fower yeres
in manner and forme as is aforesaid forever, Item I give and
bequethe to Julyan Bonham of Stalesffeld iij^l of good and lawfull
monie of England to be payd vnto her immediatly after my
discease, Item I give and bequethe vnto the ij° childeren of my
sayd sister Julian Bonham xl^s apeese to be payd vnto them within
one yere next after my discease. Item I give and bequeth to the iij
children of my sister Johan Wells xl^s a peese to be payd to them
within one yeare next after my descease Item I give and bequethe
vnto Stephen Glover Josua Glover Richard Glover Nicholas
Greneleafe and John Greneleafe the childeren of Margaret Greneleafe my kynswoman now wief of the sayd Thomas Greneleafe
xl^s a peese of good and lawfull mony of England to be payd vnto
them within one yere next after my sayd decease, Provided alweis
and my will is that if anie of the said childeren shall chaunce to die
before his or their portion shalbe due to be payd, then my
meaning is that my sayd executor shall have his and their portions
so dyeing to his owne vse for ever, Item I give and bequethe to the

sayd Margaret Greneleaf my kinswoman xl^s of good and lawfull monie of England to be payd her within one yere next after my sayd decease. Item I give and bequethe to Margery Drawnam my kinswoman xl^s of good and lawfull mony of England to be payd her within one yere next after my sayd decease. Item I give to John Benchkyn my late husbond Jeames Benchkyns brothers sonne xl^s to be payd vnto him imediatlie after my decease, Item I give vnto Margaret Fusser my daughter in lawe xl^s to be payd vnto her imediatlie after my discease, Item I give unto Haywardes wief my late husband Jeames Benchkins kynswoman xl^s of good and lawfull monie of England. Item I give to the five childeren of John Fusser vj^s viij^d a peese, Item I give to my daughter in lawe John Wevells wief xl^s Item I give to her ij^o childeren vj^s viij^d a peese, Item I give to my sonne in lawe John Hart xl^s, and I give to his sonne George Hart vj^s viij^d, Item I give to Agnes Post widowe my kinswoman xx^s, Item I give to my cosen Harris wief of Pluckley xx^s. Item I give to Fordes widowe of the parishe of St Mary Northgate xx^s to be payd imediatlie after my decease. Item I give to Aunsells widowe of St Mildredes aforesayd xx^s, Item I give to Crowder of the same parishe xx^s Item I give to Joane ys [sheet 3] of the same parishe xx^s. Item I give to Adams widowe xx^s Item I give to Drables widowe xx^s. Item I give to my cosen Agnes Poyser xx^s. Item I give to Agnes Aunsell the daughter of the foresayd widowe Aunsell xx^s, Item I give to Johan Aunsell her sister xx^s. And my will and meaning is that all those aboue named where noe time of payment is expressed shalbe payd presentlie after my descease. Item I give to Mr Hills parson of St Mildredes aforesayd xx^s to be payd him within one yere next after my said decease. Provided that if anie here mencioned in this my will shall fortune to dye before the payment of the monie above bequethed, then I will that the legacie of him her or them so dyeing shalbe and remaine unto the aforenamed John Benchkyn my executor his heyres and assignes. The resydewe of all my good chattells and moveables whatsoever not bequethed my debts and legaces payd and all ordenarie charges satisfied I give and bequethe vnto the aforenamed John Benchkyn my sayd executor and his assignes for ever. Provided alweis and my will and minde is, that if the sayd

John Benchkyn shall dye before the age of xxj^{ty} yeres that then the foresayd John Benchkyn my late husband Jeames Benchkyns brothers sonne shall have v^l of lawfull monie of England out of the resydewe of my goodes given as aforesayd to the sayd John Benchkyn my executor. And also I will that if my executor shall dye, (as aforesayd), then I will that Richard Glover my godsonne shall have out of the same resydewe of goodes given as aforesayd to the sayd John Benchkyn my executor. A fetherbed and a dozen of damaske napkins, And the resydewe of that goodes to be sold to the value thereof And my cosen Thomas Greneleafe (yf he shalbe then living) to have the buying therof before another. And the monye therof comming to be payd to the mayor and cominaltie for the time being of the citie aforesayd by them to be employed towardes the maintenaunce and bringing vp of poore childeren within the same citie. Provided also and will and intent is, that yf my executor John Benchkyn dye (as is aforesayd) That then the sayd Thomas Greneleafe shal have to him and his assignes the ij leases wherof thone is of ij gardens in the parishe of St Mary Northgate aforesayd and now in the occupation of one George Jeffrey, and the other is of ij howses within the parishe of St Mildred aforesayd. In witnes wherof I the sayd Katherine Benchkyn to this my present will have sett my marke and seale in the presence of

Jhan Marley   this is Katherine Benchkins mark
Thomas Arthure
Christofer Marley
John Moore

B. *Evidence of John Moore, shoemaker, who married Jane, sister of Christopher Marlowe, in case relating to estate of Katherine Benchkin, widow, recounted 30 September 1586.*

(Kent Archives Office PRC 39/11, fo 234)

super testamentum Benchkin
examinat' vltimo Septembris 1586

Johannes Moore civitatis Cant shomaker vbi habitavit per sex annos et antea in villa de Feversham per septem annos et antea in parrochia de Vlcombe vbi habitavit per xv annos oriundus ibidem aetatis circiter xxvi annos vel circiter libere condicionis testis productus iuratus et examinatus dicit et deponit vt sequitur

Quoad testamentum et allegacionem predict' iste deponens in vim iuramenti sui prestiti examinatus dicit that some what more then a twelvmonthes agon as this deponent now remembreth aliter certum diem et tempus non recolit vt dicit hee this deponent together with Thomas Arthur John Marly and Christofer Marley beeing requested by John Benchkin the testatrix her soonne came all vnto the howse of the saide testatrix scituat in St Mildredes parishe in Canterburye where at their coming they fownde the saide testatrix in a lower parlor of her saide howse in very good heath [sic] to this deponentes iudgement and ymedyatly the saide testatrix went vpp into a chamber of her said howse and brought downe her will written in such forme as is exhibited and alsoe an other will which was made beefore the will now exhibited and towlde this deponent and the rest that shee had sente for them to bee witnesses vnto her will, and to see her owlde will burned wheruppon she cast her saide owlde will into the fire and burned the same in the presence of this deponent and the other parties afforenamed and then shee gave her saide will now exhibited vnto Cristofer Marley to bee redd, which he red plainely and distinktly and beeing soe red the saide testatrix acknowledge the same to bee her laste will and testament, revoking and disanulling all other wills and testamentes by her beefore made and in witnes of the same shee put thervnto her hande and seale in the presence of this deponent and the partyes afforesaide and requested this deponent and the saide partyes to sett to their handes wheruppon this deponent and the saide partyes subscribed their names with their owne handes to the saide will as witnesses to the same, and this deponent saith that the saide testatrix was by all the tyme afforesaide not onely in good remembrawnce but in perfect health to this deponentes iudgement and this deponent very well knoweth that the will wheruppon hee is now examined beeing viewed and red by him at his examinacion is the self same will soe acknowledged by the testatrix as is afforesaide as well for that hee seeth his name subscribed to the saide will with his owne hand as alsoe for that hee remembreth divers legacies given in the saide will and amoungest the rest that she named and appointed John Benchkin her sonne executor of the same and one Greenleafe of Cant her overseer and further willed as in the saide will executed is deduced et aliter nescit deponere.

Repet' and recogn' coram me
Stephano Lakes officiali 30 Sept 1586.   John Moore

Documents relating to the fight at Canterbury
in September 1592 between Christopher Marlowe
and William Corkine, tailor and musician

A. *Entry under date 26 September 1592 in the Plea Roll of the
Canterbury Civil Court*

(Canterbury Cathedral Archives and Library BAC J/B/392)

Manucapcio	Willelmus Corkyn (ponit loco E(gidium) W(inston)
xij d.	[interlined]) queritur versus Christopherum
	Marlowe (ponit loco J(ohannem) S(mith)
	[interlined]) in placito transgressionis plegii de
	prosequendo Johannes Doo et Ricardum Roo
	defendens captus est et manucaptus per Johannem
	Marlowe iiij^d iiij^d secundo Octobris querens narrauit
	defendens habet licenciam loquendi ix° Octobris non
	pros' ex assensu

B. *On 25 September 1592 in the Canterbury Civil Court, Narrative of
plaint submitted by Giles Winston, attorney, on behalf of his client,
William Corkine, alleging assault on 15 September 1592 by Christopher
Marlowe, gentleman*

(Canterbury Cathedral Archives and Library BAC J/B/S/392)

Ciuitas Cantuar'
Willelmus Corkyn queritur de Christophero Marlowe generoso in placito transgressionis Et sunt plegii de prosequendo scilicet Johannes Doo et Ricardus Roo Et vnde idem querens per Egidium Wynston attornatum suum queritur quod predictus defendens quinto decimo die Septembris anno regni domine nostre Elizabeth Dei gracia Anglie Francie et Hibernie regine fidei defendoris etc. tricesimo quarto hic apud ciuitatem Cantuar' predictam in parochia sancti Andree et in warda de Westgate eiusdem ciuitatis vi et armis videlicet baculis et pugionibus in ipsum querentem insultum fecit et ipsum querentem adtunc et ibidem verberauit vulnerauit et maletractauit Et alia enormia dicto querenti adtunc et ibidem intulit ad graue dampnum ipsius querentis et contra pacem dicte domine regine nunc vnde idem querens dicit quod deterioratus est et dampnum habet ad valenciam quinque librarum et inde producit sectam.

C. *Grand Jury indictment at Canterbury Quarter Sessions held 26 September 1592 against William Corkine, tailor, for assault on 10 (15?) September 1592, upon the person of Christopher Marlowe, gentleman*

(Canterbury Cathedral Archives and Library BAC J/Q/392)

Ciuitas Cantuar'
Jur' present' pro domina regina quod Willelmus Corkyn de ciuiate Cant' predicta tayler decimo die septembris anno regni domine Elizabethe dei gracia Anglie Francie et Hibernie regine fidei defensoris etc. tricesimo quarto hic apud ciutatem Cant' predictam in parochia sancti Andree et in warda de Westgate eiusdem ciuitatis in quendam Christopherum Marlowe generosum insultum fecit ac ipsum Christopherum Marlowe adtunc et ibidem verberauit ['et' cancelled] vulnerauit et male tractauit et alia enormia dicto Christophero Marlowe adtunc et ibidem intulit ad graue dampnum ipsius Christopheri et contra pacem dicte domine regine nunc etc.

[Endorsed:] Ignoramus [and slashed diagonally three times]

Entries relating to administration of goods
of Eleanor Bull of Deptford, widow (1596) in whose
house Christopher Marlowe was slain

Act Book of the Ecclesiastical Court, Diocese of Rochester,
deposited in Kent Archives Office, Maidstone. (NB: there are two
versions of the Act Book, one a rough version and clearly done in
court, the other a fair version. The entries below are taken from the
fair version (DRb, Pa 15), with notes of any variations in the rough
copy (DRb Pa 16). The volumes are unfoliated and the first entry
appears under date 20 March 1595-6.)

Deptford.
Cave ne aliquid in [sic] fiat in bonis Elenore Bull vidue nuper dum
vixit parochie de Deptford Roffen' dioces' defuncte priusquam
vocatur Johannes Whitney de Lamheth avunculus dicte defuncte
qui hanc cautionem per nuncium suum [famulum] suum intravit.

Under date Saturday 12 June 1596.

Deptford.
Commissa fuit administracio bonorum Ellinore Bull vidue nuper
cum vixit parochie de Deptford Roffen' dioces' defuncte Georgio
[Bull] proximo consanguineo dicti defuncti [sic] primitus de bene
&c. Jurato &c. Saluo iure cuiuscumque &c.
[in margin] Pro inventario Michaelis prox. Obligentur Georgius
Bull de Harlow in comitatu Essex yeoman et Georgius Hanger
ciuitatis London clothworker et Robertus Savedge de eadem
ironmonger.

The wills of John and Katherine Marlowe
parents of Christopher Marlowe (1605)

A. *The will of John Marlowe*

(Kent Archives Office PRC 16/125 (original will) and PRC 17/52, fo. 373 registered copy)

In the name of God Amen, 1604 [i.e., 1605 by modern reckoning] the 23rd day of January, I John Marlowe being sick of body but thanks be to Almighty God of good and perfect remembrance do make constitute and ordain this my last Will and Testament in manner and form following. First I give and commend my soul into the hands of Almighty God my maker and redeemer, and my body to be buried in the churchyard of the parish of St George within Canterbury. As touching my temporal goods my debts and funerals discharged and paid I give and bequeath wholly to my wife Katherine, whom I make my sole executrix. In witness whereof I John Marlowe have to this my last Will and Testament set to my hand and seal the day and year above written.

The mark of John Marlowe

In the presence of those whose names are here underwritten

James Bissell the writer hereof
Vyncent Huffam
Thomas Plesynton

B. *The will of Katherine Marlowe, widow of John Marlowe, shoemaker*

(Kent Archives Office PRC 16/127 (original will) and PRC 17/54, fo. 267 registered copy)

In the name of God, amen. I Katherine Marlowe widdowe of John Marlowe of Canterbury late deceassed, though sicke in bodye yet in perfect memorye I giue God thankes, do ordayne this my last will and testament, written one the 17 of Marche in the yeare of our Lorde God 1605 [i.e., 1605] in manner and forme as followethe. First I doe bequeathe my soule to God my sauiour and redeemer, and my bodye to be buryed in the churcheyarde of St Georges in Canterburye neare where as my husbande John Marlowe was buryed. I do dequeathe vnto my daughter Margaret Jurden the greatest golde ringe.

I doe bequeathe unto my daughter An Cranforde a golde ringe which my daughter Cradwell hath which I would haue her surrender vp vnto her sister An. and another siluer ringe.

I doe bequeathe vnto my daughter Doritye Cradwell, the ringe with the double posye. she [*sic*]

I doe bequeathe vnto my daughter Jurden my stuffe gowne and my kirtle.

I doe bequeathe vnto my daughter Cranforde my best cloathe gowne and the cloathe that is left of the same.

I doe bequeathe vnto my daughter Cradwell my cloathe gowne which I did weare euerye daye.

I doe bequeathe vnto my daughter Jurden one siluer spoone and vnto her eldest sonne John Jurden one greate siluer spoone, and vnto her son William one of the greatest siluer spoones of the sixe, and to Elisabethe Jurden one spoone.

I doe bequeathe vnto my daughter An Cranforde one siluer spoone and to her sonne Anthonye one of the greatest spoones, and to John an other of the greatest siluer spoones, and vnto Elisabeth Cranforde one spoone.

I doe bequeathe vnto my daughter Dorytye Cradwell one siluer spoone and to her sonne John Cradwell one of the greatest siluer spoones.

I doe bequeathe vnto my daughter Jurden two cushions and vnto my daughter Cranforde 2 cushions of taffete. and to my daughter Cradwell two cushions.

I do bequeathe my christeninge linnen as the kearcher, the damaske napkin, a face cloathe, and a bearinge blanket to be vsed equally betweene them, and to serue to euerye of theire needs but if my daughter Jurden doe goe out of the towne, my daughter An Cranforde to haue the keepinge of the same christeninge linnen. I doe bequeathe to euerye one of them one tablecloathe, and the fourthe, to goe for an odde sheete that he [*sic*] which hath the odde sheete may haue the table cloathe.

I doe bequeathe vnto euerye one of my daughters sixe paire of sheetes to bee diuided equallye. and instead of the sheete which is taken awaye, there is one tablecloathe added.

I doe bequeathe to euerye one of my daughters a dosen of napkins to be diuided equallye because some are better than other.

I doe bequeathe vnto my daughter Jurden three payre of pillowe coates, vnto my daughter Cranforde three payre of pillow coates, vnto my daughter Cradwell three payre of pillowe coates/ one payre of pillow coates I doe bequeathe vnto Katherine Reue. and vnto Goodwife Morrice one pillowe coate.

I do bequeathe vnto John Moore fortye shillinges, and the ioyne presse that standeth in the greate chamber where I lye.

I do bequeathe vnto Mary May my mayde my red pettitcoate, and a smocke.

I do bequeathe vnto Goodwife Morrice my pettitcoate that I doe weare daylye and a smocke and a wastcoate.

I doe beequeathe vnto Goodwife Jurden fortye shillinges.

I doe bequeathe vnto my daughter Cradwell twentye shillinges.

I would haue all these porcions to be paied within one yeare after my deceasse.

I doe beequeathe vnto my sonne Cranforde all the rest of my

goodes payinge my debts and legacyes and excharginge my funeralls, whoome I doe make my whole executor of this my laste will and testamente.

In witnesse whereof I haue heerevnto set my hande and seale.

Witnesses these names that are heere vnder written, and I [*sic*] Thomas Hudson. the writer hereof.

The marke of Katherine Marlowe [a roughly
   formed mark with a pen, with seal, device not
   readily identifiable, on turned–down tab at side
   of document]
the mark of Katherine Marlowe
the mark of Sarai Morrice
the mark of Mary Maye
[written on 17 March]

Inventory of the goods of John Marlowe, shoemaker,
compiled 21 February 1604–5

(Kent Archives Office PRC 3/26, fo. 105)

Marlow
An inuentorye of the goodes of John Marlow taken vppon the 21
daye of Februarye Anno Domini 1604. Prized by Mr Crispe
Thomas Pleasington and Robert Lyon.

Imprimis his girdle and his purse – iiij^s

In the litle parlour next the streete
A litle table with a frame and 3 ioyne stooles – v^s
Item a court cubborde with a carpet, a greate cushion, and
5 other – v^s

In the halle
Item a litle table with a frame – iij^s
Item one chest 3 chayres, and a glasse cage – iij^s iijd
Item one payre of brandirons, a payre of tonges, and a fire shouell,
a payre of bellowes, a fire rake, and a payre of pothangers – iiij^s
Item the paynted clothe – xij^d

In the kitchen

Item a litle table with a cubbord in it, an olde ioyne stoole and an olde form and one cushion a dressinge borde and an old coupe – ij^s

Item one olde plate cubborde and brine tubbe – iiij^s

Item one brandiron, one creeper, one spitte, one gridiron, one drippinge panne and a choppinge knife – iiij^s

Item 6 ketles 2 brasse pots, 2 stupnets, 2 iron pots, one chafinge dishe, 6 brasse candlestickes, and a morter with a pestle, one chafer of brasse a skimmer and a bastinge ladle, and a warminge panne – xx^s

Item a payre of reckes, a fryinge panne, a triuet, and a tostinge iron – ij^s

Item 3 basons x greate platters, two chamberpots, 3 small dishes, 5 porrengers, 7 spoones, x saucers, 2 pewter cuppes, 2 salt sellers, [? number] pewter pots – xx^s

In the sellar

Item 3 stellinges, and a litle table – v^s

Item for pots and glasses – xij^d

In the greate chamber

Item a playne bedstedle, matte and rope, and a flocke bed and one blanket and a rugge, two boulsters, 5 curtaines and roddes – xxxx^s

Item one presse, and 3 chests – xx^s

Item one wicker chayre – viij^d

Item one truckle bed, and a boulster, and a bagge of feathers – ij^s

Item eighteene payre of sheetes – iiij^{li}

Item 4 fine tablecloathes, and 4 course ones, and 2 dosen of napkins and a doson of course ones – xxvj^s iiij^d

Item 4 payre of fine pillowcoates, and 3 payre of course – xij^s

Item halfe a dosen of course hande towells – ij^s

In the litle chamber

A litle standinge bed without a testerne. and a truckle bed with two flocke beds, 2 boulsters, 2 blankets and a couerlet – xvj^s

Item 3 blankets more and 2 kiueringes and a rugge – xv^s

Item 4 pillowes – v^s

Item 6 cushions – vj^s
Item his wearinge apparell – xxxx^s
Item an olde cheste, and olde presse, a buntinge hutche and a meale tubbe – ij^s
Item 4 payre of bootes – xx^s
Item a bible – vj^s
Item for X siluer spoones – xxxx^s
Item 3 loade of woode – xv^s
Item for olde lumber about the house – ij^s vj^d

The whole summe xxi^l xiiij^s ij^d

Thomas Crispe
Thomas Plesyngton
Robart Lyon

Instances of signature of John Marlowe, shoemaker

(Kent Archives Office; Canterbury Cathedral Archives and Library)

Reference	Date	Document	Signature
KAO PRC 39/5, fo. 55	1566	Evidence in Applegate scandal case	'Jhan Marley'
CCAL BAC J/Q/370	1570	Canterbury shoemakers' petition	'John Marley'
CCAL BAC J/Q/380	6 June 1581	Bond for appearance at Sessions of W. Key of Croydon, shoemaker	'Johannes Marlowe' (not signature)
CCAL DAC Y.3.18, fo. 146	July 1581	In Act Book, probate court acknowledging receipt of cash from estate of J. Gresshop, headmaster of King's School, for footwear.	'receued by me John Marley'
KAO PRC 16/36	Nov. 1585	As witness to Mrs Benchkin's will	'Jhan Marley'
KAO PRC 39/11, fo. 237	Sept. 1586	On evidence relating to Mrs Benchkin's will	'Jhan Marley'

Reference	Date	Document	Signature
CCAL DAC s.n.	6 Oct. 1592	Return of baptisms, etc. ('Transcript') for parish of St Mary Breadman, as churchwarden	'Jhan Marley'
CCAL DAC X.11.6, fo. 147	3 July 1593	Evidence in case concerning *Leonard Doggerell v. Parfitt*	'Jhan Marley'
CCAL DAC, s.n.	Nov. 1593	Return to interrogatory *re* parish of St Mary Breadman, as churchwarden	'Jhan Marle'
CCAL BAC J/Q/393	3 April 1594 (or 11 Aug.?)	Bond for appearance of W. Jessop, glover, at Sessions	'Jhan Marle'
CCAL CAC, s.n.	16 July 1594	Bond for payment of rent by N. Atkins to dean and chapter of Canterbury	'Jhan Marle'
CCAL DAC	Autumn 1594	Return of baptisms, etc. ('Transcript') as churchwarden	'John Marley'? (MS damaged)
CCAL BAC J/Q/394	25 July 1595	On bond for appearance of W. Jessop, glover, at Sessions	'Jhan Marle'
KAO PRC 39/26, fo. 17	1603	On evidence relating to tithe case, St Mary Breadman	'John Marle'
KAO PRC 16/125	1605	On will	(cross only, as he could not write)

In no place did John or Christapher Marlow write their names other than with the a after the M.

For convenience the following archive and bibliographical sources are referred to in the notes in abbreviated form:

Bakeless: J. Bakeless, *The Tragicall History of Christopher Marlowe*, vols I and II (Harvard, 1942)

BL: British Library

Canterbury Marriage Licences, I and II: J. M. Cowper, ed., *Canterbury Marriage Licences*, First Series, 1568–1618 (Canterbury, 1892) and Second Series, 1619–60 (Canterbury, 1894)

CCAL: Canterbury Cathedral Archives and Library

Cowper, *St Alphege*: J. M. Cowper, ed., *The Regyster Booke of the Chrystenyngs Marryages and Buryalls of the Parish of St Alphaege in the Cyttye of Canterburye* 1558–1800 (Canterbury, 1889)

Cowper, *St Dunstan*: J. M. Cowper, ed., *The Register Booke of Christeninges, Mariages and Burialls in Saint Dunstan's Canterbury, 1559–1800* (Canterbury, 1887)

Cowper, *St George*: *The Register Booke of the Parish of St George the Martyr within the Citie of Canterburie of Christenings Mariages and Burials 1538–1800* (Canterbury, 1891)

Cowper, *St Mary Magdalen*: *The Names of Them that were Chrystened Marryed and Buryed in the Paryshe of Saynt Mary Magdalene in Canterbury 1559–1800* (Canterbury, 1890)

Cowper, *St Paul: The Register Book of Christenings Marriages and Burialls in the parishe of St Paule without the walles of the citie of Canterburie, 1562–1800* (Canterbury, 1893)

Cowper, *St Peter: The Book of Regester of the Parish of St Peter in Canterbury for Christninges Weddinges and Buryalls. 1560–1800* (Canterbury, c 1887)

DNB: Dictionary of National Biography, vols I–LXIII (London, 1885–90)

KAO: Kent Archives Office, Maidstone

PCC: Prerogative Court at Canterbury

PRC: Ecclesiastical Records for Canterbury Diocese deposited at the Kent Archives Office

PRO: Public Record Office

INTRODUCTION

1. W. Sanders, *The Dramatist and the Received Idea* (Cambridge, 1968), pp. 1, 17.
2. M. Kelsall, *Christopher Marlowe* (Leiden, 1981), pp. 2ff.
3. *Ibid.*, p. 11.
4. D. Palmer, 'Marlowe' in *English Drama (excluding Shakespeare): Select Bibliographical Guides*, ed. S. Wells (Oxford, 1975), pp. 43ff.
5. S. Shepherd, *Marlowe and the Politics of Elizabethan Theatre* (Brighton, 1986), ch. 6 *passim*.
6. J. Wolff, *The Social Production of Art* (London, 1985), p. 129 and ch. 6, *passim*.
7. P. Clark, *English Provincial Society from the Reformation to the Revolution: Religion, Politics, and Society in Kent, 1500–1640* (Hassocks, 1977), esp. chs. 1–8; 'Josias Nicholls and Religious Radicalism, 1553–1639', *Journal of Ecclesiastical History*, vol. 28, no. 2, April 1977, pp. 133–50. See also P. Collinson, *'Jerusalem is Built as a City': The Protestant Reformation and the English Towns* (Canterbury, 1986), *passim*. For the description of

religious and political change in Canterbury I have followed Clark's work closely.

8. Clark, *English Provincial Society*, *op. cit.*, p. 84.

9. Clark, 'Josias Nicholls', *op. cit.*, p. 133.

10. *Ibid.*, p. 137.

11. H. C. Porter, *Reformation and Reaction in Tudor Cambridge* (Cambridge, 1958), esp. chs. 5–10.

12. Textual references to Marlowe's works are given here according to R. J. Fehrenbach, L. A. Boone, and M. A. Di Cesare, *A Concordance to the Plays, Poems and Translations of Christopher Marlowe* (Ithaca and London, 1982).

13. P. H. Kocher, *Christopher Marlowe* (New York, 1946), p. 191.

14. *Ibid.*

15. S. Greenblatt, *Renaissance Self-Fashioning* (Chicago, 1980), p. 194.

16. Kocher, *op. cit.*, p. 300.

17. C. F. Tucker Brooke, *The Life of Marlowe and The Tragedy of Dido, Queen of Carthage* (London, 1930), p. 41.

18. Kocher, *op. cit.*, pp. 303–4.

19. *Ibid.*, p. 304.

20. *Ibid.*, p. 309.

21. *Ibid.*, pp. 310–12.

22. *Ibid.*, p. 315.

23. *Ibid.*, pp. 33, 68; J. B. Steane, *Marlowe: A Critical Study* (Cambridge, 1964), pp. 23, 339–45.

24. Kocher, *op. cit.*, pp. 320–1.

25. *Ibid.*, p. 321.

26. C. Belsey, *The Subject of Tragedy* (London, 1985), p. 29.

27. S. Shepherd, *Marlowe and the Politics of Elizabethan Theatre* (Brighton, 1986), p. 156.

28. J. Weil, *Christopher Marlowe: Merlin's Prophet* (Cambridge, 1977), ch. 5.

29. Shepherd, *op. cit.*, p. 139.

30. *Ibid.*, p. xvi.

31. *Ibid.*, pp. xvii–xviii.

32. For the description of the cases of *Edmundes v. Hocking, William Darrell* and *Oudart v. Jackson* I have made use of early drafts of

x R heard from this man in 1994, he became editor of Medieval Texts

See File

William Urry's MS. The cases are to be found in CCAL DAC
X.10.12, fos. 116ff.
33. CCAL DAC X.10.16, fos. 10–65*v*.

CHAPTER ONE

1. R. W. Bond, ed., *The Complete Works of John Lyly*, vol. II
(Oxford, 1967), pp. 35–6.
2. For returns of 1562–3 see L. E. Whatmore, 'Parochial Statistics
in East Kent 1557–63', *Southwark Record*, vol. XXXIV, pp.
330ff., using Archbishop Parker's report, BL Harleian MS 594,
fos. 63–5*v* (see also J. and P. Clark, 'The Social Economy of the
Canterbury Suburbs: the Evidence of the Census of 1563', in A.
Detsicas and N. Yates, eds., *Studies in Modern Kentish History
Presented to F. Hull and E. Melling* (Maidstone, 1983), pp. 65–
86). For 1563 there are the remains of a census compiled at
Canterbury in unparalleled detail, including householders,
wives, children (with ages), servants, dogs and pigs (CCAL City
MSS E/Q/1).
3. CCAL Visitation Returns 1569, fos. 33–5, conducted by Bishop
Richard Rogers, Andrew Pierson and Thomas Lawse, commissioned by Archbishop Parker (see also J. and P. Clark, *op. cit.*).
4. Early-morning milking in the fields by housewives is often
mentioned, e.g., CCAL X/10/7 and PRC 39/5, fo. 52. For
gleaning in Barton Fields about 300–400 yards from Marlowe's
childhood home see CCAL X/10/7; and see also PRC 39/11, fo.
261, for same at Milton Manor one and a half miles away.
5. *Pace* M. Poirier, *Christopher Marlowe* (London, 1951, 1968),
p. 12.
6. CCAL BAC J/Q/378 (1578), where two men, planning a burglary
in Welsh, were overheard by a Welsh girl. There was a group of
Welsh residents on Mulberry (Lady Wotton's) Green, outside
the walls (CCAL X/11/7, fos. 103ff, in case *Williams v. Vaughan*).
7. CCAL X.10.14, fos. 18ff.

8. See CCAL BAC Canterbury City Accounts, Courts and DAC Ecclesiastical Courts, *passim*.

9. See F. W. Cross, 'History of the Walloon and Huguenot Church at Canterbury', *Publications of the Huguenot Society of London*, vol. 15; B. Magen, *Die Wallongemeinde in Canterbury von ihren Grundig bis zum Jahre 1635* (Bern, Frankfurt/M, 1973); W. Somner, *The Antiquities of Canterbury, or a survey of that ancient citie. with the suburbs and cathedrall. etc.* (London, 1640), p. 175, etc. The occupation of houses by the refugees can be detected in local taxation records, e.g., CCAL BAC B/C/S.

10. E.g., CCAL BAC J/Q/395.

11. CCAL BAC A/C/3, fo. 257. There is a vast amount of material to be recovered about topography, nuisances, sanitary conditions, etc., from sessions records (see CCAL BAC and J/Q, *passim*).

12. CCAL St Mildred's Parish Register 1; Cowper, *St George*; (and see J. and P. Clark, *op. cit.*).

13. Cowper, *St George*.

14. W. Somner, *The Antiquities of Canterbury*, with a new introduction by W. Urry (Wakefield, 1977), p. 184.

15. See CCAL BAC City Accounts, Courts, etc., and DAC Ecclesiastical Courts, *passim*.

16. W. G. Urry, 'Some forgotten schools in Tudor Canterbury', in M. H. A. Berry and J. H. Higginson, *Canterbury Chapters: a Kentish Heritage for Tomorrow* (Liverpool, 1976).

17. *Historical Manuscripts Commission*, vol. IX, app. I, p. 58.

18. CCAL X.1.2, pt ii, fo. 53 (1579); X.10.8, fo. 181. See P. Clark and P. Slack, eds., *Crisis and Order in English Towns, 1500–1700* (London, 1972), esp. chapter by P. Clark, 'The Migrant in Kentish Towns, 1580–1640'.

19. There is continuous evidence of sports indulged in by citizens in complaints made at sessions, CCAL BAC and J/Q. Cricket is mentioned in R. Culmer, *Cathedrall Newes from Canterbury: shewing the Canteburian Cathedrall to bee in an abbey-like corrupt, and rotten condition, which cals for a speedy reformation, or dissolution . . .* (London, 1644). 'Legs for a game' (stumps?) are mentioned in evidence in the lawsuit *Okeden v. Bale* in 1561 (CCAL Y.10.7).

20. CCAL Y.10.7.

21. *Ibid.*

22. See *Historical Manuscripts Commission*, vol. IX, app. I, p. 157. One of Sidney's servants, Roger Rodforth, was involved in a quarrel over hire of a horse, on which he rode off in a rainstorm with a letter for the Privy Council (CCAL BAC J/B/S).

23. CCAL BAC; CCAL FA/16, fo. 284 (*Historical Manuscripts Commission*, vol. IX, app. I, p. 156); 'the man that caeme out off the land of Babyllond' is clearly the 'straunger off the contry of Persia' to whom the dean handed 10s. on 8 September 1564 (CCAL Misc. Accounts 40, fo. 291).

24. G. S(mith), *Chronological History of Canterbury Cathedral* (Canterbury, 1883), pp. 266ff; J. Nichols, *The Progresses and Public Processions of Queen Elizabeth among which are interspersed other solemnities, public expenditures, and remarkable events during the reign of that . . . Princess . . . with historical notes* (London, 1788–1821), vol. I, p. 36.

25. CCAL, *s.n.*, Visitation (1569) conducted by Bishop Richard Rogers, Andrew Pierson and Thomas Lawse, commissioned by Archbishop Parker.

26. It was mostly destroyed in the great air-raid of 1 June 1942. See E. Hasted, *The History and Topographical Survey of the County of Kent . . .* (Canterbury, 1797–1801), p. 225, etc.; F. Summerly, *Handbook for the City of Canterbury* (London, 1843), p. 64; T. H. Oyler, *Parish Churches of the Diocese of Canterbury* (London, 1910), p. 47, pl., for view of church; J. H. Ingram, *Christopher Marlowe and His Associates* (London, 1904), pl. III, opp. p. 13.

27. CCAL MS BAC A/C/3, fo. 100. This seems to mark a renewal, for in slanderous exchanges in 1574 one parish lady remarked that another went to the belfry by night to see the ringers (CCAL DAC Y.3.17, fos. 15ff., or X.10.17, pt ii, fo. 66, or X.1.2, fo. 16).

28. It was used as a prison in Marlowe's younger days (CCAL BAC A/C, fo. 272, under date 15 Elizabeth I).

29. The topography of the area can be recovered from Cathedral Leasebooks (e.g., CCAL MS Register V, fo. 155; Register W, fo. 273); from rentals inserted annually in Canterbury City Accounts (e.g., CCAL BAC FA/19, fos. 184ff) and from many

lawsuits (e.g., *Bull v. Rose* in CCAL DAC X.10.8, which gives a lively picture of skirmishes between neighbours of the Marlowes; *Smith v. Shrubsole* in CCAL BAC J/B/S, 34 Elizabeth I, provides evidence for site of J. Smith's dwelling with those of neighbours.

30. PRC 39/11, fo. 55.

31. CCAL DAC X.10.8.

32. *Ibid.*

33. CCAL BAC J/B/S 34 Elizabeth I; BAC J/B/S, *s.a.*, *Nutt v. Marlowe*; J/B/385/v and 386/vi.

34. PRC 39/11, fo. 55.

35. L. E. Whatmore, ed., *Archdeacon Harpsfield's Visitation, 1557. II. Together with Visitations of 1556 and 1558*, Catholic Record Society, vol. XLVI, p. 294.

36. Cowper, *St George.*

37. *Registrum Matthei Parker Diocesis Cantuariensis A.D. 1559–1575*, Registers I and II, *Canterbury and York Society*, vols, xxxv, xxxvi, xxxix, pp. 342, 344, 388 (Oxford, 1928, 1933).

38. CCAL DAC X.1.5, fos. 96–7, 1564 Visitation.

39. CCAL CAC, *s.n.*, Visitation (1569) (see note 25, above).

40. PRC 42, fo. 247.

41. For the careers of Leonard Sweeting and Christopher Pashley see pp. 50 and 54.

42. CCAL DAC X.10.8, *Bull v. Rose.*

43. Johnson was one of a family of painters: see *Historical Manuscripts Commission*, vol. IX, app. I, pp. 149, 156; Cowper, *St George*, index. For William a Lee see *ibid.*, burials, 1567.

44. The burial of John Heaviside, *alias* Dygon, former monk, is noted in the MS Parish Register of St Andrew in Canterbury Cathedral Archives.

45. DNB.

46. See W. Ringler, 'Stephen Gosson, a Biographical and Critical Study', *Princeton Studies in English*, vol. XXV (1962).

47. CCAL BAC B/C/S/II, 2, 3. See Cowper, *St George, s.a.*, for baptisms, marriages and burials. The father did occasional carpentry work for the City of Canterbury, e.g., CCAL BAC FA/17, fo. 195.

48. CCAL CAC, Misc. Accounts 40, fos. 373ff. (under 1568–9).

49. W. Kelly *et al.*, eds., 'Liber Ruber Venerabilis Collegii Anglorum de Urbe', *Catholic Record Society*, vol. XXXVII (1940), p. 49; and see also H. Foley, ed., *Records of the English Province of the Society of Jesus*, vol. VI, p. 555.

50. See A. Feuillerat, *John Lyly* (Cambridge, 1910); W. G. Urry, 'John Lyly and Canterbury', *Friends of Canterbury Cathedral Annual Report*, 1960.

51. Evidence points to identification of this building with the old Sun inn, Sun Street, Canterbury (CCAL CAC, Register V, fo. 106; Register W, fo. 224); the inventory of Peter Lyly's property is in PRC 21/1/142.

52. R. W. Bond, ed., *The Complete Works of John Lyly* (Oxford, 1967), vol. II, pp. 35–6.

53. Urry, 'John Lyly and Canterbury', *op. cit.*

54. CCAL DAC X.10.14, fo. 209. The parish clerk of All Saints managed to confuse more than one baptism in the Boyle family: cf. CCAL DAC Transcripts, and MS Parish Register, deposited in Cathedral Library.

55. R. G. Usher, 'Robert Cushman', in A. Johnson and D. Malone, eds., *Dictionary of American Biography*; W. G. Urry, 'Canterbury and the Pilgrim Fathers', *Kentish Gazette*, August 1970.

CHAPTER TWO

1. Speculation about the dramatist's ancestry has centred upon a family of tanners called Marley or Marlowe who lived in North Lane, Canterbury, probably on the corner under the Westgate, backing on to the River Stour, within the parish of Holy Cross. Here on 5 March 1540, a certain Christopher Marlowe (Marley) lay dying and made his will. He had a daughter Alice or Elys, and his wife was pregnant. He owned house property which he left to his unborn child should it prove to be a boy, or to be divided equally between his two daughters should it prove to be a girl. It is unlikely that the

unborn child was John Marlowe since no proof has been found that John owned any property in Canterbury. What is more, a marriage case in the ecclesiastical courts reveals that in 1549 one William Graves believed himself to have become betrothed to Alice (Elys) Marley, a young woman whose father was dead and who possessed some house property. It is difficult to avoid the surmise that this Alice Marley was the daughter of Christopher, the tanner, who died in 1540, and that the unborn child was not a boy or did not survive.

2. PRC 39/5, fo. 55; PRC 39/11, fos. 237r–v; CCAL DAC X.11.6, fo. 147; PRC 39/26, fo. 17. For John Marlowe's age see Bakeless, vol. I, pp. 24ff. The Canterbury diocesan archives provide evidence of a family called 'Marley' at Ospringe, confirming John's testimony. In 1543 a George Marley of Ospringe was sued for personal abuse by Christopher Colson of Sittingbourne (CCAL DAC Y.2.14, fo. 35, etc., *Colson v. Marley*). It seems likely that this George was John's father. The family of tanners of North Lane in Canterbury may well have been kinsfolk of the Marlowes at Ospringe. The true form of the name Marlowe/Marley is undoubtedly Marley, evidently derived from a Kentish place-name (Marley near Maidstone or Marley south-east of Canterbury on the Dover Road). For etymology see Bakeless, vol. I, p. 5. John Marlowe/Marley calls himself 'Marley' or 'Marle' in a dozen surviving signatures. The name in either form occurs all round Kent. There was a family called Marlowe, quite distinct from that of the dramatist, in the parish of St George, Canterbury, in the 1560s (Cowper, *St George*, p. 172). Other families occur in St Mary Northgate, Canterbury, *c.* 1580 (CCAL DAC X.2.8, fo. 12), and at Eastry, near Sandwich (CCAL DAC Y.2.13). At Cambridge such forms as 'Marlin' were used. To contemporaries Christopher was 'Marley the Muses' darling'. In his solitary known signature he spells his name Marley (see Appendix III, p. 127).

3. CCAL BAC FA/16, fo. 104.
4. PRC 39/5, fo. 55.
5. CCAL BAC FA/16, fo. 270.

6. Cowper, *St George*, p. 100.

7. CCAL DAC X.4.24, fo. 108.

8. PRC 22/3, fo. 24. A William Arthur (I), who died in 1558, appears to have lived in the region of the Eastbrook, the side-stream of the River Dour, which ran along and within the shingle bank at the harbour edge beside St James's church. At the moment of his death William Arthur (I) was described as of the closely adjacent parish of St Mary.

9. Dover Borough Archives, Accounts, vol. marked 1546–58, under 'W. Arthor'; 'Arter' occurs many times, cf. fos. 37, 46, 82, 91, 105, 300, etc.

10. CCAL DAC Y.3.1, fo. 89, etc.

11. Dover Borough Archives, *s.n.*, in Maison Dieu, Dover; Plea Book marked Henry VIII, Edward VI, Philip and Mary, etc., *s.a.*; CCAL BAC J/B/357; Lambeth Palace MSS, Canterbury Consistory Court Act Book in which J. Holt sues W. Arture for debt of £10 in the Dover Court in 1556 (Dover Plea Book, as above, fo. 398).

12. CCAL BAC J/B/357.

13. CCAL DAC X.4.24, fo. 108.

14. For the parish register entries of the family see Bakeless, vol. I, pp. 12ff. For the thirteenth-century font at which Christopher and the other children were baptized see J. H. Ingram, *Christopher Marlowe and His Associates* (London, 1904), pl. IV. It was mostly destroyed in the air-raid of 1942. See A. D. Wraight and V. F. Stern, *In Search of Christopher Marlowe: A Pictorial Biography* (London, 1965), p. 4.

15. See Bakeless, vol. I, pp. 12ff.

16. *Ibid.*

17. *Ibid.*

18. *Ibid.*

19. *Ibid.*

20. *Ibid.*

21. *Ibid.*, p. 16. There is general agreement that the child must be Jane, despite the entry in the registered transcript.

22. *Ibid.* This would help to explain why John Moore had to be readmitted to the freedom on 14 September 1585 (CCAL BAC

FA/18, fo. 344, in Accounts). Only four days after John Moore's first admission by marriage with Jane Marlowe this form of entry was cancelled only to be restored on 16 February a few weeks later. If Jane had died John's position might well have seemed anomalous in the circumstances.

23. Bakeless, vol. I, pp. 12ff.

24. *Ibid.*

25. *Ibid.*

26. *Ibid.*

27. *Ibid.*

28. *Ibid.*; see CCAL DAC MS Register of Licences, under 1625; for James Gilbert, possibly her husband, see J. M. Cowper, ed., *Intrantes: a List of Persons Admitted to Live and Trade in the City of Canterbury, on Payment of an Annual Fine, from 1392–1592* (Canterbury, 1904), col. 229; CCAL BAC J/B/S, *s.a.*, *Gilbert v. Coxe*; and CCAL DAC X.4.4., pt ii, fo. 89.

29. Bakeless, vol. I, pp. 12ff.

30. Lambeth Palace MSS, Whitgift's Register, *s.a.*

31. Katherine Marlowe's will, see Appendix VI, p. 134.

32. See J. C. Hotten, *Original Lists of Persons of Quality, Emigrants, etc.* (London, Guildford, 1874, reissued 1931), p. 220.

33. CCAL DAC X.4.24, fo. 108; CCAL PRC 39/11, fo. 237, for short biography given in Benchkin case; CCAL CFC, Redemption; for action over Thomas's late father's property see CCAL DAC Y.3.1, fos. 89ff. The MS index provides other references; CCAL DAC Y.3.16 under date 15 April 1577.

34. CCAL DAC Y.3.1, fo. 158; DAC Transcripts, *s.a.*

35. CCAL DAC Transcripts, *s.a.* – St Mary Northgate, St Alphege, St Dunstan and St Mary Magdalen.

36. *Ibid.*

37. KAO, Ulcombe Parish Register; CCAL DAC Transcripts Ulcombe.

38. There was a case *Rodes v. Withers* (CCAL BAC, *s.a.*) which spilled over into the High Court of the Archbishop, held in the Palace at Canterbury. T. Arthur was described as bailiff and minister of the court in proceedings. It would be natural to run this office with that of bailiff of the archiepiscopal manor of

Westgate near by. Lambeth Palace MSS, Estate Documents nos. 1781, 1812, show Arthur as joint bailiff of Westgate.

39. PRC 44/3, fos. 12, 111, 113, etc.; for Clement Gasken see CCAL BAC FA/19, fo. 211.

40. *Acts of the Privy Council, s.a.*

41. See Cowper, *St Dunstan*, burials, 1593.

42. *Ibid.*

43. *Ibid.*

44. *Ibid.*

45. PRC 8/1, fo. 35; PRC 3/24, fo. 23; PRC 15/2, fo. 41.

46. Her will is printed in C. F. Tucker Brooke, *The Life of Marlowe and The Tragedy of Dido, Queen of Carthage* (London, 1930), app. IV.

47. Cowper, *St Dunstan*, burials, 1597.

48. See note 46, above.

49. CCAL BAC J/B/S, *Marlowe v. Quested, Taylor v. Marlowe, Marlowe v. Taylor; Boys v. Marlowe*, etc. Entries in the Plea Books occur in J/B/393, etc. (Sir) John Boys, seneschal of the Archbishop's Court, and learned counsell (later recorder) to the City of Canterbury, had had official contacts with Arthur.

50. CCAL BAC J/B/396, iv, fo. 3.

51. *Marlowe v. Beake*, Fordwich Borough Archives (deposited in Canterbury Cathedral Library), Bundle 6/23.

52. CCAL DAC X.1.2; Y.4.22; Y.4.23. References to cases may be found in MS indices in volumes.

53. CCAL DAC Y.4.23, fo. 207; DAC Y.4.22, fos. 21, 60; DAC X.3.9, pt i, fo. 187.

54. See pp. 57 and 65ff.

55. KAO, Ulcombe Parish Register; CCAL DAC Transcripts, Ulcombe.

56. CCAL DAC Transcripts, St Mary Northgate.

57. KAO, Ulcombe Parish Register; CCAL DAC Transcripts, Ulcombe.

58. CCAL CEC, col. 238, Barton first appears in the new year 1597–8.

59. CCAL BAC FA/16, 1569.

60. CCAL MS U/7, fo. 128.

61. J. Philipot, *A Perfect Collection . . . of all Knights Batchelaurs made by King James* (London, 1960), p. 18.

62. CCAL BAC J/B/S, *s.a.*, *Leeke v. Aunsell*. The story is printed in *Nurses' League Journal*, no. 31 (Canterbury, 1967).

63. Colbrand lived next door to the cathedral gate. CCAL BAC J/B/S, *s.a.*, *Aunsell v. Colbrand*; CCAL DAC X.11.2, fo. 324.

64. CCAL DAC X.3.9, pt i, fo. 79, etc. See Cowper, *St Alphege*, p. 111.

65. For Buckleys, booksellers and printers, see H. R. Plomer, *A Dictionary of the Booksellers and Printers who were at work in England, Scotland, and Ireland from 1641–67* (London, 1907), under 'Bulkley' and 'Buckley'; see also CCAL BAC J/B/391.

66. Aunsell had liaisons with 'Beverley's daughter of Wye' (ten miles away) (CCAL DAC X.1.10, fo. 67) and other women (PRC 39/11). He earned the title 'drunken knave and whoremaster knave' from a neighbour in 1584 (PRC 39/26, fo. 4). For the Fyneux family see p. 64.

67. CCAL BAC N (Musters), nos. 1 and 2.

68. CCAL BAC, Leasebook and Register, *s.a.*; CCAL DAC Transcripts, St Mary Northgate, *s.a.*

69. See p. 13.

70. CCAL BAC B/C/S/II/2; BAC J/B/353; BAC J/B/S, *J. a Pantry v. Richardson*. The date of agreement is given as 25 December 3 & 4 Philip and Mary.

71. Cowper, *St George*, *s.a.*, burials.

72. PRC Archdeaconry Act Book, 15, fo. 56; CCAL BAC, J/B/363, fo. 6.

73. *Hurte v. Applegate*, CCAL PRC 39/5, fos. 55ff.

74. Mentioned as a confraternity as early as 1489 but may be much older – CCAL BAC J/B/289, fo. 27, *Gardiani confraternitatis beate Marie et sanctorum martirum Crispini et Crispiani v. W. Marshall*.

75. CCAL Woodruff's List LIV, no. 4 (1579).

76. CCAL BAC FA/15, fo. 21.

77. CCAL BAC Woodruff's List LIV, no. 17 (1601–2).

78. Two versions of the conspectus (1576 and 1594) are bound into the 'Bunce Portfolio' in Canterbury City Archives.

79. CCAL BAC J/Q/370.

80. CCAL BAC FA/16, fo. 434; BAC, CFC, marriage.
81. Payments to Umberfield senior occur continuously in the annual cathedral accounts (e.g., CCAL CAC Misc. Accounts 40, fo. 228, etc.; Accounts, New Foundation 5, etc.); CCAL BAC FA/17, fo. 115; BAC J/Q/37.
82. Lambeth Palace MSS, V.C. III/1/6, fo. 46; Cowper, *St George*, *s.a.*, baptisms.
83. G. Townsend and S. R. Cattley, eds., *J. Foxe: 'Acts and Monuments'* (London, 1841), vol. IV, pp. 226ff.; L. H. Carlson, 'The Writings of John Greenwood, 1587–90', *Elizabethan Nonconformist Texts*, vol. IV, pp. 323–5, 331.
84. CCAL BAC FA/17, fo. 329.
85. Cowper, *St George*, *s.a.*
86. CCAL BAC J/Q/377.
87. CCAL DAC Transcripts, Fordwich, *s.a.*; Parish Register of St Peter, Sandwich, deposited in Canterbury Cathedral Library.
88. Parish Register of St Peter, Sandwich (as note 87).
89. CCAL BAC FA/18, fo. 102.
90. CCAL BAC FA/18, fo. 243.
91. PRC 39/13, fo. 74.
92. CCAL BAC FA/20, fo. 11.
93. CCAL BAC J/Q/394.
94. CCAL BAC J/B/S, *s.a.*, *Hewes v. Hales*; for monument to the Hales family see J. Dart, *Canterbury Cathedral* (1726), pl. opp. p. 79.
95. CCAL BAC J/B/S and J/B/407; BAC J/Q/405.
96. Cowper, *St Mary Magdalen*, under 19 November 1593.
97. MS Parish Register St Andrew, deposited in Canterbury Cathedral Library.
98. CCAL BAC FA/20, fo. 76; BAC FA/20, fo. 26.
99. CCAL BAC Millen's List, Dr. 40 (misc. bonds).
100. CCAL DAC X.11.2, fos. 247ff.
101. CCAL BAC N 44 and N 23.
102. *Ibid.*, N 11.
103. PRC 32/26, fo. 100, etc.
104. PRC 17/41, fo. 140. The terms of the Streater Charity are set out in CCAL BAC, Bunce MS Charity Book, p. 237; CCAL BAC FA/19,

fo. 24. Ingram, *op. cit.*, p. 130, prints a muddled version of this entry.

105. CCAL BAC J/B/S, *T. Greenleaf and the Company v. J. Marlowe*. The case was first noticed by Miss Elizabeth Campbell (Mrs Cherniak), former assistant in the Canterbury Cathedral Library.

106. CCAL BAC MS vol. relating to Poor Priests' Hospital, *s.n.*, unfoliated.

107. John Rose's will is PRC 32/37, fo. 23; for the debt assigned to the Woollen-Drapers see Woollen-Drapers' Minute and Account Book, deposited in Canterbury Cathedral Library. The debt is entered annually until 1604 (the eve of J. Marlowe's death). Four hundred years after Christopher Marlowe's birth the Marlowe Society honoured the debt to the Company of Woollen-Drapers and Tailors at the Marlowe commemorative dinner, Stationers Hall, London, in 1964.

108. PRC 17/42, fo. 231.

109. CCAL CAC files of uncatalogued bonds; BAC J/Q/372; BAC J/B/S, *s.a.*, *Knowle v. Country*; see Bakeless, vol. I, p. 27, n. 67. There are many other bonds entered in the Canterbury diocesan registers in the Cathedral Library. The long gaps between dates when John Marlowe attested a bond are not apparent from Cowper, *Canterbury Marriage Licences*, since the editor arranged names alphabetically.

110. CCAL BAC J/Q/370 i and ii.

111. CCAL BAC J/B/371, fo. 8.

112. CCAL BAC J/B/372 i, fo. 3.

113. CCAL BAC J/B/378 i, fo. 7.

114. CCAL BAC J/B/378 i, fo. 9; *ibid*. ii, fo. 3.

115. CCAL BAC J/B/380 v, fo. 1; CCAL BAC J/B/382 ii, fo. 5. And in the nine cases in the last three notes, BAC J/B/S as far as they survive.

116. CCAL BAC J/B/S, 12 Elizabeth I (12 October 1570). The case is entered in J/B/370 iv, fo. 4.

117. CCAL BAC J/B/S, *s.a.*, *Nutt v. Marlowe*; J/B/385 v and J/B/386 vi.

118. Norwood was also uncle to Rachel Flood who married Isaac Walton in 1626. She was from the Cranmer family circle.

C. J. Sissons, *The Judicious Marriage of Mr Hooker and the Birth of the Laws of Ecclesiastical Polity* (Cambridge, 1940), is of the general opinion that the Cranmers supplied an adverse picture of Mrs Hooker to Walton for his *Lives*. See pedigree in J. Strype, *Life of Archbishop Cranmer* (London, 1694).

119. CCAL BAC J/B/593.
120. CCAL BAC A/C 3, fos. 248ff.
121. CCAL BAC J/B/392 iii; J/B/S, *s.a.*
122. See pp. 17–19.
123. CCAL BAC J/B/392; J/B/S, *s.a.*
124. CCAL BAC J/B/S, *s.a.*, *Archer v. Marlowe*, with jury panel.
125. CCAL BAC A/C/3, fo. 34.
126. CCAL DAC Z.3.11, fo. 77 (1573); DAC Z.7.1 (unfoliated) (1578).
127. CCAL DAC V/V (Callbooks, etc.); DAC Z.7.2 (unfoliated, under dates in question). John Marlowe signs a routine return in November 1593 (uncatalogued returns, DAC). Samon (Salmon) and John Marlowe sign transcripts of parish registers at same date.
128. CCAL BAC A/C/3, fos. 53, 198.
129. CCAL BAC J/Q/391 iii.
130. *Ibid.*
131. There are many jury lists among uncatalogued MSS in the Canterbury City Archives. Often one panel will decide more than one case, e.g., *Lambe v. Hunt*, plus three other cases, where J. Marlowe is a juryman (27 Elizabeth I); CCAL BAC J/Q/383.
132. Plessington gave evidence several times, supplying his biography: CCAL DAC X.11.1, fo. 164, November 1587, when he said he was about thirty-nine years old; DAC X.11.1, fo. 233; PRC 39/11, fo. 85; etc.
133. CCAL CFC, marriage.
134. Plessington is listed in Newingate Ward and in St Margaret's parish, which overlap at this point (CCAL DAC Transcripts, St Margaret, and in miscellaneous sessions and taxation documents).
135. He figures in the entertaining case *Nower v. Clinton* which depicts the ponderous antics of the Canterbury constable and

watchmen (CCAL DAC X.11.1); CCAL BAC L 1/16 (in the Hovenden case, where a return is used as a file cover).

136. The house was held from the cathedral chapter and its site is clearly defined in the renewals of leases in Chapter Acts.

137. The case is related at great length in PRC 39/5, *Hurte alias Chapman v. Applegate*, CCAL DAC Y.4.12, fo. 10. See Bakeless, vol. I, pp. 24ff.

138. CCAL BAC J/Q/408 i.

139. CCAL Parish Register, St George.

140. See pp. 62ff.

141. CCAL BAC J/B/417 i (1617–18); BAC J/B/423 i, fo. 9 (1624).

142. CCAL BAC N 1 and N 2.

143. CCAL BAC N 14 and N 15.

144. *Historical Manuscripts Commission*, vol IX, app. I, p. 158. There is a considerable amount of evidence in city minutes and accounts at this time relating to arms, etc.

145. CCAL BAC N 8, v.

146. Bakeless, vol. I, p. 16.

147. PRC 16/36, and see Appendix III, p. 128.

148. CCAL BAC FA/18, fo. 344; CCAL DAC Transcripts, St Mary Northgate, *s.a.*; evidence in the case *Orledge v. Busbie*, DAC X.11.1, fo. 82.

149. Bakeless, vol. I, pp. 12ff. Both the original register and the transcript are somewhat confused as to the date of her baptism. The record of the transcript giving 18 December 1565 is preferable.

150. CCAL BAC A/C/3, fo. 163; BAC FA/19, fo. 92; CCAL Parish Register, St Mary Breadman, 15 June 1590.

151. Archives of the Woollen-Drapers' and Tailors' Company deposited in Canterbury Cathedral Library, combined account and minute book, *s.a.*

152. *Ibid.*; CCAL DAC Transcripts, St Mary Breadman.

153. See Appendix VI, p. 134.

154. Cowper, *Canterbury Marriage Licences*, II, col. 180, under 'Sampson'.

155. CCAL Parish Register, St Margaret.

156. CCAL Parish Register, St Mary Breadman; and see pp. 51–2 for Philemon Pownall.

157. CCAL Parish Register, All Saints.

158. CCAL Parish Register, St Mary Breadman; a word should be said of the name Cranford. Hitherto it has been rendered as the Caledonian 'Crawford' or 'Crauford'. This is the result of misreading 'u' for 'n', and occurrences of the name in the forms 'Cramford' or 'Crandford' show that 'Crauford' or 'Crawford' must be wrong.

159. CCAL BAC A/C/3, fo. 241 (22 January 1594).

160. CCAL DAC X.11.5 (1598), fo. 258.

161. Parish Register, Henley-on-Thames (typescript in Bodleian Library, Oxford).

162. It is unlikely that he was a student who dropped out since there is no mention of him among matriculations. But there are Cranfords in the lists.

163. L. H. Carlson, 'The Writings of John Greenwood, 1587–90', *Elizabethan Nonconformist Texts*, vol. IV, pp. 119, 322, 325, 330.

164. CCAL DAC X.11.5 (1598), fo. 258.

165. CCAL BAC J/B/397 iv; Cranford can be seen at work in court and out in the country in the court Act Books (e.g., in CCAL DAC X.9.1, *passim*).

166. CCAL BAC J/B/408 i, fo. 12.

167. CCAL BAC Millen's List, Dr. 40/E (files of misc. bonds). This is evidently a renewal in June 1613. Also CCAL BAC FA/22, fo. 188, etc.; CCAL Parish Register, All Saints.

168. Various notices and bills in CCAL BAC J/B/S, 1602–3 and other years (in cases *Dawlby v. Cranford, Sutton v. Cranford*, etc.); DAC Y.3.4, fos. 84, 91, etc.; DAC Y.3.5, fo. 154; DAC Y.5.10, fos. 190, 215.

169. CCAL BAC J/Q/408 (July Sessions), where the 'Wyndmyll' in St Mary Breadman parish is mentioned as in the hands of the 'Craufords'.

170. CCAL BAC J/B/404, where cases are entered.

171. See CCAL BAC J/B/404 i, fos. 3–19; CCAL BAC X.5.10, Y.5.11.

172. CCAL DAC X.4.4., pt ii, fo. 46.

173. CCAL BAC J/Q/425, 426.
174. For Katherine Marlowe's will see Appendix VI, p. 134; CCAL Parish Register, St Margaret, Canterbury.
175. The family seems to have dwelt close by in the Greyfriars. Entries of their baptisms, etc., occur in St Mary Breadman Parish Register.
176. CCAL Parish Register, St Mary Breadman.
177. CCAL CFC, marriage; CCAL Parish Register, All Saints.
178. Cowper, *Canterbury Marriage Licences*, II, col. 24, 'Anthony'.
179. CCAL CFC, marriage.
180. Cowper, *Canterbury Marriage Licences*, II, col. 912, 'Smithet'; CCAL CFC, marriage.
181. Transcripts embodied in Cowper, *St George*, *s.a.*; called glover in CCAL DAC, Register of Licences, under 22 March 1591 (in marriage licence Clipwell and Thatcher). Cowper does not give Graddell's name and trade in the printed version. (*Canterbury Marriage Licences*, I. 'Clipwell'); CCAL BAC A/C/3, fo. 251; CCAL BAC FA/20, fo. 75.
182. CCAL DAC X.11.9, fo. 101; CCAL DAC X.9.3, fo. 302.
183. PRC 18/3, 4 (Ecclesiastical Suits).
184. Various stages of the case *Browne v. Graddell* are entered in CCAL DAC Y.5.2, Y.5.3.
185. CCAL DAC Y.5.2, fo. 269.
186. CCAL DAC Y.5.3, fo. 79.
187. CCAL DAC Y.5.4, fo. 105.
188. For his will and inventory see PRC 17/64, fo. 109 and PRC 10/56, fo. 114.
189. CCAL BAC J/B/S, *s.a.*, *Colbrand v. Graddell*.
190. CCAL BAC J/B/S, *s.a.*, *Buckley v. Graddell*.
191. CCAL DAC X.3.9, pt i, fo. 151.
192. CCAL BAC J/B/S, *s.a.*, *P. Watson v. D. Graddell*.
193. CCAL BAC J/Q/415, T. Graddell and Dorothy, his wife, are named in a list of witnesses (10 June 14 James I, 1616).
194. CCAL BAC J/B/S.
195. CCAL BAC A/C/3, fo. 352, where a fine of £4 for such an offence was remitted; CCAL BAC J/B/S; CCAL BAC J/Q, *passim*.
196. CCAL BAC J/B/S.

197. CCAL BAC J/B/S, *s.a.*, *See v. Graddell*. Sale was made 20 December 1617.
198. CCAL BAC J/Q/405 viii. Graddell was subpoenaed in June 1612 to give evidence against another butcher in some shady transaction (CCAL BAC J/Q/411).
199. CCAL BAC J/Q/422.
200. CCAL BAC J/B/S, *s.a.*, *Graddell v. Alder*.
201. CCAL BAC J/B/S, *Graddell v. Laurence*, alleging slander on 20 (23?) March 1 James I.
202. CCAL BAC J/B/S, *s.a.*, *Peeling v. Graddell*, alleging assault 9 August 43 Elizabeth I.
203. CCAL DAC X.10.11, where the slander story *Spritewell v. Howe* is recorded.
204. CCAL DAC Y.5.7, fos. 95, 108, etc. (with other references in MS index).
205. CCAL DAC Y.5.12, fos. 4, 64, etc.
206. CCAL DAC Y.5.13, Y.5.14. Entries are given in MS indices to volumes.
207. PRC 17/64, fo. 109.
208. PRC 10/56, fo. 114.
209. CCAL DAC Y.6.1, fo. 74.
210. CCAL DAC MS Register of Licences, under 1625.
211. CCAL BAC J/Q/402; CCAL BAC J/Q/403.
212. Cowper, *St George*, burials.
213. Brooke, *op. cit.*, app. V, prints the will from the registered copy (PRC 17/52, fo. 373). The original will (PRC 16/125) was found later. The transcript is very good, but for '*sol. seod.*' at end, read '*soluta feoda*', and for the equally unintelligible '*infirmatum*', read '*insinuatum*' (fees paid and will entered).
214. See Appendix VII, p. 137, and PRC 3/26, fo. 105.
215. Brooke, *op. cit.* The will is printed from the registered copy (PRC 17/54, fo. 267). But again read '*soluta feoda*' for '*sol. seod.*', etc. The original will is PRC 16/127.
216. CCAL Parish Register, All Saints.

CHAPTER THREE

1. The King's School was re-established at the re-foundation of the cathedral in 1541 by Henry VIII (hence its name). It was usually known as the Queen's School in the time of Elizabeth I. There is an inaccurate history, C. E. Woodruff and H. J. Cape, *Schola Regia Cantuariensis* (London, 1908). D. Edwards, *A History of the King's School, Canterbury* (London, 1957), is a more scholarly publication.

2. L. E. Whatmore, ed., 'Archdeacon Harpsfield's Visitation, 1557. II. Together with Visitations of 1556 and 1558', *Catholic Record Society*, 1951, p. 335; CCAL DAC X.2.8, fo. 46.

3. *The Statutes of the Cathedral and Metropolitical Church of Christ, Canterbury* (Canterbury, 1925), Statute xxvii.

4. Revd J. E. Cox, ed., *The Works of Thomas Cranmer*, 2 vols., Parker Society 1844–6; and see Appendix I, pp. 99ff.

5. CCAL CAC, Dom. Economy 80, printed in part (with many inaccuracies) by Woodruff and Cape, *op. cit.*, pp. 96–7.

6. CCAL CAC Misc. Accounts 40.

7. *Ibid.*

8. *Ibid.*

9. See Appendix II, p. 110.

10. See Woodruff and Cape, *op. cit.*, pp. 55–6; Edward, *op. cit.*, pp. 60ff, citing a version of statutes in Bodleian Library (MS Gough, Kent 3).

11. See J. Foster, *Alumni Oxonienses, 1500–1714* (Oxford 1891, 1892), vol. I, p. 606.

12. MS Accounts, Corpus Christi College, Oxford, *s.a.*

13. Woodruff and Cape *op. cit.*, p. 91.

14. Felle(s) appears continuously in the records. As a sideline he collected cathedral rents (BL Stowe MS 122, a receiver's account of Canterbury Cathedral, 29–30 Elizabeth I). He acted as escort for prisoners taken to the Privy Council (*Proceedings of the Privy Council*, May 1579). He was involved in the case *Kempe v. Juxon* (CCAL DAC X.10.21). Esther Kemp had a quarrel with Bridget Felles, wife of James. Felle was born at Dalton, Lancs. (CCAL DAC X.11.2, fo. 247).

15. Will of W. Browne, 20 August 1581 (PRC 32/34, fo. 160).

16. PRC 21/4, fo. 169.

17. CCAL DAC Y.3.18, fos. 146ff.

18. See S. Jayne, *Library Catalogues of the English Renaissance* (Berkeley, 1956).

19. See Appendix I, pp. 99ff. The principal source for a list of scholars is the Cathedral Accounts though they only provide the names of boys on the foundation.

20. I am grateful to Dr W. E. Church of Bethersden for help with Samuel Kennett's pedigree. See G. Anstruther, OP, *Seminary Priests – I – Elizabethan, 1558–1603* (Woodchester, Glos., 1966) p. 195. It is clearly he who is called 'terrible puritan' in *Calendar of State Papers, Spanish, Elizabeth* (London, 1892–9), III, p. 336, under date April 1582. John Hart is said to have converted Kennett, but he himself was a waverer and is said at one point to have offered to go to Rheims as a spy (*ibid.*, p. 154). For the standard-bearer, see J. Foster, ed., *Pedigrees Recorded at the Visitations of the Country Palatine of Durham* (London, 1887), pp. 196–7. The Kennett family arms were 'quarter gules and or, a label of three points in chief, each point charged with as many bezants in pale'. There is an elaborate crest. The same arms were borne by Blackley Kennett, Lord Mayor of London, 1780. *Obit Book of the English Benedictines 1600–1912*, ed. Abbot Snow, revised by H. N. Birt (privately printed 1913), pp. 4, 246. Kennett was a member of the 'Cassinese' congregation.

21. For Leonard Sweeting's father see p. 50. L. Sweeting's evidence (January 1585), is in CCAL DAC X.10.9, fos. 167–8, and X.11.1, fo. 123, etc. The MS account of the church courts is Z.3.25 with the list of books *ibid.*, fos. 327ff. Soon after leaving school he was engaged in probate work, and was called '*literatus*' (April 1581, CCAL DAC Y.3.20, fo. 31). See account of transmission of Marlowe material on p. 60, esp. note 53.

22. *DNB*.

23. J. and J. A. Venn, *Alumni Cantabrigiensis* (Cambridge, 1929), pt I, vol. III; the butcher's stall owed rent to the Canterbury Corporation (CCAL BAC FA/19, fo. 22). The boy's mother seems

to have carried on the business after her husband's death (*ibid.*, fo. 63).

24. *Substitutus* in CCAL CAC Misc. Accounts 41, fo. 89. He was an orphan, for his father died in 1571, *Parker's Register, Canterbury and York Society*, p. 881. Cowper, *St Alphege*.

25. Robert Pownall is no. 328 in C. H. Garrett's list in *The Marian Exiles* (Cambridge, 1938). Pownall senior occurs for years a 'Six Preacher' and/or minor canon, as does Jonas the chorister (CCAL CAC Misc. Accounts, Accounts, New Foundation, *s.a.*). See R. Hovenden, ed., *Register of Canterbury Cathedral* (London, 1878), index. Clerical appointment in the family can be traced in Frampton Collection (Canterbury Cathedral Library). Philemon's licence to teach is in CCAL DAC Register of Licences, *s.a.* He gives Dover as his birthplace in CCAL DAC X.11.11, fo. 169, etc.

26. See *DNB*. Study grants are entered in CCAL CAC Accounts, New Foundation 9; Chapter Acts 1582, etc. H. Oxinden's note is in Capel-Cure Notebook, deposited in BL, under 14 August 1640.

27. See Bakeless, vol. I, ch. III; R. Masters, *The History of the College of Corpus Christi and the B. Virgin Mary (Commonly Called Benet) . . . Cambridge*, (Cambridge, 1753); A. D. Wright and V. F. Stern, *In Search of Christopher Marlowe: A Pictorial Biography* (London, 1965), pt II.

28. Bakeless, vol. I. p. 47.

29. J. and J. A. Venn, *op. cit.*, pt I; financial support is recorded (for example) in CCAL CAC Accounts, New Foundation 9 (20–21 Elizabeth I); PRC 39/16 fo. 15; CCAL DAC X.11.3, fo. 72, he said in 1598 that he was about forty-two years old; incumbencies are recorded in Frampton Collection, Canterbury Cathedral Library.

30. See Masters, *op. cit.*; Wraight and Stern, *op. cit.*; Bakeless, vol. I, ch. III.

31. *Ibid.*, and see Wraight and Stern, *op. cit.*, p. 61, for the entry of Marlowe on Mr Johnes' list mentioned below.

32. See F. S. Boas, *Christopher Marlowe: A Biographical and Critical Study* (Oxford, 1940), pp. 10ff.

33. Scale of charges set out in College MA Register, *s.n.*, marked

1590–1698 (unfoliated), under heading 'Certayne fees belonging to the porter'. Other charges are registered in the volume.

34. J. and J. A. Venn, *Book of Matriculations and Degrees . . .* (Cambridge, 1913), p. 447; and see J. H. Ingram, *Christopher Marlowe and His Associates* (London, 1904), pl. IX, for extract from Corpus Christi College Archives, Registrum Parvum, *s.a.*, viz. 'Marlin electus et admissus in locum domini Pashly', recorded on 7 May 1581 and clearly retrospective.

35. See Boas, *op. cit.*, and C. G. Moore Smith, 'Marlowe at Cambridge', *Modern Language Review* 4 (1908–9), pp. 167–77.

36. See Appendix III, p. 123 (PRC 16/36).

37. Benchkin's salaries for his various offices may be found in CCAL CAC Accounts, New Foundation, Treasurer and Receiver, Misc. Accounts 40–41, *temp.* Mary and Elizabeth. See also *Registrum Matthei Parker Diocesis Cantuariensis A.D. 1559–75*, *Canterbury and York Society* (London, 1907), pp. 335, 632, 908, 918, 932–5.

38. CCAL BAC Corporation Leasebooks, *s.a.*

39. See Corpus Christi College, Cambridge, Archives, Registrum Parvum, *s.a.*; J. and J. A. Venn, *Book of Matriculations*, *op. cit.*; and see notes 34 and 35, above.

40. See Moore Smith, *op. cit.*, and Boas, *op. cit.*

41. J. Venn, ed., *Grace Book Delta* (Cambridge, 1910), p. 375.

42. Bakeless, vol. I, p. 77, citing MS *supplicats*, 1586–7, no. 65.

43. See Appendix I, pp. 99ff.

44. J. R. Dasent, ed., *Acts of the Privy Council*, XV. 141, where there is an inaccurate version. See Bakeless, vol. I, p. 77.

45. J. Venn, *Grace Book Delta*, *op. cit.*

46. *Ibid.*, Introduction, pp. viii ff.

47. See Boas, *op. cit.*, and Moore Smith, *op. cit.*, also J. and J. A. Venn, *Alumni Cantabrigiensis*, *op. cit.*

48. CCAL BAC J/B/391 iv, under date 29 June 1592. He was admitted freeman of Canterbury in November 1592 (BAC FA/20, fo. 9); Cowper, *Canterbury Marriage Licences*, vol. I, 'Benchkin', under date 29 May 1594.

49. Corpus Christi College, Cambridge, Archives, Buttery Book, and see J. and J. A. Venn, *Alumni Cantabrigiensis*, *op. cit.*

50. See C. L. Kingsford in *DNB*, and L. H. Carlson, ed., 'The Writings of John Greenwood, 1587–90, together with the joint writings of Henry Barrow and John Greenwood, 1587–90', *Elizabethan Non-Conformist Texts*, vol. 4 (London, 1962), Introduction.

51. For a useful short account of Johnson and his circle see G. F. Willison, *Saints and Strangers . . .* (London, Toronto, 1946).

52. J. and J. A. Venn, *Book of Matriculations, op. cit.*, p. 250. Fyneux paid the standard fee within the year 1586–7 (Corpus Audit Book, under Michaelmas 1587).

53. D. Gardiner, 'Henry Oxinden's Authorship', *Archaeologia Cantiana*, vol. LVII, pp. 13–20. Oxinden was born 18 January 1608 in the house of his grandfather (Sir A. Sprakeling) in St Paul's, Canterbury (Capel-Cure Notebook in BL). He married Ann Peyton in 1632. She died in 1640. His mother's family (the Sprakelings) must have known the Marlowes at fairly close hand. One of Oxinden's notebooks is in Folger Shakespeare Library, Washington; one is the Capel-Cure Notebook (see above); another is BL Add. 20812; and Dorothy Gardiner, ed., *The Oxinden Letters, 1607–42* (London, 1933) and *The Oxinden and Peyton Letters, 1642–70* (London, 1937). Oxinden's printed books passed into the hands of a kinsman, Lee Warley, the eccentric lawyer, from whom they passed into the parish library of Elham, Kent. The circumstances in which the Folger Notebook and the copy of *Hero and Leander* left the collection are obscure. The latter book, the so-called Prideaux copy, is now lost.

54. For confusion over identity of Aldrich see C. J. Sisson, *The Judicious Marriage of Mr Hooker and the Birth of the Laws of Ecclesiastical Polity* (Cambridge, 1940), pp. 83–4.

55. *Calendar of Wills Proved in Vice-Chancellor's Court at Cambridge, 1501–1765* (Cambridge, 1907), p. 25. For the monument to Francis Aldrich (II), see P. Parsons, *The Monuments and Painted Glass of upward of one hundred churches, chiefly in the eastern part of Kent* (Canterbury, 1794), p. 264. For the will of F. Aldrich (I) see PRC Archdeaconry, 52, fo. 294. He gave evidence in court several times recounting his brief biography (e.g. CCAL DAC

X.11.1, fo. 62). He came from Norwich.

56. Bakeless, vol. I, pp. 116–19, making extensive use of M. Eccles, 'Marlowe in Kentish Tradition', *Notes and Queries*, vol. CLXIX (1935), pp. 20–3, 39–41, 58–61 and 134–5. Thomas Fyneux was a member of an ancient and distinguished Kentish family. I am very grateful to Mr Peter Lyons of Dover for much help with the pedigree of this family.
57. N. Purdon, 'Quod me nutrit', *Cambridge Review*, 1967.

CHAPTER FOUR

1. M. Eccles, 'Christopher Marlowe in London', *Harvard Studies in English*, vol. 10 (Cambridge, Mass., 1934); Bakeless, vol. I, pp. 98ff; F. S. Boas, *Christopher Marlowe* (Oxford, 1960), pp. 101ff; A. D. Wraight and V. F. Stern, *In Search of Christopher Marlowe* (London, 1965), pp. 117ff.
2. Various maps of the area are reproduced in Wraight and Stern, *op. cit.*, pp. 106–7 (the map of *c.* 1560), and p. 118.
3. W. W. Braines, 'The Site of "The Theatre", Shoreditch: London's first playhouse', *London Topographical Record*, vol. II (1917). L. Hotson, *The Times*, 24 March 1954. It is curious that Dr Hotson made so little use of Braines' work in this article and in *Shakespeare's Wooden O* (London, 1959). For a map of 1560 see *Archaeologia*, vol. 100, pp. 105ff.
4. *DNB*.
5. F. S. Boas, *Christopher Marlowe: A Biographical and Critical Study* (Oxford, 1940), pp. 101ff.
6. For William Fleetwood, see *DNB*.
7. The surviving funerary inscription addressed to the memory of Sir Roger Manwood, Chief Baron of the Exchequer, has been assigned to Marlowe. Oxinden records it twice in his notebooks and it was said to have been written into a lost copy of *Hero and Leander*, where it was attributed to Christopher 'Marlo'. The twelve lines of ornate Latin eulogizing Manwood as a judge are

a sufficient distortion of a cruel, greedy and corrupt man to cause one to seek an author indebted to him. Marlowe might have been overcome with relief when liberated by the Bench which included Judge Manwood after the Hog Lane killing in 1589, and penned the epitaph in gratitude. It is, indeed, just possible that Manwood commissioned and paid for the verses. Son of a Sandwich draper, Manwood served as MP for Canterbury as well as other places and, as his prosperity grew, he built a dwelling for himself in St Dunstan's Street in Canterbury, outside the Westgate, and later raised for himself a mansion at Hackington, in the parish of St Stephen's a mile away. He died on 14 December 1592 and was buried at St Stephen's church where his elaborate monument is still to be seen, though the inscription is not that attributed to Marlowe.

8. Eccles, *op. cit.*, p. 105, etc.; Bakeless, vol. I, pp. 104–5; F. S. Boas, *op. cit.*, p. 236; Wraight and Stern, *op. cit.*, p. 121.

9. For the documents in the case see Appendix IV, p. 130.

10. There are various MS maps in existence in Canterbury City Archives showing this area. Names of rooms in the Chequers are mentioned more than once, as in the probate inventory of John Marlowe's acquaintance, Hugh Jones the landlord (PRC 10/12/173). See also CCAL CAC Inventories no. 38 and City Chamberlains's Accounts.

11. Cathedral Accounts are available for 1597–8, 1598–9 – CCAL Misc. Accounts 41, *s.a.*; MS Lambeth Palace, roll no. 94. William Corkine, senior, first appears as a member of the choir in the Canterbury Cathedral account roll at Christmas 1597 but there is a long gap in the surviving accounts back to 1590 and he may have been there before. The choir at this date consisted of a body of twelve *clerici laici* (lay clerks) and ten *choristae* (choir-boys). Minor canons, six in number, were regarded as essentially part of the choir. Between the minor canons and the lay clerks stood an indeterminate and intermittent body of varying size called *substituti* to whom was sometimes added another group called *tibicines* or cornets. William Corkine, senior, was among the *substituti*, a group which, judging from the wording of the Cathedral Statutes, were intended to be singers. At the

close of the sixteenth century the minor canons at Canterbury received £13 6s. 8d. each year, lay clerks £10 and choristers £4. *Substituti* received 40s. each and the *tibicines* 25s. The training was carried out by one of the lay clerks acting as organist and choirmaster, receiving extra pay (£5 a year) on that account.

12. For the career of William Corkine, senior, see CCAL BAC J/Q/ 384; CCAL Parish Register, St Mary Northgate, *s.a.*; CFC, redemption; Woollen-Drapers' and Tailors' Company Archives, deposited in Canterbury Cathedral Library, minutes, *s.a.*; CCAL BAC J/Q/395; Cowper, *Canterbury Marriage Licences*, vol. I, e.g., 'Milles', col. 287, and see index of stray names (but the editor does not print all names of bondsmen occurring in MS volumes, CCAL DAC Registers of Licences); *Canterbury Marriage Licences*, vol. I, col. 107; CCAL BAC J/Q/396.

13. William Corkine (II) appears as choirboy in 1597–8 but may have been present earlier (see above, note 11).

14. See F. W. Sternfeld, 'Come live with me and be my love', in *The Hidden Harmony, Essays in Honor of Philip Wheelwright* (New York, 1966), pp. 173–92; C. M. Simpson, *The British Broadside Ballad and its Music* (New Brunswick, 1966), pp. 119–21; and P. J. Seng, *Vocal Songs in the Plays of Shakespeare* (Cambridge, Mass., 1967), pp. 164–5.

15. For documents see Appendix IV, p. 130.

16. The rosebud is now kept in a special container and filed with the plea book: CCAL BAC J/B/392, 'Nower'.

17. For Robert Poley see Boas, *op. cit.*, pp. 65–8, 116–28, 273–6, 288–93, etc., and Bakeless, vol. II, pp. 340–42, for bibliography of this character and his associates. For Paul Ive see his *The Practise of Fortification* (London, 1589); CCAL BAC Chamberlains' Accounts, *s.a.*; and Bakeless, vol. I, pp. 210–11.

18. Bakeless, vol. I, p. 114.

19. R. Greene, *Perimedes the Blacke-Smith* . . . (London, 1588); Boas, *op. cit.*, p. 70.

20. See Wraight and Stern, *op. cit.*, pp. 132ff, and J. B. Steane, *Marlowe: A Critical Study* (Cambridge, 1964), pp. 18–19. See also R. Parsons, *Responsio ad Elizabethae edictum* (1592).

21. Wraight and Stern, *op. cit.*, pp. 251, 318.

22. See J. W. Shirley, ed., *Thomas Harriot, Renaissance Scientist* (Oxford, 1974). The material below is largely drawn from this collection of essays. See *Times Literary Supplement*, 23 October 1969.

23. For this and the rest of this paragraph see Wraight and Stern, *op. cit.*, pp. 132–80.

24. Shirley, *op. cit.*

✗ 25. R. B. Wernham, 'Christopher Marlowe at Flushing in 1592', in *English Historical Review*, vol. XCI (1976), pp. 344–5.

26. Eccles, *op. cit.*

27. For what follows see Bakeless, vols. I and II; Boas, *op. cit.*, Wraight and Stern, *op. cit.*

28. Bakeless, vol. I, p. 109.

29. Shirley, *op. cit.*

30. Boas, *op. cit.*, p. 251.

31. For what follows see Bakeless, vols. I and II; Boas, *op. cit.*; Wraight and Stern, *op. cit.*

32. See Wraight and Stern, *op. cit.*, p. 354 and see P. H. Kocher, *Christopher Marlowe* (New York, 1946), p. 36.

33. *Ibid.*, pp. 308–9.

34. See Boas, *op. cit.*, pp. 241–4; for texts of Kyd's letters see Wraight and Stern, *op. cit.*, pp. 310–20.

35. S. E. Sprott, 'Drury and Marlowe', *Times Literary Supplement*, 2 August 1974, p. 840.

36. J. R. Dasent, ed., *Acts of the Privy Council* XXIV.244; Wraight and Stern, *op. cit.*, p. 284.

CHAPTER FIVE

1. See K. Muir, 'The Chronology of Marlowe's Plays', *Proceedings of the Leeds Philosophical and Literary Society*, V (1938–43), pp. 345–56; Bakeless, vol. I, chs. vii–ix, *passim*, and II, chs. x–xiv, *passim*; L. C. Martin, ed., *Marlowe's Poems* (London, 1931) and M. MacLure, ed., *The Poems of Christopher Marlowe* (Cam-

✗ R. Sidney wrote the name Marlowe in the letter, "Marly"; endorsed January 26, 1591 [

bridge, 1968), and F. Bowers, ed., *The complete works of Christopher Marlowe* (Cambridge 1981), 2 vols.

2. See Introduction, pp. xxv–xxvii.

3. J. R. Dasent, ed., *Acts of the Privy Council*, XXIV.244. For Maunder's activities see *ibid.*, 1590–1601, indices.

4. For movements of the Privy Council see *Acts of the Privy Council, op. cit.*

5. See V. J. K. Brook, *Whitgift and The English Church* (London, 1957).

6. A. B. Groshart, ed., *The Life and Complete Works in Prose and Verse of Robert Greene, M.A.*, vol. XII, The Huth Library (London, 1881–3), pp. 142–3.

7. See p. 59, note 50; V. J. K. Brook, *Whitgift and the English Church* (London, 1957), pp. 141–2.

8. See J. L. Hotson, *The Death of Christopher Marlowe* (London, 1925).

9. Evelyn MSS, deposited at Christ Church College, Oxford. The map was printed in black and white in H. Drake, ed., *Hasted's History of Kent . . . Pt. I, The Hundred of Blackheath* (London, 1886). This rendering misinterpreted details in the original. Part of this version is reproduced in Hotson, *op. cit.*, p. 43.

10. W. Lambard, *A Perambulation of Kent* (London, 1596), p. 429.

11. Ashmolean Museum, Oxford. The water-colour bears ref. C IV* 267.

12. For what follows see Hotson, *op. cit.*, pp. 18ff. He makes use of the amusing article of J. Le G. Brereton, 'The Case of Francis Ingram', *Sydney University Publications*, no. 5, pp. 3–8.

13. For the survey of 1609–10 see PRO L.R. 2/196, fos. 166–8.

14. KAO MS, Rochester Diocesan Act Book, sixteenth century.

15. W. Bruce Bannerman, ed., 'The Registers of St Mary le Bowe . . . London', *Harleian Society*, vols. 44, 45 (London, 1914, 1915). Credit for noticing this entry belongs to Miss Jane Apple of Lewisburg, Pa.

16. MS Deptford Parish Register deposited in the Greater London Authority Record Office, Westminster Bridge.

17. There are two versions, one rough and the other a fair copy. The probate documents are printed in Appendix V, p. 132.

18. George Hanger's will is PCC Windebank 71. A substantial amount of biographical material is recoverable for him from his company's records (the Clothworkers). He commissioned voyages to the Canaries (i.e., he engaged in illicit traffic with Spain in time of war). I am much obliged to Dr G. Ramsay, fellow of St Edmund Hall, Oxford, for collecting notes when working in the Clothworkers' Company records. For Robert Savage's will see PCC Windebank 20.

19. See MS Deptford Parish Register, Greater London Authority Record Office, Westminster Bridge. For George Bull's nuncupative will see PCC Drake 61. I am much obliged to the then Archivist of the Essex County Record Office, Mr F. G. Emmison, FSA, F.R.Hist.S., for communicating points about George Bull in Harlow.

20. Box marked 'Deptford' among Evelyn MSS. There are several chests of uncatalogued documents now at Christ Church College, Oxford.

21. The original of the Subsidy Roll is in private hands, see PRO Catalogue shelves.

22. The important discovery of the draft of the will was made by Miss Jane Apple. For the will and pedigree of Blanche Parry and family see PCC Drury 16; BL Lansdowne MS, 62, fo. 123.

23. See W. Page, ed., *Victoria County History of Herefordshire* (London, 1908), index; there is some confused material about the family in J. Duncombe, *Collections towards the History and Antiquities of Hereford*, vol. VI, p. 80, etc. Their arms were 'azure, a cross chequy, or and sable'.

24. See F. S. Boas, *Christopher Marlowe* (Oxford, 1960), pp. 265–6.

25. See Hotson, *op. cit.*, pp. 42ff. Frizer appears as an intermediary in some complex land deals in Wales between 25 and 39 Elizabeth I, *Calendar of State Papers, Domestic Series, of the Reigns of Elizabeth and James I, Addenda, 1580–1625*, ed. M. A. E. Green (London, 1872), p. 536.

26. D. Galloway, ed., *The Elizabethan Theatre* (London, 1969): see pp. 45–73, H. Berry, 'The Playhouse in the Boar's Head Inn, Whitechapel'.

27. See Boas, *op. cit.*, pp. 268ff; Bakeless, vol. I, pp. 181ff.

28. E. Hasted, *The History and Topographical Survey of the County of Kent* . . . vol II (Canterbury, 1782), p. 747; and see *Archaeologia Cantiana*, indices, vols. XIX, LII, LXVII, XC (London, 1892, 1940, 1954, 1975).

29. T. Beard, *The Theatre of God's Judgements: or a Collection of histories out of sacred, ecclesiasticall, and prophane authours, concerning the admirable iudgements of God upon the transgressours of his commandments. Translated out of French, and augmented . . . by T. Beard* (London, 1597); W. Vaughan, *The Golden-grove, moralized in three Bookes* (London, 1600).

30. E. Rudierde, *The Thunderbolt of God's Wrath against hard-hearted and stiffe-necked sinners, or an abridgement of the Theater of God's feareful judgements executed upon notorious sinners* (London, 1618).

31. F. Meres, *Palladis Tamia. Wits Treasury being the second part of Wits Commonwealth* (London, 1598).

32. Beard, *op. cit.*, ch. XXV.

33. Cited by Hotson, *op. cit.*, pp. 14–16.

34. Printed (with one or two minor inaccuracies, such as '*sacrum*' for '*sacramentum*') in Latin and English by Hotson, *op. cit.* See E. K. Chambers' review of the above in *Modern Language Review*, vol. 21 (1926), pp. 84–5.

35. Evelyn MSS, Christ Church College, Oxford, inventory of Sayes Court *temp.* Christopher Browne and wife, on long parchment roll, *s.n.*

36. See the valuable article by Gavin Thurston, MRCP, DCH, DMJ, 'Christopher Marlowe's Death', in *Contemporary Review*, March/April 1964. The author, not only a medical man but also a barrister-at-law and, like William Danby, a coroner, remarks: 'The nature of the wound as a cause of death is so wildly improbable that it alone sets a seal of authenticity in the inquest. A hired assassin . . . would stab in the back, or the chest, or cut the throat.' I am much obliged to Dr Brian Matthews, fellow of St Edmund Hall and professor of clinical neurology, Oxford, for engaging in a discussion of the problem. Dr S. A. Tannenbaum, *The Assassination of Christopher Marlowe* (Connecticut, 1962), claims that Marlowe could not have died from the dagger thrust.

See p 39 of
The Murder of Christopher Marlowe.
20 x 15½ CM bound note book on shelf
with Hotsons book.

37. See unpublished portion of Patent Rolls under dates 26 March 18 Elizabeth I (1576) and 6 October 31 Elizabeth I (1589); W. P. Baildon, ed., *The Records of the Honorable Society of Lincoln's Inn. The Black Books, Vol. I, 1422–1586* (London, 1897), p. 304; *The Records of the Honorable Society of Lincoln's Inn: admissions, 1420–1893, and chapel registers* (London, 1896), vol. I, p. 53; Hotson, *op. cit.*, p. 38, refers to William Danby of Woolwich without citing a reference.

38. L. L. Duncan, 'Extracts from some Lost Kentish Registers', *Archaeologia Cantiana*, vol. XXXI (1915), p. 182.

39. Hotson, *op. cit.*, p. 38.

40. E. G. Vine Hall, 'Christopher Marlowe's Death at Deptford Strand, 1593. Wills of Jurors at the Inquest and some other Wills', *Testamentary Papers* III (London, 1937).

41. Based on deeds among the Evelyn Papers, *s.n.*, Christ Church College, Oxford.

42. Hotson, *op. cit.*, pp. 34–7; and see Wraight and Stern, *op. cit.*, pp. 296, 356.

43. The quarrels of Mr Macander, etc., are noted in the Rochester Act Book of the period (KAO). He died in 1597 (H. Drake, ed., *Hasted's History of Kent . . . Blackheath* (London, 1886), p. 42).

44. Hotson, *op. cit.*, pp. 20–21; Boas, *op. cit.*, p. 303; A. D. Wraight and V. F. Stern, *In Search of Christopher Marlowe* (London, 1965), p. 305.

45. See C. F. Tucker Brooke, *The Life of Marlowe and The Tragedy of Dido, Queen of Carthage* (London, 1930), app. XIV; G. Harvey, *A New Letter, of Notable Contents with a straunge Sonet, intituled Gorgon, or the Wonderfull Yeare* (London, 1593) and see A. B. Groshart, ed., *The Works of Gabriel Harvey, The Huth Library* (1884, 1885).

46. T. Nashe, *The Unfortunate Traveller, Or The Life of Jacke Wilton* (London, 1594); R. B. McKerrow, ed., *The Works of Thomas Nashe* (London, 1904), vol. II, pp. 264–5; A. L. Rowse, *William Shakespeare: A Biography* (London, 1963), p. 113.

47. See Bakeless, vol. I, pp. 171–82; Boas, *op. cit.*, pp. 288–93; Wraight and Stern, *op. cit.*, pp. 300–1.

48. C. E. Woodruff, 'Notes on the Municipal Records of Queen-

borough', *Archaeologia Cantiana*, vol. XXII (1897), pp. 169–85, esp. p. 183; Hasted, *op. cit.*, p. 659 gives 'Sir' Robert Poley as MP for Queenborough in 21 James I but reverts to 'Esquire' for his title in 1 Charles I; B. Willis, *Notitia Parliamentaria* . . . (London, 1715–30), p. 211, calls R. Poley 'Esquire'.

49. See Hotson, *op. cit.*, pp. 41–51; Boas, *op. cit.*, pp. 286–8; Wraight and Stern, *op. cit.*, pp. 296–8. In his now more respectable years Frizer received a bequest of £20 and 'black' by the will of Sir Julius Denne (d. 1608), see *Miscellanea Genealogica et Heraldica*, series V, II, p. 39. I am obliged to Dr A. L. Rowse for this reference.

50. PCC Skinner 99. The account in Boas, *op. cit.*, p. 288, seems to be slightly muddled.

51. See Boas, *op. cit.*, p. 286; Bakeless, vol. I, pp. 180ff.

52. See Wraight and Stern, *op. cit.*, pp. 295–306; Tannenbaum, *op. cit.*; Boas, *op. cit.*, pp. 265ff; C. Hoffman, *The Murder of the Man who was Shakespeare* (New York, 1955), pp. 76–98.

Morley of Trinity omitted